RESISTING TEMPTATION

"My car's over there." Jaunie pointed to her blue Honda in the corner of the parking garage.

Trent turned off his ignition. "I'd better walk you over."

Jaunie unlocked her car door, then turned around to say goodnight. Trent removed his hands from his pockets and opened his arms. She moved into his embrace. For a long time he just held her, squeezing gently. She needed this—a hug between friends.

Slowly Trent's hands began to move up and down her back. His hands moved over her hips, and she began to notice the change in the embrace—and in her body.

She raised her head. "Trent, I . . . mmm."

Trent's mouth stole her words. His hands smoothed over her slim skirt, stopping at the hemline. Each time she breathed his cologne, a new ribbon of desire curled in her abdomen.

She was immersed in these sensory pleasures. His lips worked their way up her throat with gentle nibbles. Finally his mouth found hers again.

The sound of elevator doors opening jangled her nerves like a fire alarm. Quickly Trent jogged to the passenger side as Jaunie scrambled behind the wheel.

"Whew, that was close, huh?" Trent's voice faded into nervous laughter.

She nodded trying to calm her internal fizzing.

After a long silence Trent turned to her. "It's not working, is it?"

"What's not working?"

"We agreed to keep our hands off each other."

"No . . . I guess it isn't working." Jaunie stared at her lap, not really sure why that was a problem.

LOOK FOR THESE ARABESQUE ROMANCES

PRIVATE LIES

Robyn Amos

Pinnacle Books
Kensington Publishing Corp.
http://www.arabesquebooks.com

PINNACLE BOOKS are published by

Kensington Publishing Corp.
850 Third Avenue
New York, NY 10022

Pinnacle and the P logo Reg. U.S. Pat. & TM Off.

First Printing: March, 1998
10 9 8 7 6 5 4 3 2 1

Printed in the United States of America

Prologue

Hanging out in bars and picking up men for money was getting really old.

Jaunie Sterling smoothed a strand of her long auburn hair behind one ear and gave Trenton Douglas, that night's pickup, full view of her stunning profile.

"I voted for Senator Maxwell, too." As she spoke, her Plum Paradise–colored lips fell naturally into the seductive smile she'd perfected during her days as a model.

That night she was Dominique. According to Trent's fiancée, he preferred beautiful, politically aware women. And of course Dominique was both.

She fingered the wispy hem of her Versace cocktail dress. Purple—his favorite color. Just as the scent she wore, Escape, and the wine she sipped, Cabernet Sauvignon, were his favorites.

Poor Trent didn't stand a chance.

The trap had been set. Erika Maxwell lured her fiancé to the hotel lounge supposedly to meet for a date. Then, after he'd arrived, she called from a cellular phone outside, claiming she couldn't make it after all. Before Trent could leave, Dominique made her move.

Now regarding her prey through the thick fringe of her lashes, Jaunie tried not to sigh. For months she'd been losing enthusiasm for this job. Helping women catch their cheating lovers was disheartening work. She no longer relished the cool flavor of revenge that came with sending stray dogs back to the pound. Her salvation was that her boss at Intimate Investigations, Alan Warren, and Erika were in the car, listening to every word. Thank goodness this would be over soon.

Trent changed the subject from politics to his work as a contractor. And as the rich, animated tones of his voice vibrated over her, Jaunie's gaze fell on his fingers tapping absently on the bar. He had beautiful hands. The hands of a creator.

Distracted, she stared into sable eyes warm enough to melt butter and mentally raised an eyebrow. He seemed like a genuinely nice guy. The way he cocked his head when he talked had an endearing, little-boy quality that made him likable on sight.

She blinked as a wave of acute disappointment washed over her. Under normal circumstances, she probably *would* have liked him. But unfortunately, *no one* passed this test. She'd been working as a decoy for four years, and no matter how long the men held out, they all gave in eventually. She needed only to make the right offer.

And *all* she had to do was offer. As soon as the men accepted, the game was over. The unlucky man's wife or girlfriend would come inside, mad enough to lynch their lying lovers.

Usually Jaunie had no problem sympathizing with the women she worked for. Most had strong provocation backing their suspicions. Their men either had a history of cheating or were outrageous flirts. But in this case, Erika claimed that Trent had never so much as smiled at another woman. Since he stood to gain a lot of money and some important political connections after they were married, she had to be certain of his fidelity beforehand. Hence the test.

Maybe if she'd liked Erika Maxwell more, Jaunie wouldn't have found herself hoping her feminine wiles would fail. She almost wished Trenton Douglas would pass Erika's little test just to confirm that the woman didn't deserve him.

But it was already too late.

Sparks crackled between them. The unmistakable heat in his gaze told her all she needed to know—he wanted her.

Suddenly Jaunie wanted the whole scene over as quickly as possible. He made her wish for things she had no right to want.

Casually she propped her elbow on the bar, pretending not to notice as her gauzy strap slid over her shoulder and halfway down her arm. And as she'd expected, his gaze traced the trail of the delicate strap.

She stared at him until he raised his gaze to hers. It was time to make her move. "I have a room upstairs, 607. I'd hate to go back alone."

Desire flamed in his eyes as if she'd struck a match. And as sure as matches burned fingers when held too long, Jaunie knew if she didn't look away, Trent's gaze would burn her with its intensity. But in an instant the flame died, and his eyes became smoky.

He took a somewhat shaky breath. "I—I'm sorry, Dominique. This is my fault. I must have led you on . . . but that wasn't my intention. You see, I'm engaged."

Dominique caught her breath in surprise while Jaunie secretly applauded. But she had to play this out to its end.

She placed her hand on his arm. "I won't tell, if you don't tell."

Trent shook his head, gently but firmly removing her hand. "I'm sorry, Dominique, you're very beautiful and . . ." He sighed with what sounded like frustration.

"I don't have a good excuse for not telling you sooner. I guess I just enjoyed talking to you, and I didn't want to spoil it. But don't take this the wrong way. You're beautiful, you're intelligent, and if I wasn't in love with someone else . . ."

She tried to read his eyes, searching for a sign that he would give in if she pressured him. Instead, she saw nothing but sincerity and genuine regret. Something shifted inside her— the part of her that had been afraid to trust, to believe this was possible. Jaunie had never been so happy to be rejected in her life.

"I understand," she whispered. "Whoever your fiancée is, she's a lucky woman."

Jaunie set one foot on the floor, already halfway off her bar stool. She hoped she could slip away, and this uniquely faithful man would never know that his fiancée had set him up.

She reached for her purse lying on the bar. "Goodbye, Trent. You'll never know what a pleasure it was to meet you."

She turned around and came face to face with Erika Maxwell. Jaunie held her breath, praying that the woman wouldn't acknowledge her.

Erika looked straight past her. "Trent, I knew you weren't like the others."

Jaunie didn't turn around to see Trent's face, but she could hear the confusion in his voice when he asked, "What are you doing here?"

Jaunie felt Erika's hand on her arm. She wanted to pull away but instead was frozen to the spot. She pressed her eyes closed, waiting for the ax to fall.

"I hired this woman to test you. At the agency they said few men could resist such an ideal temptation, but I thought you'd be different. I just had to be sure before the wedding."

Jaunie heard nothing but silence behind her, and with trepidation rising in her stomach, she turned around.

Trent laughed softly. His dark eyes were cold and hard, conveying his lack of humor. "Did I hear you correctly? You hired *her*"—his voiced dripped with disdain—"to hit on me so you could see if I would be faithful after we were married?"

"Yes, baby." Erika moved to his side, reaching for him. "But you passed."

"Really?" Trent pulled away, shaking his head. "Then *you* failed. Everyone warned me about you. I should have listened."

The woman sputtered in cold outrage, but Trent had already dismissed her. His gaze was now on Jaunie.

Her heart skipped. The loathing in his eyes made her feel almost dirty.

"Dominique? What are you ... some kind of high-priced hooker?"

Numbly she shook her head. "No, I'm not. I just—"

"Doesn't matter," he said in her ear as he passed. "You might as well be."

He left both women without a backward glance—Erika in a seething rage and Jaunie stunned silent.

Jaunie had never felt so low in all her life. She saw her boss, Alan, at the end of the bar, watching the entire scene.

She met his eyes silently as she realized that she'd come to a pivotal moment in her career. Jaunie had vowed that if she ever came across a man honest enough to pass this test, she'd quit working for Intimate Investigations.

Trenton Douglas had restored her faith in the opposite sex. Unfortunately, at that same moment, she may have destroyed his.

Chapter One

Tearing down the old and rebuilding from scratch was nothing new.

Trenton Douglas pushed through the doors marked Payne Contracting, soon to read Payne & Douglas Contracting, and came to a halt. This was it. He'd reconstructed his life five years ago when he'd left D.C. behind and moved to New York. But now he was back, starting over. Again.

He cocked his head as he looked around. The office was nice enough. Kind of plain, not much furniture, but Trent didn't really care. Not much fazed him anymore.

Through an open office door, he saw his new partner darting around, swearing, and shuffling through a deskful of papers. Trent leaned against the door frame. "Some things never change, I see."

Robert Payne's office resembled his side of the college dorm room the two had shared years ago, minus the empty pizza boxes and dirty laundry. Robert spun around. "Trent, you old dog. How the hell are you?"

He stopped long enough to embrace Trent and slap him on the back, then resumed lifting folders and feeling through drawers. "I was wondering when you'd finally get here."

"I had to pick up my equipment and supplies. They were in storage."

"Oh, that's right." Robert's mustache went slightly awry as he stroked his goatee. "You've been in the city for months, but you couldn't give a brother a call."

"You know I spent all my time working on the house. Besides, I foolishly thought Cecily would keep you amused for longer than two months. But I'll say this, man, divorce has been good to you." Trent admired his old friend, who still maintained a basketball player's physique and a roll-with-it attitude after three failed marriages.

Robert held up his jacket and felt through the pockets for the third time. "Hey, that doesn't mean I've given up looking for number four. We're not getting any younger, buddy. When are *you* going for number one?"

Trent held up a hand, shaking his head. With women, he and Robert seemed to have the same rotten luck. The only difference was that Robert had *married* all his mistakes.

"Sorry, unlike you, my man, I know when I've been licked. I just don't see it happening."

Robert looked up from under his desk. "Don't tell me you're still hung up over that near miss with—"

"Nah, man, it's not a hangup. Just call it maturity."

At long last. Trent wished he could say that he'd learned his lesson after his engagement fiasco with Erika, but unfortunately there had been other lessons to be learned.

Ally from Philly taught him to read between the lines— between her lines had been a husband in Chicago whom she'd never bothered to divorce. And Sara had taught him that things weren't always what they seemed. She'd been so sweet, but she needed a steady dose of Prozac to stay that way.

Trent had finally come to terms with the fact that he was a sucker for a pretty face and a good neurosis. When it came to women, he and Robert had one thing in common: bad judgment. He couldn't make his friend wise up, but Trent sure had. Women were like alcohol, a man had to know his limit, and Trent had reached his.

"I give up." Robert flopped down behind his desk. "They're not here!"

Trent leaned against the wall next to a tall potted tree. "What are you—"

Trent squinted as something shiny in the base of the plant caught his eye. He felt around on the soil and his fingers closed around a key ring. He held out his hand. "Could these be what you're looking for?"

Robert jumped up and grabbed the keys. "Aw, man! How did they get in there?" he asked, shaking off the dirt.

Trent just laughed and shrugged.

Robert grabbed his jacket and forced a stack of folders into his briefcase. "I'm sorry I can't stick around to help you get settled, Trent, but I have to be on a job site in ten minutes. When I get back, I'll take you out for a drink."

"No problem, man, I'll be fine. I've got some boxes in the car to unpack."

Robert paused in the doorway. "Cool. Your office is next to mine, and if you have any questions or need anything while I'm gone, Johnny and Jerry run the investigation agency across the hall."

"A detective agency?" Trent raised his eyebrow. "Do I have to worry about dodging stray bullets when I go out in the hall?"

"Nah, man, they're good people. I told them my new partner was moving in today, so when you're done unpacking, go over and say hi. They'll look out for you."

After Robert was gone, Trent retrieved his boxes from the car and unpacked. That took him less than an hour, and without Robert to show him around, there wasn't much for him to do. He decided to introduce himself to the guys across the hall. Working near a detective agency could be interesting.

A perky receptionist greeted him when he entered the office. "Welcome to Sterling & Treymaine. How can we help you?"

Trent shifted his weight from foot to foot. "Uh, I'm Trenton Douglas. I just moved in across the hall."

The petite blonde popped out of her seat and thrust out her

hand. "Nice to meet you, Mr. Douglas. My name's Melanie, but everyone calls me Mel. What can we do for you?"

"Um, is Jerry or Johnny around?"

"Jerry's out of the office, but Johnny's in." She pointed to an open door behind her. "Go right on in."

"Thanks." Trent went over and stood in the doorway.

Inside a woman was bent over, searching through a file cabinet. Probably Johnny's secretary. He knocked on the door frame, and the woman whipped around to face him.

"I'm sorry. I didn't mean to scare you. I'm looking for . . ." His voice trailed off as he studied her.

She looked familiar, but he couldn't quite place the face. Where did he know her from?

She obviously recognized him, too, because she blinked at him with wide eyes and slightly parted lips. "What are you doing here?"

Before he could answer, the file folders she'd been holding slipped through her fingers. She hastily gathered them up and returned them to the drawer, closing the cabinet with an awkward shove. The drawer didn't catch and popped back out, jabbing her in the hip. With a deep sigh, she slammed it shut and turned to face him.

Why would seeing him fluster her like that? She definitely wasn't an old girlfriend. He would have remembered if she had been.

He studied her face. She was watching him with what seemed to be a mixture of shock and . . . dread? Clearly seeing him dredged up unpleasant memories for her. But why? The most unpleasant memories *he* had revolved around Erika.

"Dominique!" The word erupted from his lips before he could stop it. And with the name came the memories.

That wispy purple dress . . .

The hotel lounge . . .

Desire . . .

Betrayal.

"Your name is Dominique, isn't it?" He moved forward.

His question snapped her out of her trance. She moved behind the desk and sat down. "No, actually it's not. It's—"

He stepped closer, nodding his head. "So that was a lie, too, was it? It figures."

The past was in full focus now, and his memory of her was sharp. That night she had easily been one of the most beautiful women he'd ever seen. Gorgeous thick auburn hair that had hung to the middle of her back. Clear cinnamon skin and huge tawny eyes. A vision that had never stopped haunting him.

But she looked so different now. That's why he hadn't made the connection immediately. She was still beautiful, but . . . more subdued. Her long hair was clipped at the nape of her neck, and she was dressed in loose pale gray slacks and a high-collared white silk blouse. No makeup. All she lacked were horn-rimmed glasses to complete the librarian image. Was he seeing the *real* woman now? Or—

"Look, Mr. Douglas, is there something I can do for you?"

He blinked. She remembered his name—and at a time when he could barely remember it himself, let alone why he'd come over in the first place. He certainly hadn't expected to run into the woman who'd helped his ex-fiancée test his fidelity five years ago.

"I'm looking for Johnny."

She took a deep breath. "Well, that would be me."

"What? What kind of scam is this? Did you think you'd get more cases using a man's name?"

"No. My name isn't *Johnny*. It's J-a-u-n-i-e. The J is soft, like in the name Jacques. And before you ask, Geri is short for Geraldine. So as you can see, neither of us are men. Nor do we present ourselves as such. Now was there a reason you were looking for me?"

Trent rubbed his temple. His brain was starting to hurt. "I just moved in across the hall. I'm Robert Payne's new partner. He told me to stop by."

"Oh, yes. He did mention that you were moving in today." Her head was bowed as she fiddled with a pen on her desk.

The situation was getting more awkward by the minute. He

had to get out of there. He stepped back toward the door and collided with someone behind him.

He turned around to face a small woman with frizzy brown hair and wide gray eyes. "Excuse me."

She waved her hand at him. "That's all right, sweetie, you can back into me any day. Jaunie, honey, sorry to interrupt."

"That's okay, Geri—"

"I was just leaving," Trent finished for her. Apparently this new arrival was the second half of Sterling & Treymaine. And as it was, Trent hadn't figured out how to deal with the first half.

Jaunie knew Geri was talking to her, but she could hardly hear her over the loud pounding of her heart. It beat a steady rhythm of *he's back, he's back, he's back.*

She'd thought about Trenton Douglas a lot since she'd left Intimate Investigations, and she would never forget the cold contempt she'd seen in his eyes the night they'd met—the same contempt she'd seen when he looked at her today.

Physically he looked almost exactly as he had before—with dark skin as smooth as burnished wood and a lean, muscular build—but she could see there had been a change in him. He still cocked his head when he talked, but the little-boy quality was gone. Now his eyes were old and wary. Cynical.

Jaunie sighed. Maybe that look was reserved only for her. Maybe the good-natured man she'd met before was still there. She prayed that was true.

After that night she'd tried to find out what happened to him. All she'd discovered was that he'd broken things off with Erika Maxwell and moved to New York, taking a position with a large contracting firm.

She'd hoped he'd moved on and put that night behind him. But she hadn't forgotten it. That night had changed her life.

"Girlfriend, I know you're not listening to me," Geri said in her heavy New York accent as she perched on the edge of Jaunie's desk. "Are you daydreaming about that hunk who just left? Any possibility that you—"

"No, Geri, and I wish you'd stop obsessing over finding me a man. You asked me to warn you when you were acting like your grandmother Goldbloom, so now I'm warning you."

Geri shook her frizzy mass. "Nope, I'm definitely not obsessing. This is just regular concern. Here I am telling you my exciting news, and you're not listening to a word I'm saying. Swear to me that fantastic-looking man who just left is not the reason."

"Okay, I confess, but not for the reasons you think. I promise I'll tell you about it sometime, but right now, I'd really like to hear your news."

"All right, I'll let you off the hook this time, but only because I'm so excited. But I expect a raincheck on Mystery Man."

"You've got it."

Geri leaned close, nearly knocking over a jar of pens with her knee. "The National Center for Missing and Exploited Children is presenting us with a plaque for our outstanding volunteer work."

"That *is* fantastic news." *At least something's going right today.*

"They're having a banquet at the end of the month, and they're inviting all the families that have been reunited this year."

"That's wonderful. It's about time we celebrated the Center's progress, instead of focusing on all the statistics," Jaunie said.

"Exactly, and—"

Mel interrupted over the intercom to say that Geri's daughter, Sam, was on the line.

Geri hopped off Jaunie's desk, unaware that a pad of Post-it Notes was stuck to her skirt. "Sweetie, we'll have to finish this talk later. Sammy's probably having a fit because I forgot to stop by the grocery store, and we don't have any junk food in the house. I'll teach that child to cook yet."

Jaunie snatched the yellow pad from Geri's skirt just before she raced off to talk to her daughter. Sam was actually the reason she and Geri had become partners in the first place. After Jaunie had left Intimate Investigations, she'd been determined to make a new life for herself, to make a difference.

So after a two-year internship with Alan Warren, her former

boss, Jaunie set up Sterling Investigations in a spare bedroom of her apartment. Jobs were scarce at first because she refused to traipse around in the bushes trying to photograph adulterers. She'd seen enough of that line of work to last a lifetime. That decision put finding a neighborhood boy's lost dog at the top of her caseload, a service the twelve-year-old paid for with a collection of baseball cards.

But things turned around when Geraldine Treymaine walked into her makeshift office. Geri had been a hotshot trial attorney who'd just gone through a messy divorce, after which her ex-husband disappeared with their ten-year-old daughter.

Despite her inexperience, Jaunie was devoted to helping Geri. With a little trial and error and team effort, they were able to find Sam and bring her home safely. Afterward Jaunie and Geri decided to become partners.

Jaunie never regretted that decision. She no longer had to worry about being paid with baseball cards, and they were able to rent a real office in the Meridian Building near Dupont Circle. Geri's legal connections kept them busy serving processes and checking out witnesses for many of the smaller D.C. law firms. And when business was slow, they'd agreed to volunteer their services at the NCMEC, the National Center for Missing and Exploited Children.

Jaunie stood with a sigh. The walls of her office were closing in on her. She had to get out and stretch her legs. Maybe she would run downstairs and get a soda. She grabbed a dollar from her purse and let Mel know she'd be right back. When she stepped into the hallway, she saw a workman replacing the sign on the door across the hall. It said PAYNE & DOUGLAS CONTRACTING.

Jaunie took a deep breath. Trenton Douglas was back in her life. Shaking her head, she moved toward the elevators. When would the past stop looking over her shoulder?

Trent hadn't been in a bar for five years, and from what he could see, he hadn't been missing anything. Even though this particular bar was mostly filled with well-dressed professionals who'd stopped in for an after-work drink, the atmosphere still held the same expectant air of singlehood. He could almost smell the desperation.

Women were clustered in groups, watching for hot prospects. Men were watching back, calculating the right time to go in for the kill. Drinks were passed around. Ties were loosened. Hair was let down. It was still a pickup scene—just the kind of scene he'd been avoiding.

Trent looked at his watch just as Robert slid into the booth across from him.

"Thanks for waiting for me, man. The meeting ran longer than I'd expected." He ordered a beer from the waitress, and motioned toward the glass of Cabernet Sauvignon in front of Trent. "I see you started without me, but you have to let me pick up the tab to welcome you properly."

Trent laughed. "Damn right you will. If you weren't paying, I wouldn't be here."

Robert leaned back in the booth. "I stopped upstairs, and I see they finally changed the nameplate on the door. How do you like it, partner? I'd hoped to have it done before you got here."

Trent shrugged. "Looked fine to me." He scanned the bar crowd again, shaking his head. What was he doing here?

Robert slapped the table. "You sure have changed, Trent. What is it? Has New York made you hard? I remember when you used to get hyped up about stuff like that. Right now you look like you'd give your left arm to be anywhere but here. Are you having second thoughts about all this?"

"No. I'm sorry, man, it's not you. It's just being *here.*" He indicated the general bar area. "This isn't me anymore. That combined with—" He stopped short of telling Robert about Jaunie. He didn't feel like going into that right now. He hadn't sorted out his feelings yet. Seeing her was tied up with so many bad memories.

And yet he still wanted her—with the same intensity he'd felt the first time. He resented that a lot.

"Combined with what?" Robert asked.

"Um, just starting over again, you know? I guess I just need some adjustment time."

"Well, that's cool." A wide grin spread over Robert's face. "I have plenty of work to help you *adjust.*"

"That's what I'm here for," Trent said seriously.

Robert shook his head. "Shoot, I was just kidding. I'll loosen you up yet." He rubbed his thumb and forefinger over his neatly trimmed goatee as he eyed a short-skirted beauty at the bar. "As you can see, there are plenty of gorgeous single women in this office building."

Trent frowned, noting the all too familiar glint in Robert's eye that always meant trouble. "Leave me out of this."

"Oh, Lord, Trent—don't tell me you've gone celibate."

"No, but I've learned to resist temptation." He gave his friend a casual look. "Maybe that's a lesson you need to learn."

"Oh, no. Just because you've grown old and boring, don't try to spoil my fun."

Trent just shook his head. It wasn't worth an argument. He just wanted to finish his drink and head home.

"Speaking of gorgeous women, did you meet Jaunie and Geri?"

Trent straightened in his seat. "As a matter of fact I did, briefly. Why didn't you tell me they were women?"

Robert laughed. "Oh, yeah, their names. Sorry, man, I was in such a hurry, it didn't even occur to me to mention it. What did you think? Those two are a trip, aren't they?"

"Yeah." His mind was on Jaunie again.

"I knew you'd like them. Geri is hilarious and Jaunie is so—"

"Yeah, they're great. How was your meeting?"

Trent didn't want to hear Robert talk about Jaunie. Seeing her again had caught him off guard with the same gut-slamming intensity from before.

Apparently a part of Trent still didn't know what was good for him. He drained his half-empty glass of wine and prepared to leave. At this stage in his life, he was in no mood to push his limits.

Chapter Two

Creativity was the key to being a good investigator. That was one of the first things Alan Warren had taught Jaunie during her internship, and it had come in handy more than once since then.

Jaunie got out of her Honda, grabbing a box of art supplies and the envelope containing Ray Grenada's subpoena. In less than five minutes, she'd have this case all wrapped up.

Ray had been dodging this subpoena for six days. It was bad enough that the deadbeat had stiffed his wife on child support payments, but the scum didn't even have the decency to face the courts like a man.

Ray hadn't been home in a week, and no one Jaunie had spoken to knew where he was. Since he was a comic book artist and had no formal place of business, the most useful piece of information Jaunie discovered was where Ray bought his art supplies.

From a young, inexperienced store clerk, she learned that Ray typically had his supplies delivered. So that morning she got up early to ambush the delivery boy. *She* was going to deliver Ray's order—and then some.

Dressed in jeans, a college T-shirt, and a baseball cap that made her look nineteen instead of twenty-nine, Jaunie approached room 105 of the Motel 8. She chuckled, remembering this morning's performance. She'd turned on the charm, and the poor kid hadn't known what hit him. Maybe she should have been an actress.

As soon as the thought had formed, Jaunie rejected it. She hated cameras—of any kind. She quirked her lips in self-derision. She'd probably been the world's only model with a clinical phobia toward public exposure.

With a soft sigh, she knocked on Ray's room.

After several minutes he called through the door, "What the hell do you want?"

"Delivery from Arts Unlimited, sir."

He opened the door, hair tousled, wearing only a pair of jeans. It was nine thirty in the morning, and Ray looked *just* a tiny bit grumpy.

"Are you Ray Grenada?"

"Yeah, but what are you doing here so damn early?"

"Just my job, sir." She thrust the box at him and held a clipboard. "Sign here, please."

He signed, then handed the clipboard back to her.

"Oh, and Mr. Grenada?" She handed him the envelope. "Don't forget this."

He looked down at it with a frown. "What is it?"

"Your subpoena. Have a nice day."

As she left, Ray Grenada was swearing loudly and kicking the door with his bare feet. His swearing quickly turned to howling after he stubbed a toe. He made so much noise, a neighboring door opened. A man holding a pillow over his private parts told him, in very colorful language, to quiet down.

Jaunie grinned as she walked back to her car. No one said justice wasn't painful.

Still in good spirits, Jaunie stopped at Mickey's Cafe for breakfast before returning to the office. She was starving and was looking forward to a leisurely meal of scrambled eggs, toast, sausage, hash browns, coffee, juice and maybe a danish— outdoing lowlifes always made her hungry.

She entered the cafe, humming. Today would be a good day. She could feel it. She approached the counter, studying the blackboard menu and thinking that she *would* have that danish, when something made her turn her head. Her gaze fell on Trent, who was having coffee at a corner table.

Immediately Jaunie's spirits dropped. She quickly turned away, not wanting to see the rejection in his eyes—not wanting to face the fact that he still thought so little of her.

Why did she feel so guilty? She'd only been doing the job she'd been paid to do—the same job she'd performed many times before. But Trent had come to represent something else in her life. He symbolized all the things she'd never had much faith in before, but now valued dearly. That night he'd aroused feelings in her she hadn't known she could have. She'd actually wondered what it might be like to be loved by a man like him. Physically and emotionally. Eternally.

Seeing him now only made her heart ache. She still wondered, and she knew she'd never know.

When the clerk took her order, she asked for a blueberry muffin and coffee to go. Suddenly she wasn't so hungry any-more.

Trent watched Jaunie at the counter. Was it always going to be this awkward?

Since the day he'd moved in, he'd seen her in passing several times, despite the fact that they were blatantly avoiding each other. It was most obvious when they ended up on an elevator alone. They both became fascinated with watching the floor numbers light up. Even now, from across the room, the tension between them was evident.

She'd come in with a pleasant smile on her face, but as soon as she'd caught sight of him, she'd withdrawn into herself. He didn't know what was going on inside *her* head, but when he saw her, he felt about as stable as the crumbling walls of an abandoned building.

He didn't know how to sort through the range of emotions she put him through. How did he separate his attraction for her from his resentment toward her involvement in Erika's scheme?

From his table in the corner, he had a perfect view of her profile as she stared rigidly forward, waiting for her order. Her beautiful brown skin was flawless. Even dressed casually in jeans and a T-shirt, with her ponytail pulled through the back of a baseball cap, she was above-average gorgeous. She had one of those faces he could stare at for hours and never tire of the view.

She turned her head slightly, and for a brief moment, their gazes locked. Then she turned away. In that instant Trent saw her vulnerability. She'd looked like a lost child: innocent.

He massaged his temple, trying to remember why he was holding a grudge against her anyway. Erika was responsible for their fiasco of an engagement, not Jaunie. She'd been paid to do a job, and that's all she'd done. Why was he holding her responsible for all that was wrong in his world?

The fact was, he didn't know her at all. He'd projected all kinds of immoral traits on her without any knowledge of who the real woman was. She was a private investigator—not a hooker.

That night Jaunie had forced him to face a side of himself he hadn't wanted to admit existed. Sure he'd passed Erika's little test, but no one would ever know how close he'd come to failing. For a moment he'd wanted nothing more than to forget Erika and go upstairs with Dominique—*Jaunie.*

Trent frowned. That was his problem. Jaunie had been playing a role. His father raised him too well for a night with "Dominique" to go any farther than his fantasies. But those feelings Jaunie had stirred up, the feelings that had tempted him, were obviously one-sided. And even though Jaunie had been acting, Trent's fantasies were real.

He'd felt a genuine connection with her. They'd seemed to have so much in common. But of course they had. Erika had spoon-fed Jaunie his preferences from his favorite scent to his political views. He should have known better than to believe any woman could come that close to perfection.

Trent sighed as Jaunie left the cafe. What was the *real* Jaunie Sterling like?

Twenty minutes before her lunch hour, Jaunie tapped on Geri's door.

"Yeah, what?" Geri's irritated voice penetrated the solid oak.

Jaunie poked her head in. "Excu-use me! Where's all this attitude coming from?"

Geri's head popped up from behind her computer monitor. "Sorry, honey. I'm having one hell of a morning."

Jaunie stepped into the office and shut the door behind her. "What's going on?"

"Oy!" She slapped her forehead, causing her wild hair to bounce around her head like the fronds of the fern plant on her desk. "What's *not* going on? First of all, I'm trying to write the speech for our awards dinner Friday night, and trust me, I am *not* feeling inspired right now."

Jaunie sat down. "Come on, Geri, this should be a snap. This can't compare to writing the closing arguments for a trial."

Geri shook her head. "I've got other things on my mind right now."

"Like what?"

"You'll never believe what Sam, *my* little Sammy, asked me last night."

Jaunie grinned. "Judging by the look on your face, it must have been about sex."

"Yes! Can you believe it?" Geri hunkered over the keyboard again, muttering, "Thirteen! My baby's only thirteen, and already she wants to know how old you have to be to have sex!"

Jaunie snickered. "What did you tell her?"

Geri pounded on the keyboard viciously. "I told her thirty! Whattaya want me to say?"

"Thirty, huh?" Jaunie nodded, contemplating that answer. "That works for me. It means I've still got another year before I have to worry that I'm missing something. Sam, on the other hand, might not be satisfied with that answer for too long."

Geri rolled her eyes heavenward. "Don't I know. I thought I'd already taken care of this. Sam and I had the old 'birds and the bees' talk a couple years ago. Then her reaction had been 'Eew, Ma, I'm never doing *that!*' Bless her heart. I was so proud of her."

Jaunie laughed. "Well, I sympathize. Kids are growing up so fast these days. The amount of useful information my mother gave me about sex wouldn't fill a thimble. I got the unabridged version from my best friend, Nina, in junior high. She was such an exaggerator, it was two years before I believed her."

"Oh, my God." Geri slammed her fist on the desk. "Who knows what those hellions at that school are filling her head with? My poor Sammy. I wish I knew what to tell her."

"You know, there's this great book to help parents with just that kind of thing. It's called *Let's Talk About Sex,* just like the Salt-N-Pepa song."

"Salt and pepper? What do seasonings have to do with me telling my child she's too young for sex?"

"Salt-N-Pepa is a female rap group, but never mind that. I saw the author of this book on the "Dirk Preston Show" last week. He wrote *Let's Talk About Sex* to help parents give their kids the right message about sex."

Geri raised her eyebrows. "Sounds good. At this point I'll try anything."

"Great. There's a bookstore on the other side of Dupont Circle. I'm meeting my sister for lunch, and if you join us, we could pick up the book on the way."

Geri typed as she talked. "Sorry, sweetie. I wish I could, but I have to finish this speech in record time. I need to pick Sam up from summer school. Then I have to chase down a witness in a hit-and-run case for H&B."

"Okay, then I can stop in and pick up the book if they have it. You can pay me back later."

"Oh, you're a dear. That would be fabulous," Geri said, not lifting her head as she continued to type.

"I think it should be really helpful. On the show Dr. Marino—I think that's his name—said the book helps parents bridge the generation gap so that children can explore their questions about sexuality in a safe environment."

Jaunie saw Geri's head bob from behind the monitor. "Great, Jaunie. See ya later, honey."

"I'll be back in a little over an hour." She was turning to leave the office when Geri shrieked.

Jaunie spun around. "What's wrong? What happened? Did your computer crash? What?"

Geri slapped her forehead. "What did I just do?" She shook her head. "I'm going to stand before the representatives of the NCMEC and say, 'In closing, ladies and gentlemen, my partner and I would like to thank you for this special honor, but our true reward is knowing that *children can explore their questions about sexuality in a safe environment.*'"

Jaunie covered her mouth to stifle her laughter. "With a closing line like that, we'd be sure to make the front page of the *Washington Post*. But keep at it. I think you left out a few buzz words like 'drugs' and 'rock and roll.'"

Jaunie ducked out of the office just as Geri's pencil hit the door.

Trent stopped short at the top of the mystery aisle in Olsson's Bookstore. Was he running into Jaunie so often because she was on his mind? Or was she on his mind because he was running into her so much?

She had her back to him as she examined two best-selling thrillers. Trent grinned. Apparently they had the same taste in reading material. He'd recently read both of those books.

That would be a good way to break the tension between them. He could just walk up behind her and . . .

Why was he so nervous? Even when he'd bothered to approach women in the past, it had never been this difficult. He hung back for a moment, giving himself time to clear his head.

Jaunie was reading the back cover of another mystery now. She no longer wore the baseball cap, but her hair was still in a ponytail. As she bent her head, the ends of her ponytail curled just enough to tickle her neck.

It was a long, graceful neck. He could see his lips tracing the area where her ponytail brushed her smooth, cinnamon skin. Her hair would graze his face as he kissed . . .

Trent blinked. What was he doing lurking between book racks like some deranged stalker, fantasizing about a woman he barely knew? This was crazy.

Trent walked up to Jaunie and reached out to tap her on the shoulder just as she spun around. She smacked into his chest, the books in her arms scattering at their feet.

"Oh, my goodness." For a minute Jaunie just stared open-mouthed at Trent.

He reached out to steady her. "Sorry. I was just looking for something to read on my lunch break, and I saw you looking at one of my favorite books. I wanted to tell you, it's a must read."

Jaunie took a shaky breath. "Oh? Which one?"

"Deadly Sins, by J. D. Fitzwater. It's a great P.I. murder mystery."

"Yeah? P.I. mysteries are the only kind I read. I like to see how accurate they are."

"Well, after you read it, you'll have to let me know what you think."

"Sure. I was going to buy it anyway. I couldn't resist. I just came in here to—" Her eyes widened, then she quickly bent to retrieve her books.

Trent crouched beside her. "Let me help you."

They both reached for the book closest to his foot and both froze as he read the title, *Let's Talk About Sex.*

He raised an inquiring gaze, but Jaunie's head was bowed as she stacked the two mystery novels on top of it.

"Um, thanks," she mumbled, springing to her feet.

Before Trent recovered, Jaunie was standing in the checkout line.

Slowly he stood, watching her back as she hurried from the store. Trent cocked his head. Why was Jaunie buying a book on *sex?*

Her face still stinging with the heat of embarrassment, Jaunie plunked herself down at Simone's table in the restaurant.

She smiled brightly for her sister's benefit, but inside she cringed. Trent had actually been warming up to her, and she'd ruined everything with that stupid book. Who knew what kind of crazy thoughts were floating through his mind now? He'd already accused her of being some kind of hooker once in this lifetime.

"Sorry I'm late," she said breathlessly.

Simone eyed Jaunie's bag. "Where were you? Unfortunately that bag's too small for new clothes."

"I had to pick up something at the bookstore for Geri. It took longer than I expected."

"Look at you." Simone shook her head at Jaunie's T-shirt and jeans. "Did you actually wear *that* to work?"

Jaunie shrugged. "I had to wear this for a case." She paused, feeling a wistful pang as she took in Simone's Anne Klein pantsuit. "What's wrong with my clothes?"

"Sweetheart, have you looked in your closet lately? You're starting to dress like an old woman. Sensible shoes. Long-sleeved blouses with high necklines. Baggy pants. And I remember the days when you wouldn't be caught dead in a pair of jeans."

"So?"

Her older sister leaned forward. "So you *used* to be so stylish. You kept up with the latest fashions. You wore makeup."

Jaunie sighed. Simone had always been the more serious and

conservative of the two, so it was strange to hear her give lectures on fashion. "I was a model. I had to dress well."

"No, you had it going on even before Mother got you into modeling."

Tall, slim, and just as beautiful, Simone could have been a model herself, but with her straight A's and after-school activities, she'd been more resistant to their mother's vicarious fantasies of glamour.

Jaunie picked up her menu. "Do you know what you're going to order?"

Simone reached over and closed Jaunie's menu. "Don't try and change the subject."

Jaunie looked Simone in the eye. "I think I'll have the tortellini with creamed tomato sauce."

Simone shook her head and opened her menu. "I don't understand what you're doing to yourself. At first I thought you were going through a phase, but you're getting worse."

"Please, Simone, don't start this again."

"Look, I really admire what you and Geri are doing at the agency. I've already told you that the PTA at Maya's school wants you both to come back this year to speak to parents about child safety. But, believe it or not, there *is* life outside of work."

Jaunie breathed a sigh of relief when the waiter arrived to take their orders. She and Simone were having conversations like this more and more frequently. Jaunie always counted on Simone to keep her grounded, but now that her life had taken a more serious turn, Simone and Geri tried continuously to introduce her to men, or talk her into splurging on a new outfit, or take her out on the town. Jaunie knew they cared about her, but she was perfectly satisfied with her life the way it was— for the most part.

The waiter left them, and Jaunie spoke before Simone could pick up where she'd left off. "So what's new in *your* life," she asked, bracing herself for cute anecdotes about her sister's perfect marriage or her perfect kids. Simone had all those perfect things Jaunie thought she'd never have, things she'd thought she never wanted, until—

"I talked to Karina last week."

Jaunie perked up. Karina Warren was Simone's best friend, and the wife of Jaunie's former boss, Alan Warren. "Really? How's she doing? I haven't talked to Alan in a while."

Simone pushed her fingers through her short curls with a sigh. "Well, it's not good news. Apparently they're having marital problems. Karina didn't want to elaborate, but she did say they're trying to work things out. If you do talk to Alan, don't mention anything."

"Of course not."

She'd known Karina most of her life through Simone, and after she'd given up modeling, Jaunie had met Alan at a welcome home party Simone threw for her. That had been a difficult time for Jaunie, and when Alan approached her about working for him at Intimate Investigations, she was still trying to sort through her life.

At first she'd hated the idea of working as a decoy, but six years of modeling had changed her from a shy girl embarrassed by her mother's lifestyle, to a jaded woman who no longer believed in fairy tales. After the things she saw her mother go through, combined with her own experiences with men, Jaunie ceased to believe that any man was capable of fidelity. That fact made it easier for Alan to convince her that she was doing her gender a favor by exposing their mates as the cheats they were.

The waiter returned, placing two huge plates of pasta before them. "Guess who called this morning?" Simone asked.

Jaunie shrugged.

"Ramona. She wanted to tell me all about her new boyfriend—"

"Marcus," they both said in unison.

"I know," Jaunie said, nodding. "Mother called me, too."

The sisters always referred to their mother as Ramona when they gossiped about her. It was their way of mocking the period when she'd insisted on changing her name from Ramona to

Raven. For several years she wouldn't even answer to Mom because it didn't suit her "inner spirit."

The sudden name change and Jaunie's involvement in modeling at age fourteen had been just two of the many symptoms of her mother's midlife crisis.

Simone took a sip of her Perrier. "This week Mother would be a candidate for the *Geraldo* episode entitled 'Deadbeat Lovers and Their Middle-aged Girlfriends.' "

Jaunie giggled. "Well that beats last year's 'Women Who Date Their Chauffeurs' episode. But she dumped Trevor when her credit cards got out of hand. I think Marcus will suffer the same fate when the Saks bill comes in."

Jaunie wished she were more like Simone, but she couldn't deny that she was really more like her mother. It was no surprise to Jaunie that the past few years of *her* life could be summed up with topics like "My Mother Dresses too Sexy and Parties Till Dawn, and I Hate It," followed by "I Grew Up too Fast, and Now I Regret It," and finally "Men Are Lying Cheats So I Help Trap Them for Money."

Jaunie had come a long way since then, but she still thought she had a long way to go before she would be satisfied.

Friday evening Trent and Robert left the office together and headed for the elevators.

"I've got to admit, buddy," Robert said, slinging his duffel bag over his shoulder. "Helping you remove wallpaper is not my idea of an exciting Friday night."

Trent punched the DOWN arrow for the elevators. "What are you whining about? For weeks you've begged me to let you see the house."

Robert let out a low whistle of appreciation, and Trent turned to see Jaunie round the corner wearing an incredible ivory evening dress.

It fell to her ankles but traced every curve along the way, letting one of her shapely legs peek out from a long slit on the side. The neckline and sleeves were made of some gauzy, see-through material, giving the dress a dual image—both sexy and demure, provocative and virginal. The white dress taunted him with its purity at the same time as it crooked a finger to beckon him.

"Mm-mm-*mmm*. Lady, you look gorgeous." Robert smacked his lips.

Trent narrowed his eyes at Robert's enthusiasm, but had to admit she did look stunning. Her makeup was artfully done, and her long thick hair fell in huge waves around her face. She looked perfect—just like the night . . .

Trent's body went numb, and before he knew it, his lips were moving. "Big night? I hope you didn't forget to wear his favorite perfume." He scanned her insultingly from head to toe. "But I don't need to tell you that. I'm sure that book you bought the other day taught you everything you need for tonight."

Robert made a choking sound from behind him.

Jaunie's facial muscles tensed, and her eyes hardened, but she showed no other reaction to his cruel words.

Trent was somewhat stunned himself. Behavior like that was completely against his nature. Where had the words come from? "Um . . ." He struggled to find some way to take them back.

Behind him the elevator chimed, and the doors slid open. Trent entered, and Robert held the door. "Are you coming, Jaunie?"

She stepped back. "I think I'll take the stairs."

Robert shook his head and moved his hand to let the doors close. Neither of them punched a floor, so the elevator didn't move.

Robert slapped a hand to his forehead. "Trent, man, what the hell is wrong with you?" He continued to shake his head. "I can't even believe you said those things to Jaunie."

Trent merely stared at the closed doors. "I didn't tell you that Jaunie is the woman Erika hired to set me up five years ago. She worked for some other investigation agency then."

Robert just leaned against the wall, watching him coldly.

Trent shrugged. "What can I say? I guess seeing her all dressed up like that brought everything back."

Robert sighed heavily.

Trent pressed on, trying to rationalize his irrational behavior. "I mean she walks around here in plain clothes and no makeup. Where else could she be going looking like that?"

Robert hit the button for the lobby and the elevator began to descend. "She's going to a banquet where she and Geri are being honored for their volunteer work for the National Center for Missing and Exploited Children."

The elevator stopped at the lobby with a final dip, but Trent's stomach kept plunging.

He'd just made a very big mistake.

Chapter Three

"This is it." Trent led Robert into the master bedroom of the house he'd been renovating, where an expanse of lime green and silver wallpaper covered all four walls.

"Tacky stuff." Robert picked up a small tool with a wheel of teeth used to score the paper. "Let's do this."

Trent winced. Robert was not the type to get right down to business. The fact that he passed up the opportunity to joke about the offensive paper spoke volumes.

After they covered the wallpaper surface with holes, they used garden sprayers filled with a hot water solution to wet down the paper. Forty-five minutes passed, and Trent's best friend of sixteen years had yet to look him in the eye.

"You're still ticked off at me, aren't you?" Trent finally asked.

"Okay." Robert stopped stripping the paper to give Trent a hard look. "Since you want to talk, why don't you tell me what the hell your problem is? At first I thought you just needed time to adjust, but the fact is, you've changed."

Trent crossed the tarpaulin covering the hard wood floor and stopped in front of Robert. "I know I should have explained about Jaunie sooner, but she caught me off guard." He paced over to the window and back. "I mean, what are the odds of me moving across the hall from the woman my ex-fiancée hired to hit on me years ago? It's crazy," he said, fingering his putty knife. "Trust me, I plan to apologize for the things I said to her tonight."

Robert readjusted the backward baseball cap he wore. "I know you will. I'm sure that whole thing with Jaunie was rough, but the problem isn't just tonight. It's you. You're a completely different person. You don't seem to care about anything besides work and this damn house."

Trent released a deep sigh. He'd started this renovation project to help him get his head together. He'd been working on it since early spring, just over three months, but this was the first time he'd included Robert. That must be the problem. "I know I've been doing my own thing lately, but—"

"Did something happen in New York that you don't want to tell me about?" Robert stepped forward, lowering his voice. "Trent, we're like brothers. You can talk to me."

Trent drew his eyebrows together. Where was *this* coming from? Maybe he was a little more low-key than he used to be, but since when was that a crime? "No, nothing happened. Why are you making such a big deal out of nothing?"

Robert studied him closely. "You really can't see it, can you?"

"See what?"

"How different you are. We used to play practical jokes on each other all the time, but last week when I programmed your computer to moan in ecstasy every time your phone rings, you barely cracked a smile. Anytime I ask you to hang out, you make excuses. You never go out on dates. And when I asked you if we should go after the Grovesnor Health Food contract, you said, 'Why bother? We don't stand a chance.' A few risks never would have stopped you before." Robert shook his head. "I don't know, it's like . . . you're just going through the motions."

Robert's last phrase made Trent pause. His mother had said

something similar. And come to think of it, so had his sister, Kendall. She'd said he was watching life from the sidelines instead of getting in the game. Kendall sometimes used sports metaphors since her husband was a professional football player. But what did *she* know?

Obviously more than he did. Trent looked at Robert. "You really think I'm that different?"

Robert nodded. "Yeah. Trent, you're like an old man— tired. I was thinking about getting a rocking chair for your office."

"I guess I hadn't noticed." Trent turned to his side of the wall and began attacking the paper with his putty knife. Suddenly he felt as naked as the drywall he was exposing. "In New York it's so easy to fade into the background—and a lot of the time, that's exactly what I wanted to do. No hassles. Just go to work, come home, and do the same thing the next day. Simple. I guess a little too simple. In New York I didn't have any family or close friends to pull me back, or to keep me grounded. I guess gradually I just lost touch."

He heard Robert wrestling with the paper behind him. Trent looked over his shoulder. "Man, I'm sorry if you thought I'd been dissing you. I'm just out of the habit of being social."

Robert stopped to give him the same wicked grin that had nearly gotten them suspended many a time in college. "That's okay, my man. You've come to the right place. I'll have you back in the swing of things in no time."

"Take it easy, bro. I'm in enough trouble already." He turned to the wall again. "I can't believe I said those things to Jaunie."

"You want her, don't you?"

Trent almost dropped his putty knife. "What?"

"Admit it. A brother doesn't make that much of an ass of himself over a woman, unless he wants to get in her—"

"Hold it right there. I'm not looking for that kind of trouble. I've had more than my fair share already."

Robert snorted. "I don't believe you for one minute. But for the sake of argument, it's just as well you leave it at friends.

She's a tough nut to crack. I speak from experience. If I couldn't get anywhere with her, I don't know what she'd want with your ugly behind."

Trent just rolled his eyes.

"Seriously though, if you want me to put a word in, explain about tonight or something, let me know. Geri and Jaunie are my buddies. The three of us are pretty tight."

"Thanks, man, but I think I'd better fix this myself." *If that's possible.*

Monday morning Geri and Jaunie surveyed the reception area skeptically.

"Maybe we should hang it outside the door," Geri suggested, examining the wall next to their nameplate.

Jaunie frowned. "I don't know. That might be too pretentious."

"You two have been trying to find a place for that plaque for twenty minutes," Mel called from her desk. "Do you want my opinion?"

"Sure," Jaunie and Geri both answered.

"Why don't you hang it on the wall behind my desk? That way everyone will see it as soon as they come in."

Jaunie and Geri looked at each other.

"That sounds good," Jaunie said.

"Yeah," Geri agreed. "I think that will work."

After Geri had nailed the plaque in the appropriate spot, they all stood back to admire it.

"It looks great, ladies. How did the banquet go Friday night?" Mel asked.

Jaunie gave Geri a teasing grin. "Geri's speech was fantastic. She held everyone's attention—without mentioning sex once."

Geri playfully swatted at Jaunie's arm. "Seriously, it was such an emotional night. Everyone was hugging and crying. It reminded me of my last birthday." She tilted her head. "Never mind, that was mostly crying. Anyway the banquet was great."

"Yeah. Great," Jaunie said softly, turning toward her office.

"I've got some paperwork to finish up. I'll talk to you guys later."

She wasn't really in the mood to reminisce about Friday night. That evening had been full of surprises, and they'd started before she'd even gotten to the banquet.

She'd tried to convince herself that it didn't matter if Trent thought she was no better than a cheap hooker. She'd gone to the banquet determined to have fun and bask in the attention Sterling & Treymaine was finally receiving, but it had been harder than she'd thought.

The way Trent's eyes had raked over her dress cut her more deeply than his words. If it weren't late July, Jaunie would have worn a coat all night. She never would have bought that ivory gown if Simone hadn't talked her into it.

Jaunie sat down behind her computer and was staring at a blank monitor when Geri entered her office.

"Okay, kid, it's time for you to spill your guts. You've been out of it lately. What's going on?"

Jaunie shrugged. Where should she start?

Geri scooted onto the edge of Jaunie's desk—her favorite spot. It was a good thing Jaunie kept her desktop clear most of the time, because Geri preferred it to the office chairs.

"Look, sweetie, that look on your face says the problem has to be a man. Is it Robert's new partner? That sexy man you've been avoiding like the plague?"

It was that obvious? With a heavy sigh, Jaunie began to explain her history with Trent, starting from the night in the hotel lounge and ending with his caustic remarks before the banquet.

"That rat!" Geri pounded on Jaunie's desk. "No wonder you were in such a mood. Alan asked me what was bothering you, but I didn't know what to tell him."

"He asked me, too. I didn't mean to bring you down."

"So what are you going to do about this guy?" Geri picked up the calendar on the desk and began tearing off the extra days Jaunie hadn't gotten around to tearing off yet. "You must feel something for him, or his opinion wouldn't matter so much.''

Jaunie flopped back in her chair. "I think what I feel for him is still mixed up somewhere in the past. We connected that night, and within minutes that connection dissolved. I guess I'm just caught up wishing things had turned out differently. If I could resolve the past with him, I could put this whole thing behind me."

Geri set the calendar down, tossing her frizzy mane. "Then do it. Confront him."

"Oh, no." Jaunie sank lower in her chair. "Why go looking for trouble?"

Geri put her hands on her hips, straightening her small frame. "Jaunie, you have to look at this with your head and not your heart. You were doing a job. You are *not* a hooker. You're a successful businesswoman, and he has no right to treat you any differently!" She slapped her palm on the desk. "I say it's high time you gave him a piece of your mind for his childish behavior. After all, who does he think he is, walking around with a high and mighty attitude?"

Jaunie blinked, sitting erect in her chair. Geri was right! She didn't deserve treatment like this. "You know, Geri, you have a point. I've been letting him get away with murder. I should go over there and tell him off."

Now that she'd made up her mind, Jaunie's blood was burning. She had to confront him immediately. She was already out of her chair and headed for the door when Geri stopped her.

"Wait a second. Before you go give him what-for, we have one more thing to get settled."

"What?" Jaunie's shoulders slumped.

"The talk show offer. Are we going to take it?"

"Oh, yeah, we *should* talk about that," Jaunie said, somewhat disappointed as she sat back down. She had to take a deep breath to get her mind back on track. "Okay, what do you think?"

The banquet had received a lot of media coverage, and a representative from the *Dirk Preston Show,* a local cable show, approached them about appearing on a segment they were putting together on missing children.

"I think it could be great publicity for the Center. I was talking to Jeff Campbell last night about trying to get more people involved," Geri said.

"It does sound like a great way to help the Center, and I really think Sterling & Treymaine should be represented—but only if I don't have to go."

"What?" Geri swiveled on the desk and nearly fell off. "Why not?"

"I don't want to be in the spotlight."

"That doesn't make sense. You used to be a model."

"Exactly. I've been interviewed on TV before, and I hated it." She shook her head at the memory. "They always ask nosey, personal questions—as if they have the right to know what I wear to bed."

"I understand, but this kind of show is different. Besides, they don't care about us or our personal lives. This is about the children. We'll talk about the process of finding missing kids, what we do, and tell others how they can get involved. There won't be time to talk about anything else."

Jaunie sighed. She just didn't feel comfortable with the idea.

"Come on, Jaunie. We'll both be there. This will also be great for business."

"Okay, fine." She didn't want to be selfish and let her petty worries interfere with what was best for the children, or for business. "Let's do it."

"Great." Geri jumped down from the desk. "Now you can go. And when you get back, I want details, sweetie. Don't leave out a thing."

"You've got it." But now that Jaunie had been given some time to cool down, she wasn't sure just what she would say to Trent. She didn't want Geri to know that she'd lost her nerve, so she stood in the hallway staring at the door of Payne & Douglas Contracting.

And then it opened.

Jaunie didn't know who might walk through, but she didn't

want to get caught lingering. The elevators were to the left, the bathrooms were to the right. Which way was she headed?

She must not have made her decision fast enough, because she'd barely taken a step to the right when Robert, thank God it was *Robert,* called her name.

She turned around. "Hi, what's . . ." The sympathy in his eyes made her pause.

"Look, Jaunie," he said, patting her shoulder. "I'm really sorry about what happened Friday night."

Jaunie felt embarrassment brand her cheeks. "Oh, please don't—"

"If it makes you feel any better," he continued. "I took Trent down to the basement and smacked him around a little. He's come to his senses now."

Jaunie looked toward the door. "Is he in there?"

"Trent? Yeah, he's in there. I've got a meeting in Adams Morgan, but when I get back, I'll stop by and see you and Geri. We all haven't gotten together in a while."

"Yeah, sure. See you later," Jaunie answered, but she was no longer listening. Robert had just reminded her why she'd been so angry.

Not only had Trent humiliated her, he'd had the nerve to do it in front of a good friend. He had no right to treat her like that, and she was going to tell him so.

When she walked into Payne & Douglas Contracting, she could see that Trent's presence hadn't made much impact on Robert's haphazard decorating style. The outer office was still bare and without a receptionist.

She walked in farther, and she could see Trent in the office on the left. He was on the telephone.

Not wanting to lose her nerve, she focused her attention directly on him, walked straight into his office, and stood before his desk.

Trent looked up at her in surprise, then turned back to the phone. "I think I'm going to have to give you a call back on that, okay? Great, thanks. Bye."

The phone clicked into the cradle, but before Trent could open his mouth, Jaunie held up her hand.

"I've got a few things to say to you, and I think you'd better listen. I am a hardworking woman who runs her own business. Now *I* think that deserves some respect. But for some reason, you, Mr. High and Mighty, have on more than one occasion equated my work with some new form of prostitution."

Trent's eyes widened. "I di—"

Jaunie held up a hand to halt Trent's words. "You're entitled to your opinions, no matter how closed-minded they may be, but that doesn't give you the right to humiliate me in front of Robert. Now he feels sorry for me."

"Jaunie—"

She placed her hands on her hips. "I am sorry if your life is so dull that you can't get over the past, but five years ago I was hired to do a job, and that is *all* I did."

He held up a finger. "I—"

"And to think *I* felt guilty," she said, shaking her head. "Worrying that maybe you'd turned into this cynical jerk because of me. But now I'm starting to realize that you were probably a jerk to begin with."

Trent gave up trying to interrupt and leaned back, crossing his arms over his chest, waiting for her to finish.

Well, good, Jaunie thought, he had this coming, and she wasn't going to stop until she'd said her piece.

She put both hands on his desk and leaned in close. "So, Mr. Douglas, if it adds some spice to your life to make up wild fantasies about what I'm up to, you go right ahead. But keep them to yourself. The rest of us are busy living in the *real* world."

Trent let out a heavy sigh. "Are you finished?"

Jaunie nodded smugly, smoothing her palms over her pale blue dress. She'd done it! She'd stood up for herself, and nothing he could say now could take away that triumph.

Trent stood. "Then Jaunie Sterling, please let me introduce you to my mother, Mrs. Marilyn Douglas."

Jaunie's jaw dropped as she slowly turned to find a lovely,

copper-skinned older woman sitting on a folding chair in back of Trent's office. His *mother!*

So much for her moment of triumph. Jaunie was so embarrassed, she wanted to run from the building and keep going until she reached Montana. But such a dramatic exit would only make things worse.

When Jaunie found herself in bad situations, it helped to close her eyes and remember what it was like to walk down a runway—in the spotlight. The catwalk vibrating from the funky music that pulsed from king-sized speakers. Brilliant swirling lights. Flash bulbs exploding from every direction. All eyes trained on her. With those memories Jaunie knew she could survive any situation she needed to face.

Nothing in her life could be more God-awful or nerve-wracking than runway modeling had been.

With a bright smile, Jaunie held out her hand to Trent's mother, meeting her eyes with feigned confidence. "It's a pleasure to meet you, Mrs. Douglas."

"It's nice to meet you, too." Her brown eyes returned Jaunie's gaze with gentle humor. Those eyes held the strongest resemblance between mother and son, but Jaunie doubted she'd ever receive such a warm look from Trent.

"Forgive me for not being able to stay and visit with you longer," Jaunie continued, "but I have to get back to work. I'm sure you understand."

With a curt nod in Trent's general vicinity, Jaunie walked out of the office, holding her breath until she was safely outside the doors of Payne & Douglas Contracting.

Trent had already rounded the desk and was moving through the doorway when he heard his mother clear her throat. He gripped the door frame for a second before he slowly turned to face her.

"Not so fast, Trenton." Smiling sweetly, his mother smoothed the skirt of her green silk dress and sat back down on the chair. "Do you mind telling me what that was all about? What did you do to get that poor girl all fired up?"

With a sigh, Trent sat in a visitor's chair and spun to face his mother. "It's complicated, Mom."

Smiling pleasantly, she crossed her legs and folded her hands over her knee, waiting for him to continue. She was the picture of demure motherly grace, but Trent knew if he didn't come up with a satisfactory explanation for what had just occurred, she would let him have it.

No one would have guessed from looking at her that this delicately refined woman had a feisty streak. He'd seen her tell off obnoxious sales clerks without raising her voice or breaking her smile, but her words had maximum impact because no one ever saw the storm coming. Growing up, Trent's only warning that he was about to be scolded was the ever so slight lifting of her left eyebrow.

"Jaunie works across the hall," Trent said, watching her brows closely. "It was just a misunderstanding."

"Really?" Her smile never wavered, but her brow twitched. "And what was this about prostitution?"

Heat scorched the tips of his ears. There was no way for him to explain this without sounding like an ass. He massaged his temple, trying to choose his words judiciously. "Jaunie is a private investigator, and on occasion she has to dress a certain way for cases."

Trent looked over at his mother to see if she could tell where he was going with this. She continued to smile pleasantly as if they were discussing the advantages of knitting versus crocheting. She'd make one hell of a poker player.

"Since I'm not used to seeing her dressed that way—" He didn't bother mentioning that he was talking about an evening gown and not leather garter belts. She was going to think he'd lost his mind as it was. "—I may have made an uncomplimentary remark about her plans for the evening. I never said she was a prostitute, though."

There went the eyebrow.

"You're lucky that poor child didn't come in here with a

broomstick and crack you on the head. If she were my daughter, that would have been my advice. What's gotten into you, Trenton? Your father and I didn't raise you to act like that.''

"Mom, I know I was out of line, and I have every intention of making it up to her."

She looked at him with the same air of wisdom she'd had when she told him he and Erika would never last. "You were jealous, weren't you?"

"What?"

"You were jealous of whoever you thought Jaunie was going to visit with. Don't give me that look, Trenton. I know you. You like her."

Trent rolled his eyes. "Come on, Mom. I had a bad day. I took it out on someone I shouldn't have. Don't try to turn this into more than it is."

She smiled smugly. "Okay, son. When you're ready to listen to me, you just let me know. Your father and I have been married for thirty-eight years. I know about these things."

"Yeah, Mom. I know." He was ready for this conversation to be over.

"When Kendall brought Maurice home, I knew right away that they were perfect together. Now look at them—they've been married going on four years."

Trent nodded absently as he moved behind his desk and sat down.

"It's always in the eyes," his mother continued. "And it was there with Jaunie a few moments ago."

Trent looked up. "What did you see in Jaunie's eyes?"

She winked at him. "Not in *her* eyes, son. Yours."

Trent looked away. "If you're saying I look at Jaunie with love, then you're way off. I don't even know the woman."

"No, that's not what I'm saying. But I do see potential there. While she was telling you off—once you got over the initial shock—you were enjoying every minute of it. You were fascinated by her every move. Now we both know that this could lead to something more."

Trent swallowed hard—not if he could help it. He would

apologize to her, but that would be it. "Something more" was the last thing he wanted.

"Now about Robert." His mother leaned forward with the same excitement lighting her eyes that came whenever she started a new quilting project. "That poor boy hasn't got the good sense God gave an ant when it comes to women. You tell him to give me a call."

Jaunie was just leaving the ladies' room when Trent came out of his office. She hurried toward the doors of Sterling & Treymaine, keeping her gaze trained on the carpet.

"Jaunie, wait."

Oh, Lord. She blew her breath out through her teeth as she turned to face him. *Here it comes.*

She had to do a double-take when she found him watching her rather sheepishly. It was a good look for him. Then again, she had yet to see him with a look he didn't wear well.

"I do owe you an apology." He laughed nervously. "And believe it or not, I'd intended to offer it before you came across the hall to remind me."

Jaunie's cheeks warmed.

"Nevertheless," he said, his left hand furiously massaging his temple, "there's no excuse for what I said to you Friday. Robert explained that I had the situation all wrong. And even if I'd been right, it's not my place to judge you. You don't deserve that kind of treatment. I hope you can forgive me."

Jaunie had to force herself not to be distracted by the movement of his fingers as they circled his temple. Those *hands.* She'd always thought fetishes were weird, but at that moment, if she had to choose a body part to fixate on . . . well, Trent's hands would be her second choice. First choice would have to be his firm, round—

Oops! He was watching her expectantly.

"Um, I accept. Your apology, I mean."

"Thanks." He smiled almost shyly. "Now that I've been properly chastised in front of my mother, I hope we can call it even. She said I was lucky that you didn't come in with a broomstick and crack me over the head. Believe me, she was on your side.''

''Tell her I'm sorry for making such a scene.''

''Oh, no. She thought it was great''—Trent waved off her apology—''and I had it coming.''

Jaunie wasn't going to argue that point. They both stood looking at each other, and the silence began to grow awkward.

''I wish I could give you a better explanation for my behavior, but again, I'm sorry.''

Jaunie nodded her thanks. Trent nodded back. Then they each turned back to their respective offices.

During the course of the week, the atmosphere between Jaunie and Trent became warmer but no less awkward. Now when they met in the elevator or passed on the street, they could at least manage small talk about the weather or sports. But usually those brief conversations were exchanged while they studied their shoes or admired the wallpaper. At least the tense silences and guarded looks had disappeared, and Jaunie was satisfied with that.

Other than the typical law firm cases that kept Geri out of the office most of the week, business was fairly slow at Sterling & Treymaine—until Friday afternoon.

''Jaunie,'' Mel's cheerful voice came over the intercom. ''A Mr. and Mrs. Lincoln are here to see you.''

Jaunie's adrenaline kicked in. A new case! ''Send them in, Mel.''

When the couple entered her office, Jaunie stood and extended her hand. ''Mr. and Mrs. Lincoln, I'm Jaunie Sterling.''

''Please call me Patrice,'' Mrs. Lincoln said, reaching for Jaunie's hand. ''And this is Richard.'' Patrice nodded toward her husband, who silently took a seat in one of the chairs in front of Jaunie's desk.

Richard Lincoln appeared to be in his late forties. His crewcut style hair was sprinkled with gray, and the hard lines grooved into the dark skin around his mouth and eyes made him look rigid and intimidating. He wasn't handsome, but he was impeccably dressed. Some people knew food, some people knew cars—Jaunie knew clothes. Richard's Armani suit was the real thing, not like the cheap knockoffs she'd seen on many of the men who worked in the building.

Patrice Lincoln looked about Jaunie's age, late twenties or early thirties. Her dress was expensive as well, Donna Karan, but on her thin frame, the designer original drooped as if it were hanging from a coat rack. Her nervous shifting and fidgeting showed her discomfort in the expensive dress.

Despite the awkward fit of her clothing and careless style of her hair, Patrice was an attractive woman. Her coffee-colored skin was incredibly smooth, and her wide, expressive eyes were the color of golden honey. She had the look of an unfinished painting that could double its value with just a few thoughtful brush strokes.

Jaunie motioned to the empty chair as she sat down behind her desk. "Please have a seat. What can I do for you?"

Patrice sat, clutching her worn pocketbook tightly in her lap. She glanced at her husband, who looked decidedly bored, before she spoke. "We saw a photo of you and your partner in the paper earlier this week. You received an award for your work with the National Center for Missing and Exploited Children."

Jaunie nodded. "Yes. That's right."

Patrice looked again at her husband, who hadn't gained anymore interest in the conversation since the last time.

"Well, I was hoping you could help us find my son. He's missing."

Jaunie's heart lurched in sympathy for the woman. And she hadn't missed Patrice's careful use of the word *my* instead of *our* in reference to her son.

Before Jaunie could respond, Richard grumbled under his breath, "Missing, my ass—the little monster ran away."

Chapter Four

Before Jaunie could respond to Richard's outburst, Patrice recoiled as if she'd been struck. Her chin quivered as she faced him. "What's the difference? He's not home safe where he should be."

Richard met Jaunie's eyes for the first time. "The difference is, he's run away before, and he's come back on his own before. He's not gone for more than a few hours before he realizes that he'd have to get along without color TV and Sega Genesis and all that other crap I bought for him." He waved his arm for emphasis, then slouched back in his chair, arms crossed over his chest.

Patrice ignored her husband's comments. "It's different this time. He's taken food, and clothes, and . . . money. I don't think he plans to come home." She leaned forward, her huge dark eyes begging Jaunie to listen to her. "That's why we've got to find him. He's only twelve years old."

Jaunie had switched on her tape recorder the minute Richard started speaking, but it was now that she asked, "Do you mind if I record this conversation?"

Patrice shook her head, and Richard barely shrugged.

"Okay, let's start from the beginning." Jaunie started jotting notes on a legal pad as she spoke. "Have you contacted the police?"

Patrice nodded.

"Can you give me the name of the officer who responded to the call?"

Patrice laid her hand on Richard's arm. "His name was Barnes, wasn't it?" When Richard didn't respond, she nodded. "Yes, Officer Mike Barnes."

Jaunie smiled. She'd gotten to know several of the area police officers through her work with the Center, and luckily Mike Barnes was one of the few officers who didn't mind conferring with P.I.'s. She'd give him a call right away.

"What's your son's name?"

"Andrew," Patrice replied.

"Andrew Lincoln?" Jaunie asked, looking at Richard.

"Um, actually Andrew Montgomery. This is my second marriage."

Jaunie nodded. *Why wasn't* that *a surprise?* "Where's Andrew's father?"

"He died two years ago." Patrice tightened her grip on her purse, but Jaunie could still see her fingers trembling.

Jaunie bowed her head as her chest constricted with sympathy. This young woman had obviously lost so much already. Though her new husband sat beside her, she seemed quite alone. "How long has Andrew been missing?"

"Two days."

"When did you last see him?"

"Wednesday night when I sent him to bed. By morning he was gone."

"Did anything unusual happen in the household right before Andrew left?"

Patrice stared at her hands. "Nothing unusual."

Jaunie glanced at Richard. His face was impassive. He had his head cocked to one side, and his eyes were closed. He wasn't even paying attention, Jaunie thought with irritation

"Has Andrew undergone any personality changes recently?"

Patrice looked puzzled. "What do you mean?"

"Has he changed his style of dress or his hair? Hung out with a new group of friends? Spent more time alone? Anything like that?"

"No, I . . . no."

Jaunie got the impression that Patrice was holding back. "Patrice, you said Andrew has run away before. How many times?"

Patrice bit her lip, her eyes clouded with sadness. "Twice in the past two months."

"Why do you think he ran away?"

"He's having trouble adjusting, that's all. We just moved to a new neighborhood, and he hasn't gotten used to Richard and me being married. I think he wants things to be the way they were before."

Jaunie wanted to pursue that issue further, but Richard was getting restless, looking at his watch, and shooting Patrice impatient looks.

She moved through the rest of her questions, collecting names and phone numbers of their old neighbors and friends and information about Andrew's interests and hangouts. While Patrice answered her questions, Jaunie couldn't help resenting Richard's silence. It shouldn't matter that Andrew wasn't his natural son. Didn't he care that a child was missing? Jaunie got her answer when it was time to discuss her fee.

"What?" Richard said, scowling. "Why should I pay that kind of money for something the police can do?"

Jaunie bit her lip. She had no problem reducing her fee for parents in a financial bind, but she knew this wasn't about the money.

Patrice gripped her husband's arm and spoke to him in a low voice. "You wanted to spend thousands of dollars to send Andrew away. Why can't you spend a few hundred to make sure he's safe?"

Richard grunted.

Jaunie raised her brow but didn't comment as Richard silently wrote her a check. She had a feeling it would be a lot easier to find out where Richard had wanted to send Andrew when the man wasn't around. She planned to pay Patrice a visit the next day.

Until then, she had work to do.

"Thanks for the information, Mike," Jaunie said a few hours later when Officer Barnes returned her call. "I was relieved to hear that you're the investigating officer assigned to this case."

"No problem, Jaunie," he said in a smooth baritone flavored with a North Carolina accent. "There's no room for egos in this kind of situation. We're both after the same thing."

"Well, I appreciate your help. We've already gone over the facts, but what's your take on this?"

"Let me see here." She could picture the serious look that settled over his handsome dark features as he chose his words. "Seems pretty straightforward to me. Patrice was struggling to raise the kid after her man died, then along comes this big-shot businessman, who owns apartment buildings all over D.C. He's attracted to her because she's a pretty girl. She's attracted to him because she needs stability for her kid. He's got money, so he can help her take care of the boy."

Mike's voice took on a darker tone. "But here's the catch. The old man makes no secret of the fact that he has no use for kids. He's only interested in the woman. So the tension builds, and the kid cuts out, hoping his mother will choose him over the stepfather."

Jaunie sighed into the receiver. "Do you have any leads on Andrew yet?"

"We've checked all the area runaway hangouts, but Andrew hasn't been spotted yet. His case is registered with the Center, and, since he's only twelve, he's listed as an Endangered Runaway."

"Okay, that gives me an idea of where to start. I'm going to the house to speak with Patrice tomorrow. I had the feeling she was holding back, and I'm hoping she'll open up without Richard around. I'll let you know if I turn up anything new."

"Jaunie"—Mike's voice took on a more personal tone—"if you want to compare notes some more, I'm off duty this evening. We could meet downtown for drinks or something."

Jaunie smiled. Mike Barnes was a handsome, very eligible bachelor. She should have been more than a little bit flattered that he was interested. But she wasn't. What was wrong with her?

"I'm sorry, Mike. I need to finish up a few things, then I plan to go to sleep early."

"Come on, a beautiful woman like you shouldn't be going to bed early on a Friday night. There's a new club on K Street. Why don't you come for a little while, have some fun?"

"Sorry, I can't."

"Some other time?" He sounded hopeful.

"We'll see." Jaunie hung up the phone feeling silly. It *was* Friday night. When was the last time she'd had plans? A date?

With a frustrated sigh, she picked up her purse and headed for the door. In the hallway she saw that there were no lights on behind the door of Payne & Douglas Contracting.

Friday night. She'd bet that Trent was out having a good time at that very moment. Did he have a date?

Shaking her head, Jaunie walked over to the elevators. This was stupid. It didn't matter what Trent Douglas was doing that night. She could have had a date if she'd wanted to, but as she stepped into the elevator, she couldn't help wondering, *how come she hadn't wanted to?*

The air was thick with cigarette smoke, and the music was deafening—two features of the club scene Trent hadn't missed while he'd been in hibernation.

"Do you want a drink?" Robert shouted.

Trent shook his head, and Robert maneuvered his way over to the bar. Trent leaned back against the wall as couples tried to squeeze past him on their way to the dance floor.

He'd promised Robert that he'd get back into the swing of

things, or at least that he'd try. But times had changed since he'd last been to a dance club.

Boy, had they changed, he thought, picking his eyeballs up from the floor as a woman walked by in what looked like a bra and a tight pair of Daisy Dukes. He scanned the room: more of the same. There didn't seem to be a woman in the place who didn't have her belly button showing. Trent grinned. Not that he minded.

Robert came up to him with a curvy woman in tow. He thrust a drink into Trent's hands. "Here, hold this."

Trent stared at the brown liquid. "I said I didn't want a drink."

Robert nodded. "I know. That's mine. Hold it, will ya?" Then he was out on the floor, wedged in the crowd of gyrating bodies. Robert placed both hands firmly on his dance partner's waist and started getting his groove on.

Trent started tapping his fingers on the leg of his jeans, trying to act as if he were having a good time. A few years ago he would have been in the middle of the dance floor alongside Robert. Why didn't he feel like getting out there now?

Maybe he just needed to try harder. He glanced around the room. There were plenty of women lining the walls, waiting to be asked to dance. Now that he was paying attention, he found that several were shooting him interested looks.

And then he saw her.

She was at the bar. Her back was to him, but it had to be her: Jaunie, auburn hair curling down her back. She was even wearing a purple dress—his favorite color.

Before he knew he was moving, Trent found himself behind her. The music vibrated loudly off the walls, making it impossible to be heard at a normal volume, so he bent close to her ear. "Are you undercover?"

"What?" The woman spun to face him.

It was *not* Jaunie.

The woman gave him a dirty look and threw her drink on him. With a startled groan, Trent began wiping uselessly at his clothes. Someone tapped him on the shoulder.

A tall man with a linebacker build and skin the color of charcoal frowned down on him. He placed a meaty hand on the woman's back. "Is he bothering you, Shanette?"

"Uh, sorry," Trent said, gazing up at the giant. "I thought she was someone I knew."

"This fool said something about getting me under the covers." The woman gave Trent a cold look. "But it's okay, Mookie. I took care of this one myself." She pointed to the remains of her strawberry daiquiri dripping from his shirt.

Trent backed away and found Robert beside him.

The jerk was laughing at him.

"Hey, man, tell me again how you don't want Jaunie." Robert handed him a fistful of napkins. "Because like I said, no one makes this much of an ass of himself over a woman unless he wants to get in her—"

"Shut up, Robert."

It was a little past noon on Saturday when Jaunie drove up to the Lincoln residence. Patrice answered the door right away, looking much more comfortable in her jeans and sweatshirt, her hair pulled into a ponytail. "Have you heard anything? You have news about Andrew?"

Jaunie bit her lip in sympathy. "I'm sorry, Patrice. I don't have any news for you yet. But I would like to talk to you and have a look at Andrew's room."

Patrice stepped aside and let Jaunie enter the house. It was a large, beautiful house, but not well lived in. Many of the furnishings looked brand new, and several rooms were bare, still waiting for decoration. It kind of reminded her of Trent's office.

Patrice led her quietly to Andrew's room. Her hands trembled as she opened the door. "You call if you need me."

Jaunie touched Patrice's arm as she turned to go. "I know this must be hard for you, but I need you to stay and help me identify which things are missing from his room."

She nodded, but hung back as Jaunie stepped into the bed-

room. It seemed to be the typical room of a twelve-year-old
boy. Besides the bed and desk, there were two bookshelves,
painted blue, lining the far end of the narrow room. Instead of
books the shelves were filled with stacks of comic books, rows
of video game cartridges, and basketball memorabilia.

On the wall above his cluttered desk were posters of Michael
Jordan and Ice Cube. Jaunie had to grin when she found a life-
sized poster of Naomi Campbell behind Andrew's door. Over
his bed, running lengthwise, was a framed print of a futuristic
train streaking across the New York skyline. Jaunie raised her
brows. It seemed a bit sophisticated for a twelve-year-old's
tastes, but it added a nice touch to the simple room.

While Jaunie moved through the room, Patrice stood in the
doorway, answering questions when asked, but otherwise
remaining quiet.

Jaunie rifled through a few drawers, and inspected under the
bed and in the wastebasket. She leafed through Andrew's old
spiral notebooks but found nothing of any obvious importance.
They were filled mostly with class notes and sketches of futuristic cars and trains.

Feeling frustrated, Jaunie surveyed the cluttered shelves
again. "It looks like he left most of his things behind. Can you
think of anything else that's missing?"

"Richard bought most of these things," Patrice answered
as if that said it all.

It didn't say it all, but it said a lot. Jaunie looked down at
the list she'd compiled. "You said he took his backpack, an
extra set of clothing, and you noticed some food missing from
the refrigerator. Where did he get the money?"

Patrice pointed to an empty glass jar that stood about a foot
high on the top shelf. "After I got married, Andrew started
using a lot of bad language around the house. It really upset
Richard, so I started taking a dollar out of Andrew's allowance
for every curse word he used. I put it in the jar, and Andrew
couldn't get the money until he'd gone a full month without
cursing. I hate to tell you that it was full."

"How much do you think was in there?"

"It must have been over a hundred dollars."

Jaunie nodded and followed Patrice from the room. When they reached the living room, Jaunie put away her notebook. "I'm just about finished, but could we talk for a few minutes?"

"Of course, have a seat." Patrice sat next to her, then jumped up again. "Can I get you anything?"

"No thanks."

Patrice sat back down. "Well, first I want to thank you for taking this case. I feel like you really care about finding Andrew. You must care about children to be so involved with that Center."

Jaunie touched her hand. "I do care."

Patrice nodded. "I want the best for Andrew. I know he hated the fact that I was remarrying, but I thought he'd adjust. Here we're in a nice neighborhood, and he can go to a good school. He has all the games and expensive clothes he used to beg me for. Kids just need time . . . to adjust." Her voice cracked as tears filled her eyes.

Jaunie knew she was seeing a woman wracked with guilt and who desperately needed a friend. To give Patrice time to pull herself together, she changed the subject. "This is a beautiful house. This room has a lovely view of the backyard."

She sniffed. "Thank you. I've never had so many nice things in my life. I haven't gotten down to decorating yet, because it's a bit overwhelming. But I bought some new curtains . . ."

For a while Jaunie and Patrice chatted about everything from furniture to soap operas. And later when Patrice was relaxed and ready, they began to talk about Andrew. Jaunie learned that Andrew had ridden the King Cobra roller coaster six times in a row on his first trip to an amusement park, that he'd gotten his hand stuck in an elevator when he was five because he wanted to see where the doors went, and that he had an aversion to haircuts.

After a few more minutes of reminiscing, Jaunie brought the subject back to what she needed to know. "I couldn't help overhearing something you mentioned to your husband yesterday. You told him that if he were willing to spend thousands of dollars to send Andrew away, he should be willing to spend a few hundred to see that he gets home safely. Can I ask you what you meant by that?''

''It's nothing, really.'' Patrice bowed her head to stare at her lap, clearly embarrassed. ''Richard tells me that it's customary to send a boy away to school at this age. It's just that I would miss him so. My boy and I haven't been separated since his father died.''

Until now was unspoken but understood.

Jaunie nodded as the pieces fell into place. ''I take it Andrew wasn't too thrilled with the idea of boarding school, either. Could that be why he ran away?''

Patrice gripped her hands tightly. ''Could be. Richard says that Marshall Hall Military Academy is just what Andrew needs and—''

''Excuse me, did you say Marshall Hall? In Annapolis?''

Patrice nodded. ''Yes, you've heard of it?''

Jaunie wished to heaven that she hadn't. ''Uh . . . yeah.''

''Richard says it has a very good reputation. I was hesitant, but if you've heard good things, too—''

''Well, not exactly.''

''What do you mean?''

''Marshall Hall is surrounded by controversy. Many people disagree with the militant temperament they instill in young boys. I've heard about kids who've had difficulty fitting into society after leaving the school.''

She gasped. ''Are you sure? Richard says Marshall Hall will teach Andrew discipline, help him be more organized.''

Jaunie grimaced. ''I'm sure that's possible. But I think the problem with this particular school is that some kids take the mind-set that's taught there a bit too far. After leaving, some have shown signs of paranoia and instability.''

Patrice went pale. ''My God. I had no idea.''

''Well, it's something to think about. In the meantime I'll do my best to find Andrew.''

Patrice had withdrawn into herself, her face tight with sadness. ''I'll talk to Richard about this Marshall Hall. He couldn't possibly have known.''

Jaunie wasn't so sure about that. "I'm going to go now, but I'll be in touch. Take care," she said, squeezing Patrice's hand as she left.

Anxious to get back to work, Jaunie headed to Silver Spring, where Andrew and Patrice used to live. Hopefully old friends and neighbors would be able to help her. Jaunie couldn't stand to see the sun set on another day with the boy out there alone.

The sun had just begun to set when Trent walked into his apartment Saturday night. Without turning on the lights, he let the basketball fall onto the couch and went to the kitchen. He pulled a bottle of spring water out of the refrigerator and finished it in one chug. *Damn,* he thought, tossing the water bottle in the recycling bin. *It's still there.*

That restless feeling—the same feeling that had prompted him to call Robert a few hours ago and challenge him to a game of one-on-one. They played for hours, running each other ragged. Trent had been certain that he'd come home too beat to do anything but shower and hit the sheets.

But that feeling was back—the one that made him want to crawl out of his skin. He was frustrated, dissatisfied—and he didn't know why. He'd spent his Saturdays casually, without formal plans more often than not over the past few years. Then today, suddenly, he couldn't stand it anymore.

It didn't help that every time he stood still for a moment his mind returned to his foolish mistake the night before. Stupid! He slammed his hand down on the counter, shaking his head.

Worse than his embarrassment over seeing female mirages, was the disappointment. She hadn't been Jaunie.

Trent pushed away from the counter and left the kitchen. He had to get out of the house. Sexual frustration was rising, and now it threatened to choke him.

He entered the bathroom and turned on the shower. Then he leaned against the sink and took a deep breath, trying to relax. Wasn't he past those days of being a slave to his gonads? He wasn't a monk, but his need for female companionship had lessened over the years. Now out of the blue, his sex drive was back with the full force of an eighteen-year-old's.

Trent's hand shot out and turned off the water. A shower wasn't going to help. He needed to do something physical, something with his hands. He shut his eyes against the suggestions his body had come up with.

He left the bathroom to find his tool belt. He wasn't going to handle this like a teenager. A few hours working at the house would take care of his problem. But for the first time, he could sympathize with addicts and alcoholics. He knew what it was to want something that was no good for him.

Women were his weakness. He fell in love far too easily for his own good. And why not? They were pretty and soft and smelled so good. Their utter femininity worked on his brain, making it impossible for him to see their lies and ulterior motives.

It had taken him years to admit he had a problem, but now that he'd faced it, he had a chance of controlling it. He'd cut back to small doses until he needed them less frequently. He wasn't yet immune, and he probably never would be. He'd been taking it one day at a time.

But now the cravings were back. Now his addiction had a name and a face and a body. Now he couldn't get his fix from any beautiful woman with soft skin and a sweet smile. She had to be tall and slender with perfect curves. She had to have full pouty lips and haunting tawny eyes, and hair so long and thick he could wrap it around those cinnamon curves . . .

Trent groaned, quickly gathering his tools and heading for the door. A little hard work and food—that was all he needed. Because whatever he did, he had to stay away from that woman. She'd made her living telling lies. All she'd have to do was look at him with those wide tawny eyes and tell him the sky was green . . . and he'd agree. And if she touched him . . . he'd believe her.

Trent grabbed his keys and locked the door, his body still tense with restless energy—the first symptoms of withdrawal.

Yes, his addiction had a name, and it was Jaunie.

Chapter Five

As soon as Trent crossed the threshold, he knew something was wrong. It wasn't the first time in the last few days he'd come to work on the house and sensed things weren't quite as they should've been. Only this time the feeling was stronger.

From the entryway, he could see that nothing was noticeably out of place, but there were subtle differences. Instead of lining the wall as he'd left it, the orange extension cord connected to the electric sander now looped out into the middle of the floor as if someone had tripped over it. And the lid of his tool chest was open. The catch was loose and popped whenever bumped or jarred, but it had been closed when he left.

Trent flipped on the lights in the kitchen, setting down the box of Kentucky Fried Chicken he'd picked up on the way over. He was nearly finished with the house, and all the appliances had been installed.

He looked at the microwave. Instinctively he pulled it open and saw telltale stains on the bottom. Someone had broken in—to nuke a TV dinner?

Trent went over to the refrigerator, where he kept a modest supply of food so he wouldn't have to break when he worked at the house on the weekends. His supply had been discreetly sampled. The lemonade was down an inch, one of his oranges was missing, and a few centimeters had been shaved from his roll of salami. A hungry burglar?

Trent frowned. He thought this neighborhood was too suburban to attract the homeless. Apparently he was wrong.

Moving quietly, he crossed the room and began to tiptoe up the cherry-wood steps he'd stripped of faded gray carpeting and polished himself. When he reached the top of the landing, he flicked on the light switch, and the hallway lit up. He could see into three of the four upstairs bedrooms. They seemed empty.

The bedrooms on the right were the only rooms Trent hadn't finished remodeling. He moved forward to inspect the master bedroom, and the linen closet door flew open. Before Trent realized what was happening, a streak of color shot past him and down the stairs.

It was a kid!

Trent took off down the stairs, nearly tripping and breaking his neck as his shoes slid on the well-polished wood.

"Hey! Hold it," Trent shouted uselessly. The kid was already at the door. In a last-ditch effort, Trent dove from the bottom step and grabbed the hood of the windbreaker knotted around the kid's waist.

Trent hit the floor hard, but held tight to the boy's jacket. Within seconds the boy had wriggled free of it and was once again lunging for the door.

Trent jumped up and grabbed the boy's arm. "Not so fast. What are you—"

The kid immediately started screaming obscenities, a couple of which made Trent blink twice. He thought he'd heard it all on construction sites, but this kid really knew how to cuss.

Trent pulled him away from the door. The kid had been screaming so loudly the neighbors could probably hear him. "You need to watch that mouth."

"Fu—"

Trent clamped his hand over the boy's mouth. The kid was

obviously in trouble and had an attitude. He had to find a better way to handle this.

The boy couldn't have been more than eleven or twelve, but his eyes were hard with fear and anger. Trent's gaze dropped to the convenience store hot dog the boy clutched in his hand. Ugh! Those things were toxic, a step above rubber.

"Okay, never mind what you're doing here." Trent dropped his hand from the boy's mouth and picked up the windbreaker from the floor. "Obviously you don't have anywhere else to go," he said as he guided the kid into the kitchen.

The boy pulled his arm from Trent's grasp, puffing up his stance. "I got places!"

With a grin, Trent backed off, reaching for the box of chicken he'd left on the counter. "Hey, then don't let me keep you. I just thought you might help me eat this chicken." He tilted the box so the kid could see it.

The boy looked at the half-eaten hot dog in his hand and then back to the chicken. No contest. His hand shot out, reaching for the box.

Trent grabbed his hand before it made contact. It was filthy. "Hold it. I may not have a table or chairs, but I have soap." He pointed toward the sink. "Wash 'em!"

The kid twisted his brown face into a scowl but did as he was told. While he scrubbed his hands, Trent studied him. The boy looked small and thin, but who could tell with his oversized Ice Cube T-shirt and baggy jeans swallowing his body. His hair had grown out of its style and was borderline nappy. But a kid on his own wouldn't feel pressured to comb or cut his hair.

Trent filled two paper cups with lemonade and spread a double layer of paper towels on the counter. He laid out two drumsticks and a breast for the boy. Who knew how long it had been since the kid had had a decent meal? Hopefully he could find out tonight where the kid belonged. If not, Trent sighed, well there was plenty of room at his apartment. It might be easier to straighten everything out in the morning.

"So, kid . . . I can't keep calling you kid. What's your name?"

The boy was devouring the chicken. Between bites he said, "None of your damn business."

Trent grinned. "Whoa, that's a long one. Mind if I call you 'business' for short."

The kid rolled his eyes, giving Trent a "you're so corny" look, but the tension in his stance eased.

Trent smiled to himself. It had been a long while since he'd been a kid, but he wasn't doing too badly.

Trent went to the refrigerator to refill the kid's cup, and he heard something hit the floor behind him. Turning, he saw his own cup had spilled when the boy reached for another piece of chicken.

Trent smiled at the kid's guilty look. "It's okay. I'll clean it up." Grabbing a wad of paper towels, Trent crouched to blot the lemonade. "You know, when I was your age, I was accident prone. I used to spill, drop, or break anything in sight. But now—"

Trent stood up. The box of chicken was gone—and so was the kid.

Jaunie woke up with a start Sunday morning. The phone was ringing. Eyes still closed, she reached for the receiver. Geri was the only person with enough nerve to call this early. "What do you want, Geri?"

"Is this Ms. Sterling?" a male voice asked.

Jaunie bolted straight up in bed, her drowsiness evaporating as she recognized the voice. "Yes, it is."

"This is Richard Lincoln."

"Oh, Mr. Lincoln. I don't have any news on Andrew yet, but I do want to assure you that I've—"

"That won't be necessary. I just called to let you know that your services will no longer be required."

The cold words slammed into her. Jaunie clutched the phone to her ear. "Was Andrew found, Mr. Lincoln?"

"No. Patrice and I have decided to go about this another way."

"But, Mr. Lincoln—"

"Send me a bill for your expenses, and I'll see that you're compensated for your time. Goodbye, Ms. Sterling." The hard click of the line disconnecting made her jump.

This made no sense. Why would the Lincolns fire a private investigator two days into a job when their son hadn't been found?

Jaunie picked up the phone and hit star sixty-nine. The Lincolns owed her a better explanation. She breathed a sigh of relief when Patrice's quiet voice answered the phone.

"Patrice? This is Jaunie Sterling."

"Oh, uh, hello." She sounded uncomfortable.

"Could you please explain to me what's going on? When I talked to you yesterday, everything was fine. Today your husband called to fire me."

A weary sigh came from the other line. "I'm sorry it turned out like this, but Richard says he knows what's best. He was very upset when I asked him about Marshall Hall. The things you said about the school really upset him. You see, he graduated from Marshall Hall Military Academy himself."

Jaunie gazed heavenward. *It figures.*

Patrice continued. "So of course any school that was good enough for Richard is good enough for Andrew."

Jaunie's heart dropped to her toes. Was she in the Twilight Zone? After their long talk yesterday, she'd thought they understood each other. Just because she'd been less than complimentary about Richard's old school, suddenly Patrice didn't care about finding her son anymore?

Clearly that man had her brainwashed. Arguing would do no good. "I'm sorry you feel that way, Patrice. Goodbye."

This time Jaunie replaced the receiver first. There was a twelve-year-old boy alone on the streets, and once he was found, he was headed for a school that was no less dangerous.

Jaunie couldn't give up.

* * *

"Hello! Anybody in there?" Robert asked Monday morning, knocking on Trent's forehead.

"Yeah. I'm listening." Robert had been trying to go over a set of construction drawings with him, but Trent's mind kept wandering back to the kid he'd found at the house.

"The hell you are. What's on your mind this time? A woman? Are you still upset about what happened at the club?"

"No." Trent sighed. "This is a bit more serious than that."

Robert propped up his feet on the new conference table Trent had insisted they buy for the spare office. "Fire when ready. I'm listening."

Trent told Robert about finding the runaway kid in the house. ". . . So when I'd finished wiping the spill, both the kid and my dinner were gone."

Robert raised a brow. "Aw, man, that sucks! Was it extra crispy?"

Trent glared at his friend. "Stop acting stupid. I took a sleeping bag over to the house last night, hoping the kid might come back for the jacket he'd left behind. No such luck."

"So what are you going to do now?"

"Well, I feel like dirt knowing that kid's still out there. I mean, I just turned my back for a second and he disappeared. I have no idea how to find him, other than staking out the house. But now that he's seen me, he might not come back."

"This is perfect."

"What?"

"You work across the hall from two P.I.'s who know all about missing children. Go over and talk to them."

Trent raised his eyebrows. "That's not a bad idea." He looked at the collection of blueprints spread out before him. "Do you mind if we take care of this later? I don't think I can concentrate until I get this off my mind."

Robert grinned wickedly. "That's fine, Trent. You go ahead. I'm used to carrying you on my back."

Trent crossed the hall and found himself facing Mel, who was brightly dressed and perky. "Uh, is Geri in?"

"Sure, she's in her office. You can go ahead and knock on her door."

Trent knocked, and Geri's harried voice answered, "Come in."

He opened the door and did a double-take. Geri stood in the middle of the room.

"Oh, hi, Trent. What do you think?" She twirled around, modeling her purple leotard and tutu, accessorized with red and blue striped tights and big floppy shoes. Her wild, springy hair and red clown nose completed the image.

"Uh, you look . . . like a clown."

Geri laughed. "That's right, sweetie. Today's the last day of the Summer Festival at the Baltimore Harbor, and there's a certain clown performing there who's an elusive witness for a hit-and-run case. I think I've finally got that sucker cornered."

She grabbed a duffel bag from her desk. "I'm sorry. Did you want to talk to me about something?"

"Yes, actually—"

"Well, if it's something quick, you can ride the elevator down with me. Otherwise, hon, I'm afraid I'm gonna have to talk to ya later."

Trent stepped aside so Geri could pass. "Oh, that's okay. It can wait."

Geri turned. "If it's really important, talk to Mel about my schedule and have her pencil you in. Wish me luck." Geri waved goodbye and popped out the door.

Trent shook his head. He'd been hoping to catch Geri with a free moment. He'd thought it might be easier to talk to her instead of Jaunie, but now it seemed he didn't have a choice.

When she heard a knock at her office door, Jaunie called, "Come in," but Trent was the last person she'd expected to see.

"Uh, hi," he said, swinging the door closed behind him,

then he hastily jerked it back open. "Um, how do you want this?"

Jaunie was amused to see him acting as nervous as she usually felt around him. "You can leave it open. What can I do for you?"

He stepped forward, wiping his palms on his jeans. "Well, I kind of had a question and I thought maybe . . ."

"Yes?" He looked so good. Normally she saw him in long-sleeved shirts or jackets, but today he wore a black T-shirt with his jeans. The short sleeves showed off his powerfully corded arms.

"You and Geri volunteer at the National Center for Missing and Exploited Children, right? I was just wondering what's involved in something like that?"

A smile spread over her face. The Center always needed more help. "What's involved in volunteering? Well, that depends on how much time you can contribute. You can take calls for the hotline anytime that fits your schedule or—here, let me show you." She reached into her bottom drawer and started pulling out brochures.

She spread the pamphlets out on her desk. "The Center's doing so much right now. Besides the hotline, they train law enforcement officers, have a home page on the Internet, and—"

"Actually I kind of wanted to know *how* they go about finding missing kids."

He was rubbing his temples again. Either she had some weird effect on him, or he was prone to migraines. Jaunie wasn't sure which would be worse.

"How?" Jaunie sighed. "Well, they have a poster and photo distribution program. I'm sure you've seen those little cards with blue photos along with coupons for the cleaners or restaurants, right?"

"Yeah," he said, resting his forearms on the back of the chair opposite her desk.

She could see she hadn't hit the mark yet, so she tried again. "And they also have age-progression technology, where they can take the photo of a child who's been missing for a long time and manipulate the image to show what that child might look like today.''

Trent leaned forward. "Wow, that's incredible. Have you actually seen that done?''

She still wasn't sure what he was after, but at least he sounded interested. ''Yeah, the actual process takes hours—but when it's done, the results are astounding.''

Partly because he seemed interested, and partly because she was afraid he would leave if she didn't, Jaunie continued to talk. And while she did, he asked questions. It made her feel good to know that, despite their differences, they could share this interest.

''How did you get involved in all this?''

''My first big case was a missing child case, and I didn't have a clue what I was doing. The Center sent me information and put me in contact with the right people.''

''Your *first* big case? That must have been rough.''

Jaunie nodded. ''It changed my life. The missing child was Geri's daughter, Samantha.''

His eyes widened. ''Geri? Your partner Geri? You're kidding?''

''Well she wasn't my partner then. At the time she was a big-shot trial attorney. She'd just gotten divorced from her husband, and he was ticked because she got custody. He took their daughter and headed out of state.''

''So how did she end up here? Were you friends already?''

Jaunie laughed. ''Nope. Geri had been to two other investigation agencies before me, and at the time I'd been working out of my apartment in Georgetown. The police and the other agencies had wanted her to sit around and wait. You've seen Geri—she's got too much energy to sit still. She burst into my office and laid down her ground rules. She said she came to me for two reasons—one, because I was a woman, and she thought I'd be able to sympathize and, two, because she wanted to be in on the search from start to finish. I told her I didn't have a problem with that.''

"So how did you finally find her daughter?"

Jaunie couldn't believe she and Trent were having a real conversation. He was surprisingly easy to talk to.

"We tracked Geri's ex to New Mexico and brought Samantha back ourselves."

"So you and Geri have been partners ever since."

"Yep." Jaunie watched as his brow furrowed. "Trent? You look like you still have something on your mind. Is there something else you wanted to ask me?"

He leaned back in the chair. "This is going to sound stupid. That's why I didn't come right out and ask. What I really want to know is . . . what do you do when you know a specific kid is missing, but you don't know his name or where he belongs. You just know he isn't where he's supposed to be?"

Jaunie frowned, trying to follow his train of thought. "You know he isn't where he's supposed to be. Does that mean you know where a missing child might be staying?"

Trent shook his head, clearly embarrassed. "Not exactly. I think I saw a kid who *could* be a runaway, but I don't know where the kid is now."

"Where did you first see him?"

"I only saw him once. There's this house I've been remodeling, and for a few days I'd been noticing certain things weren't as I'd left them. Finally Saturday night I found out why. A kid had gotten in somehow, and I think he'd been sleeping there."

"What happened when you found him?"

"He tried to run, and I grabbed him—tried to get him to talk. He wasn't interested. Finally I figured he was hungry and settled him down enough to offer him some food. But as soon as I turned my back, the kid was gone. I haven't seen him since."

Jaunie nodded her head. "Well, you could always go file a report with the police. They'd try to match the description you give them with any kids who have been reported missing. What did he look like?"

"I guess he was around eleven or twelve. Black . . . and uh, I don't know, short."

Trent wouldn't last a day in the P.I. business with that kind of attention to detail. Jaunie resisted the urge to remind him that most twelve-year-olds were short. Jaunie sighed. "Well, I hope you can remember more than that for the police. That isn't much to go on."

Trent's face fell. "Damn. I knew this was stupid, but I had to give it a try."

Jaunie felt bad for him. She knew when it came to kids, the old adage "You win some, you lose some" just didn't apply. She wished she knew of a better way to help him. Lord knew, she didn't have any leads on the Andrew Montgomery case. Even though it was officially closed, she had no intention of letting it go.

"Let's think about this. Did the boy tell you anything? Something that might give you a clue as to where he's from or what he was doing in your house?"

Trent frowned. "No. He didn't say much, and what he did say . . . believe me, it isn't repeatable."

"Had a bad mouth on him, did he?"

"For real. I tell you, I think *I* learned a few new words that day."

"And where exactly did you last see him?"

"In the kitchen of the house I'm fixing up. It's in Silver Spring near the Metro station."

Jaunie nodded. "I know that area. I was conducting some interviews in that neighborhood the other day."

"I spent the night there last night, hoping he'd show, but no luck."

"Well, what about his clothes? Was he wearing anything distinctive—something with a sports logo or a catchy phrase?"

"Yes! He had on an Ice Cube T-shirt. He's a rapper."

Jaunie cut her eyes at him. "I *know* he's a rapper. Do I seem that out of touch?"

Trent frowned. "No, I'm sorry. I guess—you just seem like the type who would rather listen to Bach or something."

Jaunie raised an eyebrow, but didn't pursue it. "Okay, so now we have an eleven- or twelve-year-old, African-American

runaway with a foul mouth, wearing an Ice Cube T-shirt.''
Jaunie's heart beat sped up. That sounded just like . . . no,
nothing in life was *that* easy. ''We still need to narrow it down.
Think carefully. Is there anything distinctive you can remember
about his appearance?''

Trent sighed heavily with a shrug. ''He just looked like any
kid you'd see on the street. Besides the fact that he was in
desperate need of a barber . . . I don't know what else to tell
you. He ran off before I could get any information out of him.
He wouldn't even tell me his name.''

Jaunie touched Trent's arm, feeling his frustration. ''Look,
this isn't your fault. I'm a professional, or at least I'm licensed
to be, and sometimes I can't do any better than that. For instance,
just yesterday I was thrown off a case because I insulted my
client's alma mater.''

She reached into her drawer and pulled out Andrew's picture.
''This boy is still missing because his stepfather can't get
beyond—''

Trent snatched the picture out of her hand. ''That's him!
That's the kid I saw!''

Chapter Six

Trent stared in amazement at the picture in his hand.

Jaunie grabbed it back. "What? This is the kid? I've been looking for him for days."

He moved behind her to get another look at the photo. "I'm sure. He's the one."

She slapped her hand to her forehead. "Of course—this all makes sense. Andrew and his mother used to live in Silver Spring before she got married. He would know the area well enough to know that the house you've been working on is empty. No one would think to look for him there."

Trent nodded, going back to his chair. "You know this kid. What's his story? Why isn't he home with his parents?"

A corner of Jaunie's pretty mouth turned downward. "From where I stand, things were fine until Andrew's mother married some wealthy land developer. Apparently Andrew and his stepfather don't get along." Her dark eyes narrowed. "It's no surprise—the guy's a complete jerk, and Andrew has been acting up. He's run away before, but this time it seems he doesn't plan on going back. Now I have evidence that he's still in the area."

"I thought you said you were thrown off the case."

She gave him a sheepish look. "I was. But that doesn't mean I'm giving up. Richard Lincoln, Andrew's stepfather, wants to send him to Marshall Hall. That must have been the final straw that sent Andrew running."

"Marshall Hall? That sounds familiar."

Jaunie nodded. "Richard fired me because I had a long talk with his wife about that school. I told her about the controversy generated by the school's teaching methods, but I guess when she confronted her husband, he cajoled her with the news that he went to Marshall Hall when he was a boy. And look how well *he* turned out." She sneered. "The man is completely cold. My first meeting with them, he said he resented hiring a P.I. because the kid was a troublemaker. He didn't want to waste money on something the police could do."

Trent scowled. "He sounds like a jerk."

"That's why I haven't given up looking for Andrew. I'm not so sure Richard cares if the kid is found."

Trent admired her persistence. Her commitment to helping missing children had been clear when she'd talked about the Center, and now her face was glowing with an energy and confidence he hadn't seen before.

"But what about his mother?"

"She loves him—I can see that, but Richard has a strong hold over her. She seems to believe whatever he tells her."

He shook his head. "No wonder the kid left."

"I know. At least now I have a lead." She took out a notebook. "You said you spent the night at the house, hoping that he'd show?"

He shrugged. "Yeah."

"Well, how long has it been since you found him?"

"Two days."

"Okay," she said, smacking her hand on the desk. "Then there's still a chance he could come back if he's desperate."

"I don't know," Trent said, frowning. She looked so determined, but he didn't want to get her hopes up. "Now he knows someone's on to him."

She was scribbling furiously in her notebook. "Well, I've got to give it a shot. It's all I've got."

His raised his brows. "Give what a shot?"

She dropped her pen, giving him a matter-of-fact look. "Staying at the house tonight. There can't be too many places a kid his age can crash at night. His picture has been on the news, and I've been covering the entire area, alerting anyone who might come across him. He might take a chance and—"

He held up his hands. "Wait a minute. I can't let you stay at the house."

She crossed her arms. "Why not?"

"Why not?" He froze. "Because . . . um, it isn't safe."

"What?" She stood, placing a hand on her hip. "I'm a private investigator. Believe me, spending the night in an empty house, waiting for a twelve-year-old kid to show up is not the most dangerous situation I've ever been in."

He knew he wasn't making sense, but he just didn't like the idea of her staying there alone. It was a testosterone thing. "Look, it's my house, and I'm not going to let you stay there by yourself. I spent the night there last night, I can stay there again tonight."

"You want to stay there *with* me?"

"I was thinking *instead* of you."

"Oh, no. This is *my* case—or at least it was. Despite her jerk of a husband, Patrice is worried sick about her son. I want to be able to let her know what's going on—tell her that I've at least seen him. You weren't able to get through to him the last time. If he does show up tonight, what makes you think you can do any better? At least I've worked with runaways before."

"Fine. Then we'll both stay. At least he's seen me before, and it might be easier for him to talk to a man." As soon as the words were out of his mouth, Trent had already begun to have his doubts about the situation. Spend the night in an empty house with Jaunie? That was like locking up an alcoholic with a fully stocked stocked bar.

"Great. Then it's settled. You can give me directions to the house, and I'll meet you there after work."

Trent sighed, rubbing his temples. "All right, then that's the plan." But resisting temptation had never been one of his virtues.

After stopping by her apartment to pick up a few things, Jaunie parked her car a street over from Trent's house. She recognized his four-by-four farther down the street where she'd suggested he park. Andrew might not have shown up when Trent stayed at the house because he saw the truck in the driveway.

As she hauled her sleeping bag, a small overnight case, and a pizza box up the street, she noticed the sky had darkened and was crowded by storm clouds. By the time she reached the house, it was drizzling. Trent stood in the doorway waiting for her.

She dropped her things in a heap in the front hall. Placing her hands on her hips, she looked around. "This is a beautiful house. Do you mind if I take a look around?" She knew Andrew wasn't there now, but she might come across something that could help with the search.

"I'll give you the tour." He walked through the foyer, past the kitchen, into a room with a hardwood floor covered with sheets of plastic. "This is the dining room," he said, spreading his arms wide.

"It's so huge." An ornate crystal chandelier hung from the ceiling, and directly in front of Jaunie were two wide French doors that opened to a deck in the backyard.

He walked over to the doors. "I'd take you outside, but it's raining pretty hard. I don't know if you can see it, but there's a hot tub on the deck."

The deck, overlooking an expanse of lush green grass and trees, wrapped around the house in the shape of a polygon. A sunken hot tub was in the far corner. "This is incredible. How much did you do yourself?"

"I built the deck and installed the hot tub." He turned and led her into the kitchen through a doorway that connected with the dining room. "Most of what you see, I've done myself. The previous owners didn't take very good care of it. I had to practically gut the thing and start over."

She followed him upstairs, opening every closet and peeking in every corner as he told her little secrets about drywall and moldings. Half the time she didn't understand what he was talking about, but that didn't matter. She hadn't heard him speak with such enthusiasm since the night they'd first met. And most importantly, the little-boy quality she admired was back.

Jaunie was genuinely impressed with his work. He'd gotten the best of everything. All the bathrooms had pedestal sinks with gold fixtures and wide tubs with air jets. The master bedroom was enormous, with a skylight and a walk-in closet.

She watched Trent's hands as he pointed out the detailing on an antique mirror he'd found at an auction. His fingers caressed the head of a delicate brass angel, and Jaunie couldn't help imagining his hands caressing—

Swallowing hard, she stepped back, trying to rechannel her thoughts.

Bad idea. Now she had a clear view of the black T-shirt stretched over his muscles, emphasizing his back, which, though broad at the shoulders, narrowed at the waist of his jeans. Jaunie sighed . . . and the fit of those jeans. None of the male models she'd worked with had anything over Trent.

When he turned around, he caught her staring. Even though she glanced away, she knew he'd interpreted her look correctly.

He stepped into the hallway. "The two bedrooms on the right are the only rooms I haven't finished. Once they're painted, I can have the carpet installed."

"This is a dream house," Jaunie said, anxious to forget that awkward moment. "What are you going to do once it's finished?"

"Sell it."

"Really? You don't want to live here?" she asked, twirling around. "I don't think I could let go of a house this beautiful."

"You'd have to if you wanted to make money. If it wasn't beautiful, no one would buy it."

Jaunie shrugged. She didn't know how he could remain so detached. She hadn't invested any time in it, and already she hated the idea of someone else living there.

Finally he took her downstairs to the basement-level family room. The best room in the house. A large stone fireplace stood grandly in the center, and behind it two rows of steps led to a wet bar made from dark wood panels. The room was inviting. She could picture herself relaxing in front of a fire on a cold winter night.

"We should sleep down here because it has carpeting," Trent told her. "Trying to sleep on a hardwood floor can be murder on your back."

"Fine with me." The gray carpet was so thick and plush, she ached to take off her shoes and curl her toes in it.

"I think Andrew came in over here." He pointed across the room. "Those sliding glass doors aren't very stable. They can be pushed off track from outside and then opened. I decided not to fix it until the kid's been found."

Jaunie looked through the doors. They opened to a small patio area just underneath the deck. "In this weather he may be driven back here to take shelter. There aren't too many places that would protect him from the rain all night."

Trent came up behind her. "We can only hope. If he's made his way to D.C. by now, there's no telling what kind of trouble he's gotten himself into."

Jaunie turned around to face him. "Don't be so . . ." She hadn't realized how close he was. He didn't move back. ". . . negative."

"I wasn't trying to be negative," he said, reaching out almost casually to touch a tendril of hair that rested by her ear. "I just wanted you to be prepared for the possibility that he might not show up tonight."

Jaunie barely heard him. The beating of her heart, his breathing, the whisper of his fingers near her ear were distracting. She raised her gaze to his, and her heart lurched. She *knew* that look. She saw it every night in her dreams, but she never thought she'd see it again in daylight.

He wanted her. His head bent toward hers.

Bells chimed softly in her head.

Trent's head jerked back, and he looked over his shoulder.

Did he hear the bells, too? Jaunie blinked as she realized the bells weren't in her head, they were coming from the doorbell upstairs.

"Someone's at the door." He turned, taking the stairs two at a time.

Jaunie followed at a slightly slower pace. Andrew wouldn't ring the doorbell. Who could it be? By the time she'd caught up to him, Trent was standing in the doorway, talking to a gray-haired older woman clutching an umbrella.

The woman looked over Trent's shoulder to Jaunie. "Is that your wife?" She collapsed her umbrella and slipped past Trent. She held out her hand. "I'm Irma Wilson. Your neighbor. I saw you walking up the drive and came to welcome you both to the neighborhood. Are you newlyweds?" Her eyes darted around, taking in the empty rooms.

Trent shifted his weight. "Uh—"

"Where are you from?" she said, leaning forward to peek into the kitchen. Irma Wilson seemed to be searching for gossip to share with her bridge partners.

Trent looked at Jaunie from over his shoulder, clearly unsure how to react.

Jaunie decided to take advantage of the nosey neighbor's presence. Searching through her bags, which were still in the front hall, she pulled out Andrew's picture. "Mrs. Wilson, I'm Jaunie Sterling and I'm a private investigator." She smiled when Irma's eyes lit up. "I'm searching for a runaway who was last seen in this area. Have you seen Andrew Montgomery?" She handed her the picture.

"Nooo, I haven't." Irma gave her a sly look. "Are you on a stakeout?"

Jaunie winked at the woman. "Well, as a matter of fact—"

"I knew it! I just knew it!"

Jaunie gently guided the woman back to the door. "We have to get back to work, Mrs. Wilson, but I'd appreciate it if you'd take that picture and keep your eyes open for Andrew."

She nodded eagerly. "I'll get right on it. I'll get the girls in my gardening club to keep an eye out, too."

Well, she'd been close. Gardening, not bridge. At least this was one situation where a wagging tongue would come in handy.

Mrs. Wilson winked on her way out. "Have fun, kids."

Trent shut the door behind Irma. "She was a character, wasn't she?"

"Yeah." Jaunie searched his face for signs of discomfort, but he showed no reaction to their near-miss kiss or Irma's assumption that they were married.

As they grabbed napkins and a couple of sodas and headed downstairs to eat the pizza she'd brought, Jaunie tried not to feel hurt by the fact that Trent was behaving as if their special moment had never happened.

One empty pizza box later, Trent looked over at Jaunie through the dim glow of the flashlight beam. The room was dark now, and she'd instructed him not to turn on any lights for fear of alerting Andrew to their presence.

She was meticulously tearing strips from the plastic label on her soda bottle. They'd already laid out their sleeping bags side by side in the far corner of the room, away from doors and windows, and they'd changed into comfortable clothes. Now all they had to do was wait.

Trent stretched out on his sleeping bag. The flashlight she'd brought was between them, pointing toward the ceiling, and she lay on her back staring at the circle of light as if she were stargazing.

The flashlight barely made a difference as darkness overtook the huge room, but it was enough light for him to see her. Safe in the shadows of the night, Trent admitted that he couldn't ignore it any longer.

He wanted her.

Tension, attraction, the past—all stood between them like a dense fog. It was time to clear the air.

He propped his head on his fist. "There's something I think we should talk about."

Jaunie rolled onto her side, facing him. "What is it?"

All in all, things had been going well between them. He hated to ruin it by raising a sensitive subject, especially when he'd rather raise the hem of her T-shirt. Or raise the nipples on her breasts with his tongue.

Trent rolled onto his back. "Well ..." he stalled, forcing his mind away from the way her legs looked in those little shorts, or how her hair, sedately clipped at the nape of her neck, would look spread out over her naked breasts.

If he cleared the tension, settled the past, maybe the attraction would fade away with them.

Yeah, right.

"I think we should talk about the night we met." He turned his head to watch her as he spoke those last words. She looked resigned and maybe relieved that the subject had finally come up.

She turned onto her back, her face dropping into shadow. "I guess we should. Pretending it never happened obviously isn't working."

Trent rubbed his palms on his sweatpants. "I still have mixed feelings about that night. I'm glad I found out Erika didn't trust me *before* I made the mistake of marrying her. My problems with her had nothing to do with you. But I don't understand how you could make your living setting men up."

He turned to face her. The words came out more harshly than he'd intended.

Jaunie sat up, hugging her knees with her arms. "I didn't think of it like that. Most of the women who came to Intimate Investigations were nothing like Erika Maxwell. Their men were cheaters and they already knew it. They just needed to prove it. I thought I was *helping* them.''

She sounded as if she weren't so sure now, Trent thought, staring at the back of her pink T-shirt. It was a lot easier than staring into her eyes. This wasn't easy for her to talk about. He wished he could let it drop, but he had to know.

''You may have thought you were helping some of those women, but what about the guys who were innocent? The men that didn't give in?''

Jaunie turned to look him in the eye. ''They all gave in—until you.''

Trent started. She didn't sound arrogant. She wasn't bragging, but was just stating a fact. ''You didn't come across *any* faithful men?'' he asked incredulously.

''Some of the other women who worked for Alan did, but you were my first. The agency's overall track record was high. Only thirteen percent were faithful.''

Trent shook his head, trying to place himself in Jaunie's shoes. He knew how men could be, but in his experience, a lot of women were no better. He was tired of paying for what other men had done and was about to say so when Jaunie spoke.

''Don't get me wrong. I'm not saying it's the best job I've ever had. I only got involved because I'd been hurt too many times myself. I thought I was doing the right thing, showing women what men were really like. I was bitter for a while. That's not a good reason for doing anything, but it wasn't as easy as I'd thought it would be.''

Trent rolled onto his side, watching her profile. ''What do you mean? What happened?''

''Some guys figured that since they'd already lost everything, why not try getting with me? But some of the men blamed me, even though it was their own doing. Some just threatened. Others tried to make good on their threats.''

''What?'' Trent sat up. ''You were in danger?''

''Alan did a good job of protecting us.''

''Alan is the guy that ran the agency?''

''Yes. I was never hurt, but one guy really scared me. He

would show up wherever I was and watch me. It was unsettling."

Trent clenched the sleeping bag with his fist. "What happened to him?"

"He was finally arrested for harassment. He left me alone after that."

"It sounds like a crazy business. How in the world did you get into it? I'm sure it's not advertised in the want ads, or offered in college course catalogs."

"It's just like any other specialty in the P.I. business. Alan chose it because it's profitable. Cheating never goes out of style." She played with the clasp on her watch. "He's married to my sister's best friend. When he found out I'd given up modeling, he asked me to work for him."

"You were a model?" Trent didn't know why he was surprised. She was certainly beautiful enough. He'd just never made the connection.

"Yes," she said with a heavy sigh.

He cocked his head. "Why do you sound so down about it? Don't models get paid a ridiculous amount of money to travel around the world, wearing expensive clothes and meeting all the right people?"

"That's true."

There was more, Trent could tell by the sound of her voice. "But you didn't like it?"

"I hated it."

"Why?"

"I don't like to complain about modeling. People just think you're whining. Oh, the lights are too hot, the hours are too long, etc. But it has a downside, or at least it did for me."

"What was the downside?"

"It was like being a glorified coat hanger. People reduced you to your best and worst features. One minute your eyes are exotic and your legs are statuesque, five minutes later your eyes are too dark and your legs are skinny. You can never find stability. I was fourteen when I started, and it was so hard being picked apart all the time that my self-confidence was at zero.

"It was a superficial business based on what's hot now and what looks good on the surface. And there were the drugs and the sexual harassment. I was lucky because I was with a reputable agency that stayed away from all that, but some of the things I saw other girls get into . . . I'm sure if you ask Naomi Campbell or Cindy Crawford they'll tell you different, but it just wasn't right for me."

"Then why did you do it?"

"I didn't want to. I did it because I thought it would make my mother happy. But once she'd reaped all the benefits she could from my career, she moved on to the next thing, and I was stuck living the life."

Now Trent wished he could see her face. Her voice was hollow and held a note of loneliness. Before he could find words to comfort or commiserate, she spoke again.

"Anyway, I got used to the lifestyle. I modeled for six years, but it changed me." She turned to face him. "Have you ever awakened one morning and discovered you weren't who you thought you were? Nowhere near who you wanted to be?"

Had he ever. He was living it. He'd been going through life believing he was fine only to discover he'd been walking around in a fog. But he wasn't comfortable enough with the idea himself to admit it out loud. So instead he shrugged and said, "I don't know."

"Oh," she said, sounding disappointed. "Well, trust me. It's not a pleasant feeling."

Silence stretched out between them, and Trent realized she wasn't going to say any more. "Jaunie, I'm glad we talked. Now we can put the past behind us."

She smiled. "Yes, I'd like that." After a moment, Jaunie stood. "I'm going to get some water. My mouth is dry. Do you want anything?"

"No thanks." Trent watched as she headed toward the stairs. Her life had been nothing like he would have expected. She hadn't gone around using and abusing men for her own amuse-

ment. Even when she'd said she used to be a model, he'd
assumed she'd been spoiled by life in the fast lane. But it was
clear she'd somehow managed to find her way back to reality—
which was more than he could say for himself lately.

Trent stared at the circle of light on the ceiling, feeling guilty.
He'd forced Jaunie to spill her guts all night, and he didn't
have anything left inside him to share in return.

She wasn't thirsty after all, Jaunie decided as she reached
the kitchen. She just needed some space, so she continued up
to the bathroom on the second floor.

At the top of the stairs, it was pitch black. Groping at the
first door she reached, Jaunie flicked on a light switch. Oops!
It was a closet, not a bathroom. She started to turn off the light
and shut the door, when a card on the floor caught her eye. It
was a Metro train fare card. Trent must have dropped it. She
picked it up and shoved it into her pocket. She'd give it back
to him when she got downstairs.

Thank goodness the next door she came to was the bathroom.
She glanced at her watch: eleven o'clock.

Jaunie listened to the rain's steady clatter on the roof. Had
she just lost her one and only lead? If the boy didn't come
back for shelter on a night like this, he probably wouldn't come
back at all. Maybe Trent was right. Maybe Andrew had found
his way to D.C. by now.

After splashing her face with cool water, she leaned back
against the wall, drained from worrying about Andrew. From
talking to Trent. She'd said more than she'd planned to. Even
though she felt better for it, it was painfully clear that Trent
hadn't felt the need to share in return.

Nevertheless they were more at ease with each other now
that the past had been brought to the surface. It was a start.

With a final sigh, Jaunie turned out the light and left the
bathroom. The hallway was dark. When she reached the top
of the stairs, she saw a dark shape with a flashlight moving
toward her. Startled, she tripped, her stocking feet sliding on

the polished staircase. She bumped down the first three steps before Trent dropped the flashlight and caught her.

"I'm sorry. Are you okay?" he asked, helping her back to her feet. "I didn't mean to scare you. I just wanted to make sure you were all right. I didn't see you in the kitchen."

Jaunie straightened. "I'm fine. I was in the bathroom."

They were standing halfway up the staircase, and Trent still hadn't let go of her waist. The flashlight had slid to the bottom of the stairs and was shining dimly up into the hall.

Feeling awkward about his nearness and unable to read his features, she said the first thing that came to mind. "Andrew's not coming, is he?"

Trent cocked his head. "I don't know. It's getting late."

Jaunie nodded, not sure what to say or do next. He was standing only one step below her, and he showed no sign of backing up.

The house was black other than the occasional lightning flash from the storm and the faint glow from the flashlight. It must have been the darkness that made them bold. By unspoken mutual consent, they both leaned in until their lips met.

Years of curiosity, anticipation, and imagination exploded. Jaunie gripped his shoulders, and Trent groaned as his arms tightened around her waist.

Mmm. It had been so long. His tongue slid between her lips. She leaned closer, and he lifted her until her feet no longer touched the steps. Then suddenly she was descending. Once she was sitting on the stairs, Trent knelt over her, his weight on his knees as he cradled her back and kissed her neck.

Instinctively she locked her knees around his waist. His mouth played at the neckline of her T-shirt as his hands drove under it. They moved over her rib cage until his thumbs found the edge of her bra, pushing under it and gliding over the undersides of her breasts up to her nipples.

As sensations mounted inside her, Jaunie reached out, clutching the wooden banister with one hand and Trent's shoulder with the other. He pushed her T-shirt higher, dipping his head to her breasts, teasing each with the tip of his tongue. Jaunie released her grip on the banister to give Trent's back her full attention. She wanted to touch every inch of those muscles she'd admired earlier.

Trent's hands left her breasts to grip her around the waist. He lifted her again, this time to trade places with her. He leaned back on the stairs, bringing Jaunie down on his lap.

Immediately she began tugging his shirt from his sweatpants. He helped her by stripping it off in one motion. His dark skin was like burnished wood, each muscle exquisitely defined like a fine carving—so smooth. She tested the surface with her lips. Unable to help herself, she let her lips caress his skin from his shoulder to his stomach, marveling that something so hard could feel this soft.

She was so caught up in her exploration, she didn't recognize the discomfort she was causing. When his fingers bit into her thighs, she raised her head and found his countenance twisted like that of a man tortured. He released a low groan as he arched his hips restlessly.

She gripped his head with both hands, bringing her mouth back to his, kissing him aggressively. He met her with hot aggression of his own. His hands, those wonderful, strong hands she'd ached to have on her, moved under her shorts to cup her buttocks.

Unable to control the wild heat climbing inside her, Jaunie raised up on her knees so he could access what he wanted. His fingers hooked on her underwear and began to tug downward, bringing her shorts—

Crashing!

Banging! In the basement.

"Andrew," Jaunie whispered, snapping out of her sensual haze as the private investigator took over.

Chapter Seven

Jaunie dashed down the stairs, righting her clothes and groping for the flashlight. She reached for the basement doorknob only to find Trent's hand there first. He charged into the basement with Jaunie hot on his heels.

One end of the sliding glass door had been wedged open just enough for a small boy to climb through. Jaunie aimed the flashlight's weak beam around the room, but couldn't see Andrew.

Trent hit the light switch.

"Andrew!" Jaunie saw the boy crouched in a corner freeze for a moment.

He looked bedraggled and soaked to the bone. Rivulets of water coursed down his face, and silver beads clung to his matted hair. His thin T-shirt had been poor protection from the fierce downpour, and his sneakers were covered with mud.

As Jaunie studied him, Andrew snapped out of his daze and darted behind the fireplace. Jaunie ran at him from the right and Trent from the left, hoping to trap him. Somehow the boy slipped between them, and Jaunie and Trent nearly careened into each other head-on.

While they got their bearings, Andrew zipped up the basement stairs. They both raced after him. Trent reached the stairs first, but he lost his footing in the thick carpeting, and slid down on his stomach.

"Trent, we're going to lose him!" Jaunie shouted, climbing over his body and scrambling after Andrew.

Upstairs Jaunie turned on the hall lights. Muddy footprints told her where to go. She rounded the corner and started jogging up the front hall stairs with Trent right behind her.

This time Jaunie, still in her stocking feet, slipped on some mud and lost her footing on the stairs. Trent just lifted a leg so she could slide past him as he continued to climb, calling over his shoulder, "Sterling, we're losing him!"

Knees stinging from her fall, Jaunie hobbled after them. She heard crashing and shouting coming from one of the unfinished bedrooms on the right. When she reached the doorway, she tried flicking the light switch, but nothing happened.

She scanned the room in time to see Trent climbing out the window. Her heart stopped. Oh, God! Andrew!

Jaunie stuck her head out the window, searching for Trent and Andrew, but was blinded by the pelting rain. Wiping the rain and her hair from her eyes, she squinted into the foggy night.

Andrew knelt precariously on the edge of the sloping roof over the deck. He was trying to grab a tree branch that was just beyond reach of his fingertips.

"Andrew, no!"

His slight body jerked, causing his sneakers to skitter on the rain-slick roof.

Panic stabbed her heart. *Where is Trent?*

Then she saw him. He was lying flat on his stomach, edging toward Andrew. Each time Trent reached out, Andrew made a frantic grab for the branch, forcing Trent to draw back.

Before she knew it, Jaunie had one leg over the windowsill. The sight of her own white sock jarred her back to reality.

What am I doing? I wouldn't be able to do any good there. I don't even have shoes on!

She pressed her eyes closed as every accident she'd ever heard about flashed through her brain. No, don't go there! she told herself sternly. She had to calm down.

There had to be something she could do. Who knew how much time there was before Trent or Andrew—

"Andrew," she called. "Your mother's worried about you. She'd give anything to have you safe. Please, come inside."

Andrew looked over his shoulder, surprised either by her voice or her words. She had to keep talking.

"If you come inside, everything will be okay. I promise. You don't have to—" Jaunie gasped as Trent grabbed Andrew by the waist. He'd been able to creep up on the boy while Jaunie distracted him.

Trent dragged Andrew back up the roof toward the window. Jaunie held her breath, praying that Trent wouldn't fall. He lifted the boy over his shoulders. "Grab his arms, Jaunie."

She did as she was told, pulling Andrew in through the window. She collapsed under his soggy weight, but held firm, half expecting a struggle. Andrew just sank heavily in her arms, clearly too worn out to fight anymore.

Later, Trent watched Jaunie pull a package of Mickey Mouse Band-Aids from her purse. The three of them huddled in the basement in front of the fire he'd made from some leftover wood. It was the first time he'd made a fire in the middle of July, but since he and Andrew had been soaked to the bone, and he'd given Andrew his only dry shirt, they needed the extra warmth.

Jaunie peeled the paper off a Mickey Mouse Band-Aid as she eyed the nasty scratch on Andrew's forehead.

"Hey, where'd you get those?" Trent asked.

Andrew scooted back. "Mickey Mouse is whack! You ain't putting that thing on me!"

"Geri gave them to me. She practically lives in the Disney store," Jaunie answered Trent, then turning to Andrew, said, "And this isn't for you. It's for me."

Andrew and Trent both gaped as Jaunie pulled her knees to her chest and placed a Mickey Mouse Band-Aid over the small scrapes on each knee she'd received from sliding down the stairs.

Andrew tisked, rolling his eyes, but Trent could only grin. Jaunie knew how to handle Andrew. At first the kid wasn't too responsive, and when he was, his responses weren't repeatable. He and the kid had been butting heads every time Trent tried to get him to do something, but Jaunie had known how to convince him to change out of his wet clothes and stick around at least for the night. It had taken them so long to calm him down, they didn't want to risk losing him by trying to take him home right away.

The kid still wasn't saying much, but he stopped swearing when Jaunie asked him to, and at least now they had his attention.

Trent rubbed a spot on his sternum. "Hey, you have any more of those? I think I could use one."

"What for?" Jaunie frowned, looking him over. "You don't seem to be cut anywhere."

"I think I have rug burn on my chest," Trent answered, chuckling.

Jaunie burst into giggles while Andrew just looked back and forth between the two of them muttering "whack."

Jaunie threw Trent the box as she explained to Andrew—in more detail than necessary—how Trent slid facedown on the basement stairs.

Andrew contorted his face oddly as he tried not to laugh out loud. Keeping the joke going, Trent pulled out a Band-Aid and made a big show of choosing the proper spot, carefully pasting it on his chest.

Trent returned the Band-Aid box to Jaunie. "Thanks, I feel much better now."

She held open her purse but didn't put the box away. Looking at Andrew, she said, "Are you sure you don't want one, too? There's no one here to notice how 'whack' the three of us look."

Andrew puffed and rolled his eyes, saying, "I don't care." But he sat incredibly still as Jaunie gingerly placed the Band-Aid over the scratch on his forehead.

"There," she said, smoothing it gently. "Unfortunately it's just a small scratch and probably won't leave a scar."

Andrew raised his eyebrows.

"While I was working as an apprentice to get my P.I. license, the guy I worked with used to give me a hard time because he said my skin was too perfect. I didn't have any scars. He said scars are like badges that remind you to stay out of trouble."

She gave Andrew a wry look. "I said, 'If you stay out of trouble in the first place, why would you need a reminder?' "

Andrew snickered despite himself.

"Nevertheless by now I've gotten a couple scars in the line of duty, so he stays off my back."

Jaunie went on to tell Andrew about some of the scrapes she'd gotten into while earning her license. By the time she started her third story, Trent had figured out that she was making the whole thing up. He had a feeling Andrew knew it, too, but the kid was spellbound as Jaunie regaled him with her outlandish adventures.

While Andrew listened, he suddenly didn't look so old anymore. The lines of tension around his mouth and eyes had eased, and his face was relaxed like a twelve-year-old's should be.

Trent leaned back and watched them, realizing that he'd seen that old, hard look on his own face more often over these past couple years. He shook his head. It didn't make sense. Despite his misadventures with women, at thirty-six he was three times as old as Andrew and hadn't suffered through half as much hardship as that kid had.

That fact really put his life into perspective. Trent had had a happy childhood. Growing up, he'd been one of the few kids in the neighborhood who'd still had both parents. His family was still close—when he let them be. And his sister, Kendall, had made a good marriage just like the one his parents had.

Trent didn't know where he'd gone wrong in that department,

but now he realized he had no right to complain. He'd been given the opportunity to take a big bite out of life. He couldn't regret the lingering aftertaste when he was looking at a kid who might never get the chance to taste any of the good things life had to offer.

No wonder Andrew responded so well to Jaunie—doing what she asked of him, not putting up a fight when she fussed over him. It was probably more attention than he'd received in a long time. It had to be a relief to sit back and be a kid for a while. He'd probably been on his own long before he'd hit the streets a few days ago.

The maternal instincts suited Jaunie—a little too well, Trent thought, feeling a distant ache in the vicinity of his crotch. And no Band-Aid would heal that.

He absently rubbed the place where Mickey Mouse lay on his sternum. Instead of the big production he'd made of putting it there, he'd really wanted to ask Jaunie to kiss it and make it better.

Trent flashed back to Jaunie rubbing her lips over his chest on the stairs, his hands under her T-shirt. Jaunie sitting astride him, just as he was about to—

"Hey!" Jaunie snapped her fingers in front of his face. "Snap out of it. I thought I was doing pretty well, but clearly I'm more boring than I'd thought. Andrew's out cold, and you're in a trance."

Trent blinked. "Sorry." He looked over and sure enough, Andrew, wrapped comfortably in *his* sleeping bag, was sound asleep.

Jaunie looked apologetic. "I don't want to wake him. Do you want to take my sleeping bag?"

"Nah." He rolled up his sweatpants, which had been drying by the fire, into a pillow. He now wore the jeans he'd worn earlier that day. "There's enough wood to keep the fire going if I need to. I'll be fine over here."

"Are you sure?"

"Yep," he said, rolling over and getting comfortable.

"Okay. Then I'm going to turn in, too. I want to take Andrew back home to his mother first thing in the morning. Good night.''

"Good night.'' Trent watched Jaunie's slender form move under the sleeping bag as she settled in to sleep. It had been one hell of a long day.

Turning onto his back, he threw an arm over his eyes to block his view of her. It was going to be one hell of a long night.

"Jaunie, wake up!''

She jerked awake with a groggy moan.

"He's gone.'' Trent was kneeling over her. He fell back hastily as Jaunie came to her feet in one motion.

"Where is he?'' She started for the stairs, calling, "Andrew!''

Trent stopped her with a hand on her arm. "Don't bother. I've already searched the house from top to bottom. Jaunie, he's gone.''

"No!'' She stamped her foot, feeling like a two-year-old but not caring. "He can't be gone. I thought we—''

Oh, Lord. Not now. No tears now. Private investigators didn't cry when things didn't go their way. It was . . . unprofessional. She could handle this.

Trent squeezed her shoulder. "I'm sorry, Jaunie.''

She turned away from him, blinking rapidly. Taking a deep breath, she stared at the ceiling, hoping the tears forming behind her eyes would roll back where they'd come from.

She felt Trent's hands on her shoulders, firmer this time. She tried to pull away, but he wouldn't let her.

"Look, I know how you're feeling. I feel the same way. When I woke up and found him gone, I cursed myself for having the nerve to sleep, for not waking up or hearing him leave. I tore the house apart, hoping he'd be there—knowing he wouldn't be.''

She jerked away. "I'm not surprised he didn't stay.'' The words sounded phony, even in her own ears, but she couldn't stop them. "That's how this business goes sometimes. I'm a professional. I'm used to it."

"I don't think anybody ever gets used to being disappointed," he said quietly. "We both wanted to make a difference for that kid. And it's not too late. We just have to find him again."

She turned around. "Yes, you're right. I just have to think—concentrate on where to look next."

"In a minute," he said, reaching for her. "This first."

She let herself be pulled into a hug. His arms wrapped around her, and for the moment, she relaxed. With a comfortable sigh, she let him absorb her weight.

Jaunie didn't know how long they stood like that, but it felt natural when she raised her head and his lips covered hers.

This kiss wasn't like those they'd shared the night before. This kiss wasn't hurried, intense, or carnal. It was patient, quiet, and comforting. It ended as softly and as naturally as it had begun. Then, by mutual consent, they each withdrew from the embrace.

Jaunie went to stand by the sliding glass door, and Trent sat on steps that led to the bar. They were a whole room apart, but Jaunie could still feel his nearness.

"Um." Trent cleared his throat; his voice carried without him raising it. "This is kind of like déjà vu, but I think we should talk about last night."

Jaunie held her breath. Last night. Last night had been more than she'd ever hoped to get from him, so it would have to be enough. "I think I know what you're going to say, and you don't have to. Last night we agreed to put the past behind us. Why don't we include what happened after that as setting the past straight, and pack it away with the rest? Today's a new day. We can start fresh as *friends.*"

"I think that would be best. Do you understand? I just can't do this again."

Jaunie tried to ignore the pain that sliced through her heart at his confirmation. Even though she hadn't expected him to protest, a small part of her had hoped—

"Jaunie, I'm the Titanic of relationships. I'm a disaster at romance. You know. You witnessed one of my shipwrecks."

She turned toward him. "That wasn't your fault."

"It doesn't matter. With women I make bad decisions. At my age I can't blame it all on the women. It's me—I'm just no good at this whole thing."

Jaunie cringed inside. That was a standard line, right? *It's not you, it's me. I'm just no good at love.* He was telling her that she'd just be another mistake in his long line of failed affairs. And he was right.

What could she offer him? Before she'd met him, she couldn't honestly say that *she'd* believed a stable relationship was possible. He was right. Friendship was best.

"I genuinely like you, Jaunie, and after all we've been through to get to this point, I'd hate to have it end like all the others."

She smiled at him. "Then it's settled. Now that we've gotten all that physical stuff out of the way, we can be friends."

Trent smiled back. "You're right."

"Now our minds will be free to focus on finding Andrew."

This is for the best, Jaunie thought. *And if I remind myself enough, maybe I'll actually believe it.*

For the rest of the day, Trent and Jaunie went their separate ways. Jaunie set out to find Andrew, and Trent went to work, but promised to stop by and check on her progress later.

When Jaunie got to the office, her first order of business was to call Patrice. She could at least give the woman the assurance that she'd seen Andrew and that he was all right. She just wished she didn't have to deliver the news that he'd slipped through her fingers as well.

Pulling out her electronic Rolodex, she called the number. Her fingers had already dialed the first three digits before she paused. When they did find Andrew—and they would—what would prevent him from running again? He'd be stuck in the same situation he'd run away from. Jaunie knew Patrice loved him. She could see it in her face, hear it in her voice. Richard was the problem—and Marshall Hall. There had to be some way for her to get through to Patrice.

After thinking for a few minutes, Jaunie came up with a plan. She made two phone calls: one to Patrice and one to an old friend. She'd been lucky to get all the pieces into place on such short notice. Maybe she could give Patrice a little reality check.

For the rest of the morning, Jaunie searched all the places in the area that could possibly interest a twelve-year-old. Movie theaters, arcades, malls. Nothing.

Finally at one thirty, it was time to meet Patrice for lunch. When Jaunie approached the table, Patrice stood.

"I can't believe it. You saw Andrew. Are you sure he's okay? Did he look like he'd had enough to eat?"

Jaunie, who had gone over every detail of last night's events—with the exception of the roof incident—over the phone, didn't mind going over it again.

"Patrice, there's something I want to talk to you about."

"Oh, don't worry. I'm sure that since you've seen Andrew, I can convince Richard to rehire you. The police still haven't made any progress."

"Patrice, that's not really my primary concern. It's Andrew." She spotted Jeremy Saunders at the entrance. "I hope you don't mind, but I've asked a friend to join us."

Patrice looked confused. "Who? Why?"

A tall, thin, redheaded man approached the table.

"Patrice, I'd like you to meet Jeremy Saunders. Jeremy, this is Patrice Lincoln." They both nodded politely.

Patrice's eyes darted back and forth between the two of them. "Does this have something to do with Andrew?"

Jaunie took a deep breath. "Yes, indirectly. Jeremy is a graduate of Marshall Hall."

Patrice immediately became defensive. "I already told you, my husband is a graduate of Marshall Hall. All those things you said about the school can't be true."

Jeremy had been sitting in silence until this point. He was

pale by nature, but his face had a gaunt dark-eyed look that gave him a sad, haunted appearance. "Mrs. Lincoln," he said quietly, "I don't know what you've been told about Marshall Hall, but I'm here to tell you the truth."

Patrice pursed her lips. "All I care about is finding my son. I haven't got time to listen to a few complaints about some private school. That's not important right now."

Jaunie gazed across the table. "Patrice, I think it *is* important. I believe I'm close to finding Andrew. In fact, it's just a matter of time. But once you get him home, you want him to stay, don't you? Will you please listen to Jeremy?"

"I'll listen," she answered stiffly. "But I know all I need to know from Richard."

Jeremy's lanky frame slouched in the chair as he smoothed his palms on his gray suit jacket. "My parents sent me to Marshall Hall when I was sixteen years old. I didn't want to go, but I'd been getting into trouble in public school, and finally my parents had to make good on their threats."

His voice was hollow. "I didn't think it was so bad at first. In addition to the regular schooling, we learned military techniques. We handled weapons and took combat training. That was cool. It wasn't until I got in trouble for the first time that I began to see the difference. There was no detention or extra KP duty like you'd expect. At Marshall Hall you were punished by your peers."

Patrice's eyes widened. "What do you mean?"

"You can't let your guard down because there's always someone watching. We were rewarded for turning in other students. They called it 'team learning.' I can't tell you how many times I got my butt kicked, and teachers looked the other way."

Patrice gasped, but Jeremy continued. "If you check, you'll find that the school has several unresolved complaints against it. Nothing can be done formally, because the instructors are never directly involved. Apparently you can't hold the school accountable for the actions of the individual students. There's never any proof that the teachers have encouraged this kind of behavior. They tell you to sue the parents. But that would take a lifetime. It's not just one kid—it's every kid.''

Jeremy continued to speak of the horrors he'd encountered at Marshall Hall. Jaunie had heard him tell his story before, but it was no less painful to hear it a second time. Now Jeremy was a guidance counselor at her niece's elementary school, but it had taken years of therapy to bring him to that point.

He told Patrice how he couldn't stop looking over his shoulder. Marshall Hall had taught him to strike out at society before it struck him. He described scenarios of psychological torment. The school fostered a gang mentality that was hard to break free of.

Jeremy continued to speak until Patrice, with tears in her eyes, begged him to stop.

"Oh, Lord," she whispered, shaking her head. "I just want my baby back. I just want my son." She gave Jaunie a pleading look. "If you bring my son home to me, I promise I'd lie down and die before I send him to a school like that."

Jaunie got back to Sterling & Treymaine late that evening, feeling drained. She'd left Andrew's mother distraught, but hopefully comforted by Jaunie's promise to find her son.

She entered her office to find Geri propped on the edge of her desk, chatting with Trent, who was lounging in her chair.

"Finally," Geri said, throwing her arms up. "Sheesh! I haven't seen you all day. Mel said you popped in early this morning, but she hadn't heard from you since. You didn't even call in for messages."

Jaunie dropped her purse on the desk and sank into a guest chair. "I'm sorry, Geri. I've been running around all day."

"It's all right, honey. But if Trent hadn't stopped by, I would have been worried. He said you're still trying to track down the Lincoln kid. How goes it?"

"Actually he's the Montgomery kid. His stepfather hasn't adopted him." *And hopefully, never will,* she added silently. "And it's not going as well as I'd like."

Trent groaned. "No luck, huh?"

Jaunie shook her head, then glanced at Geri. "Anything new happen here while I was gone?"

Geri bobbed her head. "Yep. We got two new cases. Surveillance for Mendleson's Deli and another process serving for H&B."

Jaunie bit her lip. "I'm sorry I couldn't be here."

Geri swung her legs. "Don't worry, sweetie. I got it covered. You just concentrate on finding this kid."

"But we're not likely to get paid for this one. I can at least help you—"

"Forget it. Don't you hear? I've got it covered. Believe me, I understand that money or no, you can't let this go. I went through this with Sammy, remember? You do what you have to do."

"Geri, you're an angel. Thanks."

"No problem. But speaking of Sammy, I gotta get home." She nodded toward Trent. "Toodles."

The door clicked shut behind Geri, and Jaunie let loose a weary sigh.

Trent leaned forward. "Uh, I think I owe you another apology."

Jaunie looked up, surprised. "What for?"

Trent looked down, clearly embarrassed. His long, well-structured fingers automatically reached for his temple. "Uh, for what I said about that book you bought."

Jaunie frowned, confused. "What book?"

His fingers pressed harder into his temple, distorting the shape of his right eye. Jaunie tried not to grin at the nervous habit. *"Let's Talk About Sex."*

Jaunie tilted her head wickedly. "You want to talk about sex? I thought we'd agreed to—"

"No! I don't want to talk about sex! I mean, not right now—oh, shoot. That's not what I meant."

"I know," Jaunie said, giggling. "I couldn't resist."

"While I was talking to Geri, she mentioned that you'd bought the book for her and why."

"How did that come up?"

Trent shook his head. "I don't know, but you know Geri—she's like the Energizer bunny. Once you get her started talking, she keeps going and going."

"Yeah, I know what you mean."

"I know I already apologized for what I said to you, but I still feel I should—"

Jaunie held up her hand. "Please, let's just forget it. We agreed to put the past behind us. That should include everything."

He let his breath out. "Okay, you've got a deal. So do you plan to start the search for Andrew up again in the morning?"

Jaunie rested her head on the back of the chair. "First thing."

"Great. Where do we start?"

She lifted her head. "What do you mean 'we'?"

He smiled at her. "I took the morning off tomorrow, so I can help you."

Chapter Eight

"So where are we headed?" Trent asked the next morning, as Jaunie turned off on the exit for Georgia Avenue.

She glanced over at him as he tapped out a drumbeat on her dashboard in time with the Mariah Carey song playing on the radio. If she didn't know better, she'd think he was actually excited about tagging along with her today.

She quirked her lips skeptically. Hopefully he didn't harbor any fantasies about participating in any of the melodramatic shenanigans he may have seen on TV. People were often disappointed to discover that the reality of her job wasn't nearly as thrilling as they expected.

"We're going to the mall," she answered.

"The *mall?*"

She didn't have to look at Trent to know that the mall wasn't exactly what he'd had in mind. "That's right."

"But why are we starting with someplace like that? Aren't we supposed to check out the train stations or bus terminals first?"

Jaunie shook her head with a wry smile. "Maybe in some cases, but we know Andrew has chosen to stay in the area, for whatever reason. He's spending his days *somewhere,* and the mall isn't an unlikely place for a twelve-year-old to hang out.''

She spared him a glance and found him studying her with mild disappointment. ''I know it sounds mundane, but the fact is, sometimes the best hiding place is right under your nose. I know of a case where a young boy ran away from home, and the parents went crazy searching everywhere they could think of.'' She looked over at him. ''He was missing for three days, and do you know where they finally found him?''

Trent shrugged. ''No idea.''

''He'd been staying in an old storage shed behind their house the entire time. He waited until his parents left for work, then went back to the house. By the time they came home, he was in the shed again. Finally one of the neighbors caught him sneaking in one morning and called his parents.''

Trent whistled. ''Okay, I see your point.''

Jaunie pulled into a parking space in front of Wheaton Plaza. ''We're here.'' She got out of the car and handed him a brown envelope.

''What's this?'' His large hands cradled the envelope gingerly as if she'd just handed him a package marked ''TOP SECRET.''

She slung her purse over her shoulder, and they started toward the main entrance. ''They're flyers with Andrew's picture and relevant information on them. We're going to stop in each store and pass them out.''

He nodded. Jaunie shot him a sidelong glance, inspecting his clothes. She was glad he'd worn khaki slacks and a tan oxford shirt. As much as she loved his jeans, she'd found that a professional appearance received the best response in these situations. She herself wore a lightweight eggshell linen blazer over a muted floral, ankle-length sundress.

Once inside the mall, Trent opened the package of flyers. ''Should we split up? I take one side, you take the other?''

''That will save time, but come with me to the first couple stores so you can get a feel for what to say.''

They agreed to start with a record store since Andrew was

clearly fond of music. Jaunie walked in and asked to see the manager.

A tall man with long hair, who didn't look a day over nineteen, approached them. "I'm the manager. What can I do for you?"

Jaunie shook his hand. "Hi. My name is Jaunie Sterling, and I'd like to ask for your help with a very serious matter." She handed him the flyer. "This is Andrew Montgomery. He's a twelve-year-old runaway, and we believe he may be somewhere in this area."

She pointed to her card stapled to the bottom of the flyer. "If you see him, would you please give me a call?"

The man's head bobbed slowly. "Sure. No prob."

Jaunie smiled. "I'd also appreciate it if you'd let your other employees see this flyer and ask them to keep an eye out."

"You got it," he answered. "Good luck."

"Thanks so much for your time."

Trent followed her to a few more stores before she gave him a supply of flyers of his own, and they split up. She instructed him to pay careful attention to stores Andrew might have an interest in, namely ones that sold basketball shoes or video games.

About an hour later, Trent rejoined her as she was talking to a man selling Day-Glo shoelaces from a cart stand. She looked up at him, and he spread his hands to show that he'd run out of flyers.

As she continued to speak to the shoestring vendor, she noticed that Trent had become preoccupied with the store across from them. The corners of her mouth twitched. The store was Victoria's Secret.

She wrapped up her conversation, shaking the vendor's hand, then turned toward Trent, who had his back to her. "I doubt Andrew has any interest in a sale on demi-bras," she said, nodding to the window display.

Trent jumped at the sound of her voice, color rising in his face as he turned toward her. "Sorry. I was just curious. I've always wondered what goes on inside those places."

Jaunie giggled. "It's not a bordello, it's a lingerie shop. You've never been inside one?"

He flinched. "Hell, no. I don't think they'd let me in on the big 'secret.' "

"Men are allowed in there." She started walking over. "It's no big deal."

"Where are you going?"

She turned back and grabbed him by the sleeve. "Come on. You may as well get this over with. Someday you're going to have to buy something for your wife or girlfriend. I may as well demystify you now."

Jaunie walked into the store and stopped before a round table covered with panties. "See, it's just underwear." She turned to look at Trent, then smiled. If she touched his face at that moment, his skin would singe her fingers.

While she went to the counter to show the saleslady Andrew's flyer, Trent stuck close to her back, trying not to look around. When she'd completed her speech, she turned back to him. "Mystery solved?"

Trent nodded but was clearly uncomfortable. Trying to ease him into it gently, Jaunie led him over to a display of hand creams, perfume, and bubble bath. Then she showed him the robes and pajamas. "See, it's just like any other store."

Her gaze drifted over the racks of intimate apparel, realizing she'd made a mistake—not because Trent was wandering around like an automation, but because lingerie was her weakness.

She slid another glance toward Trent. He was studying a lacy red teddy from the corner of his eye, then his gaze would dart around to see if anyone had noticed him noticing the garment. Jaunie chuckled to herself. If he was this uncomfortable now, how would he react if he knew she used to model for the Victoria's Secret catalog?

She shook her head. It wouldn't be pretty. That little tidbit would have to remain Jaunie's secret.

With his hands shoved deep into his pockets, he nodded and glanced around, but he seemed to relax a bit.

"Okay, I think you're ready now." Jaunie led him to the back of the store where the bras were.

Not only had he relaxed, he was starting to get into this new adventure. "Do you think this suits me?" he joked.

Jaunie turned around to find him holding a cobalt blue, lace bra up to his chest. Before she could answer him, a saleslady walked over. "Can I help you with anything?"

Trent immediately shoved the bra behind him.

Jaunie giggled. "No, thank you. We're just looking."

Trent threw down the bra, making a beeline for the exit. "Let's get out of here," he called over his shoulder.

Shaking her head, Jaunie followed.

They finished the remaining stores in the mall together, then stopped to rest at a table in the food court.

Trent leaned back, sipping his Coke from a straw. "So, boss, where to next?"

Jaunie played with the lid on her soda. "Um, actually I'm not sure."

He sat up pushing his Coke away. "What? Really? You don't have this all planned out already?"

"Well, I checked the local movie theaters and arcades yesterday. I'm just not sure where to check next." She propped her chin on her palm. "Where would you hang out if you were a twelve-year-old?"

Trent twisted his lips as he thought. "I don't know. It's been a while since I've been in tune with the mind of a twelve-year-old. My sister has a kid, but he's only two."

Jaunie frowned. "My sister has kids, too, but they're too young also." She clapped her hands together as inspiration hit her. "Jimmy is eleven!"

"Who's Jimmy?" Trent asked, crunching on an ice cube.

"Alan and Karina's son." She barely noticed Trent's confused look as her mind raced ahead. She held up her watch. "It's only eleven thirty. Alan should be in his office right now."

She started to get up, but Trent reached over to stop her,

recognition flickering in his eyes. "Is this the same Alan that—"

"That I used to work for? Yes." Heat danced on her cheeks. She felt compelled to explain. "While I was going for my license, I worked with him—as a private investigator. He still gives me advice when I need it."

Trent nodded but didn't reply.

"If you need to get back to work, that's fine. I mean, you don't have to come along."

"Oh, no. I'll go," he said in a tone that said he wouldn't miss it for the world.

Jaunie began to wind her straw around her finger. "He's been a really good friend to me. Through everything. He understood when I told him I couldn't work for him as a decoy anymore. He said he knew my heart wasn't in it. When I told him I wanted to become a private investigator, he didn't laugh at me like everyone else did."

She stared at the ceiling, remembering. "God, my mother had a field day. Ex-model turned P.I. She thought it was hilarious. But Alan said he'd do whatever he could to help me. I went back to school, and he told me what courses to take. Then he let me work with him, and he showed me the ropes."

She dropped her gaze to meet his. "Alan has always been there for me. I know you probably look down on him because of the line of work he's in, but—"

Trent reached over and gave her hand a squeeze. "You don't have to explain yourself. Really."

Jaunie blinked, laughing in self-deprecation. "Of course. I'm sorry. For some reason I seem to think talking to you is a substitute for therapy. I didn't mean to go on like that."

She tried to pull her hand back, but he wouldn't let it go. "That's not what I meant. I just meant your friendship with this guy has nothing to do with me. Just like my problems with my ex-fiancée had nothing to do with you. We agreed, remember? The past is the past."

"Right. I'm sorry. Let's go." Why couldn't she keep her

mouth shut? This was the second time she'd found herself spilling her guts to Trent. What was her problem?

At least Trent wasn't hung up about Alan. For some reason she'd been afraid he might hold a grudge against Alan because he owned the agency Erika had used to set him up. It could have been a very awkward situation, but thank goodness Trent was such a good sport. Maybe he and Alan would even like each other.

"Yes, he's adorable," Trent said halfheartedly as Jaunie held out yet another picture of Alan's son, Jimmy, for his inspection.

They'd been in Alan's office for twenty minutes, and as far as Trent was concerned, they had yet to get down to business. Instead, he'd nodded and "mmm-hmm'ed" in all the right places while Jaunie and Alan laughed, talked, and caught up on mutual friends.

At that moment Jaunie was bent over Alan's shoulder as he flipped through a stack of pictures featuring Jimmy at summer camp. She'd worn her hair down that day, and it fell over Alan's collar as she leaned in to see the photos. Periodically, when she'd pull the hair behind her ear and it would brush Alan's cheek, he would gaze up at her adoringly. Jaunie was completely oblivious to the fact that Alan, married or not, was in love with her.

Not that Trent cared. It didn't matter. But it was disgusting to watch. He couldn't stand the guy. What was he doing here anyway? Weren't they supposed to be out looking for Andrew? Instead he was sitting here watching this guy drool all over Jaunie.

She sat next to Trent again. "I'm glad Jimmy's having fun this summer, Alan, but as I told you on the phone, I need to pick your brain about something."

Alan stroked his mustache as he watched Jaunie cross her legs. "I'm all yours."

Trent watched Jaunie from the corner of his eye. How could she miss the innuendo in *that* remark?

Apparently she had, because she started to explain their situation with Andrew without blinking an eye.

Trent just shook his head. Every time Jaunie had mentioned Alan's name in the past, he'd pictured some white-haired guy who served as a father figure for her. But now, as he sat across from the man, he realized he couldn't have been more wrong. The guy wasn't a day over forty, and Trent supposed some women might find his light skin and light eyes attractive. Personally Trent thought whatever chemical process Alan used to make his hair wavy just made him look silly.

Trent narrowed his eyes suspiciously as he watched Alan and Jaunie talk. Had they ever been lovers? He remembered the way Jaunie had sung Alan's praises at the mall. She'd said he was a good *friend*. But that could still mean . . . No, she didn't look at him with the same interest Alan had for her. The attraction was purely one-sided, Trent concluded with a slight nod.

Why was he so relieved? Because he couldn't blame the guy for wanting Jaunie? Because he wanted her himself?

No! Trent crossed his arms over his chest. They settled that already. All those feelings were just remnants of the past. They were friends now.

But he still couldn't stand the guy. There was something about him—

"What do you think, Trent?" Jaunie looked over at him. "Do you want to try that?"

"Uh, I guess so," he answered, wondering what he'd just agreed to try.

"That settles it then." Jaunie got up, grabbing her purse. "Thanks a million, Alan. As usual, you're a life-saver."

Trent stood, too, and Alan came around the desk to walk them to the door. "Anytime, Jaunie. Give Simone my best." He kissed her on the cheek, then held out a hand to Trent. "Nice to meet you, man," he said coolly.

Trent appraised him with the same coolness as he shook his hand. "Same here."

Out in the parking lot, Jaunie was talking a mile a minute. "You know Alan was right. We should definitely focus on any hobbies Andrew might have. He said Jimmy is really into comic books, and there's a comic book outlet near here."

Trent frowned. So that was Alan's bright idea? Focus on hobbies? He could have thought of that. Out loud he said, "Actually I think we should check out basketball courts. The courts are always packed with kids in the summertime. I know of a few around here."

Jaunie stopped in front of her car. "That's a good idea. We can check out the courts after we go to the comic book outlet."

"Why not just—hey, what time is it?"

Jaunie looked at her watch. "It's one o'clock. Why?"

"I told Robert that I'd be in this afternoon. I'd better call him."

"Okay. I have a mobile phone in my purse. I can drop you off at the office on my way to the comic book outlet." Jaunie started digging through her purse and pulled out a cellular phone.

While Trent dialed Robert, he noticed Jaunie studying a Metro card she'd taken from her purse. When he got off the phone, she handed it to him.

It had a balance of over forty dollars on it. "What's this?"

"It's yours."

He shook his head. "I don't think so."

"Yes, it is. I found it in the closet at your house."

Trent shook his head. "It's not mine, but—"

Jaunie snapped her fingers. "Andrew! Of course! Now I know exactly where to look for him!"

Jaunie pulled over in front of the Meridian Building so Trent could get out.

"I can't believe you plan to ride the Metro all day looking

for a twelve-year-old. Thousands of people ride the Metro every day. He could be anywhere.''

"I already explained this to you. I saw a huge poster of a train in Andrew's room, and in his desk, I found several sketches of trains. You said yourself that the first time you saw him, Andrew was hiding in the closet. That Metro card is his. I'm going to start with the Red Line and talk to the attendants at the booths of each stop. They may recognize him.''

Trent shook his head as if he thought she was headed on a fool's mission. "Good luck. Let me know how it goes.'' He got out of the car and went inside the building.

Jaunie parked the car in the Meridian parking garage and then walked to the Dupont Circle Metro Station.

She got on the train heading toward Shady Grove, deciding to start at the top of the Red Line and work her way back to Silver Spring. Even though it was midsummer, and many people were on vacation or sight-seeing, there were plenty of seats for Jaunie to sit down.

She got off the train at Shady Grove and showed Andrew's flyer to the attendant. He hadn't seen the boy but agreed to hold on to the flyer just in case. She got back on the train, getting off at each station to talk to the attendants. By the time Jaunie was passing through Dupont Circle Station again, it was three o'clock.

At the next stop, Farragut North, Jaunie was just getting back onto the train when she heard someone call her name. The "doors closing'' bell chimed, and she turned around just in time to see Trent slip through before the doors shut on him.

The train jerked into motion, and Jaunie quickly grabbed on to a pole for support. Trent came to stand in front of her, holding on to the rail above his head.

"What are you doing here?'' Jaunie asked.

"Things are slow at work, so I just took the rest of the day off. I figured if I could find you on the Metro, maybe the two of us could find Andrew.''

"How long have you been looking for me?''

"Not too long. I got on at Dupont and rode a few stops

farther downtown. Then I stopped at Metro Center and talked to the attendant to see if you'd been there yet. He hadn't seen you, so I rode back until I found someone who had. I must have just missed you at Dupont.''

Jaunie raised her eyebrows, impressed. ''Well, you're turning into quite the detective, yourself.''

Trent grinned. ''Thanks. I'm glad I found you so soon, though. There are some real weirdos on this thing.''

''I know what you mean. What happened?''

''I had to stand up on the last train, and a big crush of people got on. Someone in the crowd pinched my butt.'' He leaned down to Jaunie's ear. ''And I think it was a guy.''

Jaunie giggled. ''Well, you do have a pretty cute butt. I guess he just couldn't resist.''

Trent's glare announced that he didn't find her comment funny. He glanced around. ''These trains are nothing like the subways in New York. They're cleaner, and there's no graffiti.''

''Yeah,'' Jaunie said, nodding. ''I remember the trains in New York. The Metro *is* much nicer.''

At the next stop, they got off and approached the attendant together. Again no one had seen anyone fitting Andrew's description. They got the same answer at the next several stations they stopped at.

''It's not that he may not have been here, it's just that we can't keep track of all the people that come through,'' one of the older attendants told her sympathetically.

''Thank you. We understand.''

When they were back on the train, Trent said, ''We've only got a couple stops left, and we haven't had any luck. Are you sure you want to continue?''

''Yes, I'm sure. The next stop is Silver Spring. We found Andrew in this area. We can't give up now.'' She tried to sound confident, but she was beginning to think she'd been wrong. Just because she found a Metro card with an unusually large balance, might not mean that Andrew was spending his summer days riding around on the train. While she wasted time here, his trail was probably getting colder. She'd promised his mother that she would find Andrew. She couldn't let her down.

Trent and Jaunie got off at the Silver Spring Metro Station and approached the booth. When the attendant saw Jaunie, he stepped out of the booth and reclined against the gate.

"What can I do for you, pretty lady?"

Trent moved to her side holding out a flyer. Before the man could take it from Trent, Jaunie took it and handed it to the attendant herself. "Is there any chance you've seen this boy? He's a runaway, and we have reason to believe he may be hanging out on the train."

The man studied the picture, then studied Jaunie. "Is he your son?"

"No, he isn't." She held out her hand. "My name is Jaunie Sterling, and I'm the private investigator listed on the card at the bottom of that flyer. You haven't seen him?"

The man grinned, then looked over at Trent. "Who's he? He the boy's father?"

Jaunie tried to hide her impatience behind a friendly smile. "No. This is Trenton Douglas. He's a concerned friend. I take it you can't help us?"

The man was quiet for a few minutes, then he tapped the flyer. "I think this is the same kid Renald found last week."

"Renald? Who's that?" Trent asked.

The man nodded. "Yeah, this is the kid. The train had just finished its last run to this station around midnight, and Renald, the operator, found this kid hiding in one of the cars. The kid thought he was going to sleep there."

Jaunie clutched Trent's arm in her excitement. "That must be Andrew!"

Trent nodded. "What happened then?"

"Renald brought the kid down here. We were trying to get his name out of him so we could call his parents, but he ran off. Since then I've seen him a couple times, but he doesn't stick around long enough for us to catch him."

Jaunie turned to Trent. "This is it! We've as good as found Andrew!"

* * *

At a quarter to twelve, Trent and Jaunie stood at their posts at the Metro station, waiting for Andrew. Jaunie stood at the telephone alcove behind the huge map of the Metro routes, and Trent stood before the sign, pretending to study it.

"I feel ridiculous," Trent said under his breath. "I've been staring at this sign so long, my eyes are crossing."

"You'd never make it as P.I. if your tolerance for boredom is this low," she said, holding a dead telephone receiver to her ear.

After they'd talked to the attendant who'd identified Andrew, they agreed to part company and reconvene before the Metro closed for the night. Jaunie had changed into a pair of jeans and a T-shirt, and pulled her hair into a ponytail. Trent wore the same clothes he'd worn earlier.

"Wait—I think that's him," Trent said, excitement mounting in his voice.

Jaunie casually looked over her shoulder. Sure enough, a small form was bouncing down the escalator with his nose buried in a comic book. "Don't move until he gets right up to us."

Trying to be patient, Jaunie switched the receiver to her other hand. Her heart was hammering in her chest. She couldn't lose Andrew again. She wouldn't!

Slowly she turned so she could see him approaching. He placed his card in the turnstile and walked through. Jaunie dropped the phone and reached for him.

"I got him," Trent shouted, wrapping his arms around the boy.

Immediately, Andrew started screaming and cussing. Trent's hand covered his mouth. A few people who were exiting the station with Andrew turned to look, but no one stopped them.

"Come on," Jaunie yelled, hurrying ahead. "Let's get him to the car."

She headed for the parking lot and heard a loud "ooff"

from behind her. She turned to find Trent doubled over as Andrew streaked past her.

Jaunie dashed after him with Trent on her heels. "Andrew! Andrew, stop!" she called.

Andrew began weaving through the few remaining cars in the lot. She saw him duck behind the tires of one of the cars. Keeping low, she carefully skirted around the parking lot and came up behind him. Andrew turned, but before he could move, Jaunie lunged in and locked her arms around his waist.

Andrew yelled and wriggled but Jaunie held him firmly, gripping her elbows with each hand as she clutched him to her.

Trent came running up behind them, breathing heavily. "You got him!"

"Hey! What's going on here?"

That was the first time Jaunie noticed the young couple standing in front a blue Mercedes a few feet away. The man had his arm around a woman as he walked toward them.

The little blonde looked concerned. "Can we help?"

Andrew stopped wriggling for a moment. "Help! They're trying to kidnap me! Help me!"

Jaunie blinked in shock, turning to look at the startled couple. They blanched, exchanging worried looks.

Trent was thinking quick on his feet. In a deep, authoritative voice he said, "Boy, you better stop your lyin' or I'm gonna whup your butt. You've given me and your mother enough trouble tonight, and when we get home—"

The blond woman moved forward. "Is violence really the answer?"

Trent snorted. "I should let you take him home for a night and then let *you* answer that question."

Then the man spoke up. "Missy and I have two little ones of our own, and we've found that talking—"

Jaunie decided to jump into the act. "Trent and I have tried everything: talking, grounding, restricting television privileges. Unfortunately Andrew doesn't respond to any of those things." She added an artful tremble to her voice. "We just don't know what else to do."

The man furrowed his brow with concern. "You know we've used a therapist for our son, Timmy, and he's made marvelous progress." He poked his wife. "Missy, do you have Dr. Jarvis's card in your purse?"

While Missy dug through her purse, Jaunie snuck a peek at Andrew. He seemed so completely dumbfounded by the entire exchange that he'd given up struggling. Now he just reclined against her legs in quiet resignation while they talked. Jaunie hadn't realized it, but her grip on Andrew had relaxed, and now her arms were gently draped around the boy's neck as a mother would hold her child.

Trent took the card Missy offered him. "Hey, thanks. We may as well give it a shot."

The man held out his hand. "I'm Chuck Rigowski, and this is my wife, Missy."

Trent shook his hand. "Trent. This is my wife, Jaunie, and our son, Andrew."

Jaunie nodded. "It's nice to meet you both."

Chuck smiled. "Good luck to you. Dr. Jarvis is a marvel. You'll love him."

Trent and Jaunie waved politely while the Rigowskis got into their car and drove away.

As soon as the Mercedes was out of sight, Trent looked over at Jaunie and Andrew. "Let's get out of here."

Chapter Nine

Forty-five minutes later Jaunie, Trent, and Andrew walked into Trent's apartment in Rosslyn, Virginia. Well, Jaunie and Trent walked. Andrew was carried, then dragged, and finally shoved into the apartment. Jaunie locked the door while Trent held on to Andrew, who immediately shrugged out of his grip.

"Man, get off me!" Andrew shouted, adding a few colorful expletives to the phrase.

"Hey, what did I tell you about that mouth?" Trent moved in front of Andrew, who kept turning his back.

"Andrew," Jaunie said, walking over to him. "I thought we agreed last time that using language like that doesn't encourage people to take you seriously. Trent and I want to hear what you have to say. We want to help you, but you can't get respect unless you're willing to give it."

Andrew turned away with a shrug, moving to the sofa and flopping down in the middle. "Since I'm stuck here, you got any food?"

Trent headed for the kitchen, and Jaunie tried to call Patrice. No one answered, so they decided it would be best for Andrew to stay there until they could take him home in the morning.

Twenty minutes later they were all settled down with three plates of spaghetti. Jaunie was impressed with Trent's culinary skills and with the fact that he'd proven food was a sure route to winning over Andrew.

Andrew relaxed as he ate and began to chatter without the foul language. He started asking question about the P.I. business and finally Trent and Jaunie.

He leaned back, kicking his feet up on the coffee table as he leveled his gaze on Trent. "So is she your honey dip?"

Before Trent could respond, Jaunie cut in. "Am I his *what?*" She knew she was a little rusty on the latest slang, but that phrase only made her think of doughnuts.

Andrew shook his head. "Come on. You know what I'm saying. Are you two knockin' boots?"

Jaunie felt heat rise in her cheeks as she opened her mouth and closed it again.

"No!" Trent answered. "Jaunie and I are just friends. And that's none of your business."

Andrew threw up his hands. "I'm just saying though, if you two aren't together, you need to be. You both crazy. Y'all were tripping at the Metro."

Jaunie leaned back, glaring at Andrew. "Well, you started it."

"Okay, okay." He leaned forward, looking devious again. "So have you ever—"

Jaunie stopped him with a hand on his arm. This was getting out of hand. "We can talk about whatever you want, *after* we talk about why you ran away."

His mischievous grin disappeared, and his jaw went stiff. "I ain't talking about that."

Jaunie resisted the urge to correct his grammar. For now she'd settle for no cursing.

He crossed his arms. "And if you're thinking about taking me home, you can forget it."

Trent massaged his temple. "We have to take you home. Your parents are worried."

Andrew snorted. "Fine. You take me home, but I'll just run

away again. And next time you won't find me. I'll get on a train or a bus and go so far, you'll never see me again.''

Jaunie thought about that. ''Why *did* you stick close to home, Andrew?''

''I don't know.'' He shrugged, looking away. ''Just in case.''

''Just in case of what?''

He fiddled with the nap of the sofa.

''Does it have to do with your mother?'' she pressed.

''I thought she might need me, if she ever left that ass—''

''Watch it, Andrew,'' Trent cautioned.

''You were hoping your mom would leave Richard? Is that it?'' she asked.

Andrew's lower lip poked out. ''I'm not going home until she leaves him.''

''Your mom loves you. Won't you at least sit down and talk this out with her?''

He crossed his arms over his chest. ''There's no point. She doesn't listen to me—not since she married that . . . uh, creep.''

Trent leaned toward Andrew. ''Just because your mom has married someone new doesn't mean she doesn't love you.''

''Bullshhh—'' He glanced over at Jaunie. ''Bull. She's really changed because of that dumbhead. Me and her used to be so cool, but now she does whatever *he* says. Man, it's disgusting. I won't live with them. That's it.''

Jaunie raised her eyebrows in Trent's direction. He shrugged.

''So Richard is the problem, right? Has he hurt you?'' she asked.

Andrew shook his head. ''He's just straight-up mean. You can tell by looking in his eyes. They're like Semitoid's.''

Jaunie didn't know who Semitoid was, but she knew it was an accurate comparison.

''So what is it?'' Trent asked. ''You argue? You don't get along?''

''He hates me,'' Andrew mumbled, staring at his hands. He cusses me out whenever Momma's not around. She's always mad at me because he tells her everything's my fault. I told him I would run away. He said if I did . . . to make sure I didn't come back. He said Momma would eventually forget about me because she has him now. And they'd have more children.'' Running the back of his hand across his eyes, he pretended he wasn't crying.

"That's sick . . . and it's not true, Andrew. You must know that.'' She felt moisture sting her own eyes. ''Your mother loves and misses you. If you could see how much she's suffered since you've been gone, you'd know that.''

Andrew shrugged, frequently dashing a hand across his eyes. "I'm not going back there. I'll just run away again. I swear, I will.''

"There has to be a way for us to work this out.'' Jaunie looked imploringly at Trent.

Trent gripped Andrew's shoulder. "You can't stay out on the streets, man. It's not safe. Until we work this out, you can crash here. Okay?''

Jaunie blinked. That wasn't what she'd had in mind.

Andrew looked at Trent then looked around his apartment. "I guess I'm down with that.'' His voice was deceptively casual, but Jaunie could see his shoulders slump with relief.

Fine. That bought them some time, but it didn't resolve the situation. She doubted she could talk Patrice into leaving Richard—no matter how much she wanted to. So how was she going to get Andrew and his mother back together?

"Andrew?'' Jaunie waited for him to look at her. "You love your mom, don't you?''

"Yeah.'' He stared at the floor.

"You don't want her to be unhappy, do you?''

"She doesn't care that I'm gone.''

"Yes, she does. She cries every day because you're gone.''
He raised his eyes. "Momma's crying?''

"She misses you. Why do you think she hired me? The police are out looking for you, too, but she wanted to do everything possible to try and find you. Don't you think you at least owe it to her to let her know you're okay?''

He stared at his shoes. "You'll tell her.''

"Yes, but she'll want to see for herself.''

Andrew was silent, but Jaunie could see that he was torn.

"Look, it's settled that you'll stay here with Trent for a while, right?" He nodded, and she said, "So you have nothing to lose if I set up a meeting between you and your mother."

"Not with the butthead there."

"Just you and your mother. No Richard."

He twisted his lips skeptically. "She won't come without him."

"If she promises not to bring Richard, will you agree to talk to her?"

He shrugged. "I guess."

Jaunie reached out and squeezed his hand. "Good decision, Andrew."

He looked embarrassed, but he didn't pull his hand away.

Trent rescued them from the awkward moment. "It's late, Andrew. Why don't I show you the spare room so you can get ready for bed."

"I ain't tired." His yawn said otherwise.

When Trent returned from getting Andrew settled, Jaunie was curled up on the sofa. "Still awake?" he asked, flopping down beside her.

"Yeah. Just trying to recover from this very long day."

"I'm with you on that one." He stretched his feet out in front of him.

"Is Andrew all settled?" She released a tiny yawn and blinked her drooping eyelids.

"He's knocked out," he answered, admiring her adorable sleepy expression. She looked rumpled and comfortable on his couch.

She started to get up. "If he wakes up during the night, he might try to—"

He nudged her back. "Don't worry. I locked the door. He's not going anywhere."

"Good." She sank into the cushions. "I think it would kill me to have to tell Patrice that I'd lost him again."

He reached over and squeezed her shoulder. "You won't have to this time."

She looked at him. "Thanks for all your help today—and for volunteering to take in Andrew."

"No problem. I was glad to do it. He's not such a bad kid—as long as you keep a bar of soap on hand for his mouth."

"His language is a defense mechanism. He swears like that only when he's upset or scared. He controls it just fine when he's calm."

He raised his eyebrows. That made sense. Obviously she knew her child psychology. "You made a lot of progress today. I think you got through to him. You should be proud of yourself."

Her smile was shy. "Thanks. I think we both should be proud."

Trent folded his hands behind his head. This was nice. They'd made a great team today.

"I should call Alan and let him know that we found Andrew."

He looked at the ceiling, feeling his body tense. "Oh, yeah. Alan."

"Alan seemed okay to you, didn't he?"

"What do you mean?" Like he cared.

"My sister says he and Karina are having marital problems."

"Probably because he's lusting after you," he said under his breath. Damn. He hadn't meant to say that out loud. He looked away, hoping she hadn't heard him.

Jaunie grabbed his arm. "What? What did you say?"

He faced her. No turning back now. "You mean you really can't see that guy is in love with you?"

Jaunie shook her head in confusion. "That's ridiculous. He's married to my sister's best friend."

Trent moved closer to her. "Do you think a little thing like marriage would keep a guy from wanting you? Come on. You made a living proving that men always want what they can't have."

She drew back as if he'd slapped her.

He was on a roll tonight, he thought with self-derision. "I didn't mean that it's your fault. I just mean that sometimes a man can't help wanting something, whether he has a right to or not. And if he wants it bad enough, he can't always prevent himself from taking it."

He could see color rising in her cheeks. She must have figured out that he was talking about himself now.

"But you did," she whispered.

He nodded. "I did. Once."

Without thinking about the action, Trent placed his hands on either side of her face and brought their lips together. His tongue immediately found its way into her mouth.

Her allure was mind numbing. He continued to sip at her lips, knowing with every touch he should pull away. After each brush of their lips, each caress of their tongues, he told himself, *just one more kiss.* But it was so hard to stop.

Jaunie's body had a lethargic pliancy in his arms. She curled against him, making soft noises like a purring kitten. Before he knew how they'd gotten that way, he was stretched out lengthwise over her, his face buried in her breasts.

Like a man surrendering to drunkenness, Trent let go of rational thought and sensation took over. Colors of desire. Sounds of heat. The taste of exhilaration.

His vision filled with cinnamon skin. Hot and soft. Dark nipples . . . like black pearls . . . smooth in his mouth. Wet. He cooled them with his breath.

Her back arched, and his nostrils were filled with her scent: sweet, sexy, spicy.

Mmmm. He was so hard. Straining with burning heat.

Kissing her navel. Tongue dipping, circling. Soft kisses, lower. He wanted more heat . . . more skin.

Blue jeans. Zipper. Sliding down.

Moving?

Trent blinked as he realized Jaunie was pulling away. Pushing him off.

He moved back, rubbing his temple as his brain began to

function again. "What's wrong?" *Idiot! You know what's wrong!*

She was sitting up, straightening her clothes. "It's late. I have to get home." She picked up her purse and walked to the door.

Trent followed more slowly because of the ache in his pants. He knew he should say something, but the words wouldn't come. His brain was still thick, hung over from her kisses.

Her eyes searched his, looking for something he couldn't give her. Finally her gaze dropped, and she turned to the door. "I'll see you tomorrow."

"Yeah." He could feel her disappointment. How could he explain why he pushed her away with one hand and drew her near with the other? Maybe if he wasn't still drunk with her scent, her taste, he could find the words. Instead he said good night and closed the door behind her.

Jaunie woke early the next morning, anxious to call Patrice. As soon as the woman got on the line, her first words were, "Jaunie, do you have news about Andrew?"

Nothing could have made her happier than offering her answer. "Yes, Patrice, I've found Andrew—and he's safe."

"Oh, my God!" Patrice didn't say anything else for a long time, and Jaunie could hear her sobbing on the other end.

She gave her a few minutes to absorb the good news. "Right now Andrew is staying with a friend of mine."

Patrice had a catch in her voice when she spoke. "When is he coming home? This morning? Should I pick him up? Lord, I can't wait to see my baby."

"Patrice, I'm going to bring Andrew to you—but not at home." Jaunie bit her lip. She hated this.

"Why not?"

"It's Richard. Andrew doesn't want to come home while he's there."

Patrice's voice filled with relief. "Well, that's no problem. Richard's at work now."

"It's more complicated than that. He misses you, and he wants to see you, but I'm afraid Andrew doesn't want to come home as long as you're *living* with Richard."

"That's not his choice to make. I'm his mother."

"I know that, but Andrew says he'll just run away again— so far that we won't find him next time."

Patrice was silent.

Jaunie took a deep breath. "Do you know why Andrew doesn't want to live with Richard?"

"Yes, but it's only natural that they don't get along. It's hard for Andrew to accept a new man in his life that's not his father. Richard understands. He also said that since I feel strongly about not sending Andrew to Marshall Hall, that's okay."

"Patrice, Andrew tells me that Richard cusses him out. He said when he'd threatened to run away, Richard told him to go ahead because you and he would have more children."

"No, Richard couldn't have said that."

"Is it possible?" Jaunie had no trouble believing it after witnessing Richard's attitude in her office.

"I don't know . . . I—I—"

"Does Richard have a temper? Has he ever made threats to you?"

"He's never hit me," she said quickly.

"Did he ever threaten you, Patrice?"

She was quiet at first. "Not really threats. Richard just likes things a certain way. He speaks harshly sometimes, but he's a good man."

"Patrice, I think Andrew is afraid of Richard. For some reason he prefers being alone on the streets rather than in the same house with your husband. My friend will let Andrew stay with him while we try to get this worked out."

"My poor baby. Does he hate me?"

"No, Patrice, he loves you very much. He's agreed to meet with you today at my office. He wants to talk to you, but he doesn't want to see Richard."

"Then you just have to convince him to come home."

"Patrice, I think Andrew just needs to be reassured that he's just as important to you as Richard is."

"Andrew is my heart. I'm his mother. He comes first with me!"

"I believe that, Patrice. And I think if you say that to Andrew, he'll believe it, too."

"Hey, you're a little early. We're not quite ready yet," Trent said, when he opened the door for Jaunie later that morning.

His white dress shirt was still hanging open, exposing the smooth expanse of his well-muscled chest. No chest hair. Very nice, Jaunie thought.

Searching for Andrew, her gaze passed Trent and settled on the sofa, reminding her of the long goodbye they'd shared there the night before. Her cheeks began to burn. "Where's Andrew?"

Trent closed the door. "He's in the kitchen, eating cereal." Trent raised the hair clippers he held. "When he's finished, he agreed to let me give his hair a little trim. Then we'll be ready to go."

Just then Andrew came bouncing out of the kitchen, wearing a fresh T-shirt—obviously one of Trent's—and his baggy jeans. "What's up, Jaunie?"

"Morning, Andrew."

"All right, man, you ready for your haircut?" Trent asked, spreading some newspaper on the floor.

"Dag, man, you back on that?"

"Don't you want to look sharp for your mom? You gotta learn early, kid, women don't appreciate a nappy head." Trent winked at Jaunie.

Andrew hopped onto the stool Trent had set on top of the newspaper without further argument.

"Okay, little dude, how do you want me to cut it?"

"That's on you. I don't care."

Trent ran his hand over his low-cut fade. "Well, what do you think of the way I wear mine?"

Jaunie covered her mouth, waiting for Andrew to utter his favorite word for everything: "whack."

Instead Andrew looked over his shoulder at Trent, nodding slowly. "I guess that'd be cool."

Jaunie raised her eyebrows. Clearly there was some male bonding going on here. She could see the change in Andrew already. His little body was no longer rigid with tension and defensiveness, and he seemed to honestly respect Trent's opinions.

As Trent cut Andrew's hair, the two traded jokes and quips, but all Jaunie could think was how she wished Trent would button up his shirt. The view was definitely distracting.

When Trent finished, Andrew looked very handsome. Seeing them both side by side, Jaunie almost imagined that she saw a resemblance. Trent would make a good father.

Whoa! Just because Trent and Andrew were getting along was no reason for her brain to go off in that direction. If her mind kept moving in this vein, she'd start imagining what their children would be like . . . uh-oh.

"Are you two ready to go?" Trent came out of his bedroom, shrugging on a sports coat. She didn't know why he was so dressed up, but he looked fantastic.

Get a grip, girl! "I'm ready."

"Yeah, let's jet!" Andrew darted for the door.

Jaunie smiled at his eagerness. He wouldn't admit it, but he was anxious to see his mother.

He didn't have long to wait. They reached the Meridian Building in twenty minutes, heading straight for Jaunie's office. Patrice was waiting.

"Andrew!" As soon as they opened the door, Patrice rushed to Andrew and wrapped her arms around him, sobbing.

After a few moments of hugging and rocking, she pulled him back, kissing his cheeks repeatedly. "Oh, baby, you look wonderful." She rubbed the top of his head. "You even got a haircut."

"Trent did it, Momma. He said women don't appreciate nappy heads."

Patrice looked up, her gaze resting on Jaunie and Trent.

Jaunie stepped forward. "Patrice, I—oh!"

Patrice threw her arms around Jaunie, nearly knocking the breath out of her. "Thank you. Thank you. Thank you, Jaunie."

"You don't have to thank me. I'm just happy that Andrew's okay." Jaunie stepped back and motioned toward Trent. "Patrice Lincoln, this is Trent Douglas. He helped me find Andrew and let Andrew stay with him."

Patrice embraced Trent with the same fervor. "Thank you, too."

"You're very welcome. I'm glad I could help."

Patrice turned back to Andrew, and Jaunie grabbed Trent's arm, tugging him toward the door. "We'll give you two some time alone."

Patrice looked over her shoulder. "No. Please stay. Maybe you can help. I want Andrew home with me tonight."

Andrew pulled away from his mother's grip and moved behind Jaunie's desk. "I'm not coming home as long as craphead is there," he said, sitting in the chair and propping his feet on the edge of the desk.

Jaunie and Trent exchanged a look as they moved back into the office, trying to remain inconspicuous.

"Andrew! Richard is my husband."

Andrew played with the calender on her desk. "Not my fault. I didn't tell you to marry that sucker."

Patrice sighed, looking to Jaunie for support.

Jaunie just shook her head and spread her hands.

Patrice sat in the guest chair and leaned her arms on the desk. "Andrew, is it true? What you told Jaunie about Richard? Does he curse at you? Did he tell you it was okay for you to run away?"

Andrew started spinning in the chair. "Yeah."

"Baby, why didn't you tell me?"

He stopped spinning. "What's the point? You don't listen to me anymore, and it's all because of him!"

"Sweetheart, I'll always listen to you. I love you."

"Yeah? Then you used to love me more."

"How can you say that?"

"Because you let that muckhead talk you into sending me away."

"Baby, if that's the problem, I've already decided not to send you to that school. I want you home with me. I never wanted to send you away. It's just that Richard—"

"See! See how you listen to him? He'll just find another way to get rid of me, and you'll go along with it. Doesn't matter, cause I ain't coming home."

"Andrew, are you trying to hurt me? Do you know how miserable I've been with you gone?"

He shrugged.

"If I talk to Richard about this, will that help?"

"Talking ain't gonna help."

"How do you know unless you let me try?"

"Cause if Daddy was alive, this never would have happened. You wouldn't have married the shmuckhead, and things would be like they used to be."

"Honey, I know things have been different since your daddy died. But I can't fix that. Remember? We talked about how we have to move on."

"Not with the bootiehead."

"Andrew, you can't keep calling him names."

"It's better than what I used to call him."

"Andrew, do you think I love Richard more than I love you?"

Andrew looked at her with a frozen expression. "Yes."

Patrice was silent for a moment. "Andrew, come here."

His eyes widened as if he was afraid he was in trouble.

"Please, honey," Patrice said. "Come here."

Andrew moved around the desk and stopped in front of his mother. She leaned forward and cupped his cheeks with her hands. "Sweetheart, there isn't anyone in the world more important to me than you." Her voice trembled, and Jaunie knew she was crying. "I gave birth to you. You're a part of me. Don't you understand that?"

Andrew jerked his head and mumbled, "I guess so." His words were punctuated with a huge sniff.

Patrice reached into her purse and pulled out a plastic package of tissues, giving one to Andrew and taking one for herself.

"If you aren't happy, baby, then I'm not happy. I won't force you to stay someplace where you aren't comfortable."

Andrew's brows lifted. "Then I don't have to go back?"

"Can I make a deal with you?"

His lips twisted skeptically. "Here we go!"

"Andrew, please. I haven't been married long. I can't throw it away without trying to work things out. You don't get married just to get divorced. You know that, right? Right?"

Andrew's head was bowed, and he nodded slightly. "Yeah."

"Then just give Momma some time to try to make this work for all of us. Come home with me today and help me talk to Richard. I think if we all agree to try, we can get past this."

Andrew's shoulders slumped.

"Look at me, Andrew." When he raised his head, she continued. "If you promise me that you'll come home and honestly try to make our family work, I'll make you a promise."

"What is it?"

"If after that you still aren't happy at home, then we'll both leave, together."

"You mean it?"

"With all my heart, but you have to promise to talk to me and give me a chance to work this out. Okay?"

Andrew bobbed his head but appeared to be too choked up to speak. They hugged, holding on for dear life.

Finally Patrice stood, and without words everyone began hugging. Jaunie was so happy and touched, tears of joy formed in her eyes. Looking over, she could see that Trent had been deeply moved as well.

As Patrice and her son were getting ready to leave, Trent leaned down to Andrew's level. "Hey, buddy, I'm glad you decided to go home with your mom and work things out. That's the way a man faces his problems, head-on. But the next time you feel you need some time on your own, will you do me a favor?"

Andrew listened to Trent attentively. "What?"

Trent pulled out his business card and a pen and wrote on

the back of the card. "Give me a call. You can hang out at my place while you get your head together. Then you can go back to your mom because she needs you." He handed him the card. "On the front is my work number, and my home number's on the back."

Andrew looked as if Trent had just handed him the key to the city. He couldn't seem to stop grinning and nodding. "Cool."

After Andrew and his mother left, Jaunie was still trying to get her emotions under control. No matter how many times she blinked and dabbed, the tears wouldn't stop welling in her eyes. And Trent was having a moment of readjustment himself.

He leaned against the edge of her desk, shaking his head. "I'm really glad that Andrew's going home but . . ."

Jaunie watched him furrow his brow as if deep in thought. "What's wrong?"

"This is going to sound weird . . . and selfish. But I'm kind of disappointed that the kid's not going to be staying with me after all."

Jaunie raised her brows. "That's not weird or selfish. I understand how you feel."

"I hadn't really thought it through at the time, but now that he's gone, I realize I was kind of looking forward to having him around."

Jaunie nodded, realizing that Trent had been experiencing those fatherly pangs she'd been thinking about that morning. Maybe just as she had, he'd realized that he would be a good father. Maybe Andrew made him start thinking about the things he was missing in his life.

He'd reminded Jaunie that she had a maternal time clock. She was almost thirty. Jaunie shook her head as she felt the tears welling again. Why was she so weepy? Her hormones must be out of sync.

Through her blurry vision, Trent's dress shoes came into view. His fingers were on her chin as he lifted her face. "Are you okay?"

"Yes. I'm not usually this emotional."

"It's understandable for you to be emotional. These past

few days have been full of tension.'' He wrapped his arms around her and held her.

That was just what she needed. Being in his arms was like a tranquilizer. The rest of the world faded away, and she let go of her tension for a minute.

A nagging doubt pushed at the edges of her mind, questioning whether she should be in his arms. They'd had an agreement, but his arms felt good. She wanted to savor that.

Eventually she felt his embrace loosening, and she leaned back to look up at Trent. He was giving her a heavy-lidded look. It was delicious. His lips were slightly parted. One of his hands rubbed her back, while the other had moved up to stroke the soft skin behind her ear.

Her head tilted back farther. Just one kiss and then—

''Darlin, wait till you hear—oops!''

Jaunie jumped a foot in the air then whipped around. Geri was standing in the doorway with Robert looking over her shoulder.

''Sorry, kids,'' Robert said. ''Did we interrupt a little somethin' somethin'?''

Trent leaned on the edge of her desk. ''No, of course not.''

''No. We were just—'' Jaunie started at the same time, moving behind her desk.

''Sorry, sweetie,'' Geri said, shutting the door behind her and Robert. ''Mel said your clients left, so we thought the coast was clear.''

Jaunie rubbed her palms on the skirt of her lilac dress. ''Don't be silly, Geri. You weren't interrupting. What's going on?''

Robert strutted across the room and held his hand out for Trent to give him five. ''Buddy, it's time to cel-lo-*brate!*''

Trent slapped his hand. ''What's up? Did you get the shop drawings for our two o'clock meeting?''

''Forget that, man. We just got the Grovesnor Health Food contract.''

''You're kidding. When did you find out?'' Trent asked.

''About fifteen minutes ago. Tate Architects just called. So get ready, the four of us are going out tonight!''

Chapter Ten

"Okay, everyone." Geri raised her wineglass. "I propose a toast."

Jaunie, Trent, and Robert held their glasses aloft.

"To Payne & Douglas Contracting, and the two most handsome men in the building."

Jaunie laughed. "Geri, you're an outrageous flirt."

She winked. "I just call 'em like I see 'em, hon."

"Well, I have one." Jaunie raised her glass. "Here's to Payne & Douglas Contracting . . . and the free dinner they're buying Sterling & Treymaine."

Robert, who was sitting next to Jaunie, tapped her on the shoulder. "Excuse me, *we* did all the work—shouldn't you two be treating *us* to dinner?" He gave Trent a sly grin. "Actually *I* did all the work on this one. Trent's had his head in the clouds lately." He casually looked over at Jaunie.

"Don't you believe it," Trent said hastily. "I carried you through college. This is just payback. It's about time you hauled your own weight for a change."

"Yeah, blah, blah, blah. Let's not bore the ladies with details."

When the laughter finally faded, the two couples took the opportunity to taste their food. Since they'd arrived, the four of them had been acting like silly teenagers, and Jaunie was loving every minute of it.

"Jaunie," Geri said, sawing off a bite of her salmon steak. "I talked to Eric Wilson, one of the producers of the *Dirk Preston Show* today."

Jaunie tensed. "Have they changed their minds about needing us?" She could only hope.

"Don't be silly, sweetie. Of course not. We're all set to tape the show on August twenty-third."

"Oh, I see," Robert said. "You two are trying to upstage us by becoming television stars. Well, what's the topic?"

"Man, I bet the topic is 'Women Who Go to Restaurants and Order the Most Expensive Items on the Menu.' " Trent gave Jaunie's filet mignon a comical leer.

Geri snapped her fingers to get the men's attention. "For your information, we're going to talk about missing children. The show should air two weeks later in September. We're one of the first shows of the new fall season." She winked at Robert. "But if I ever hear them planning a show on 'Men with Egos Twice the Size of Their Heads,' I'll tell them to give you gentlemen a call."

Jaunie gave Geri a high-five across the table. "You go, Geri!"

After that Geri excused herself to make a phone call. "Everyone, Sam says hi," she announced when she returned.

Trent stood to let Geri slide into the booth. "Who's Sam? Your boyfriend?"

"No, silly. Sam's my daughter. Short for Samantha."

"That's right," Trent said. "Jaunie *has* mentioned her. Let's see, we've got Jaunie, Geri, Sam, and your receptionist goes by Mel. Is it some new trend to give women names that sound like men's?"

Jaunie looked at Geri. "That's true. I hadn't really thought about our names like that."

"Well, I think it's sexy to give a woman a man's name."
Robert stroked his goatee. "It's like a girl wearing my jacket
or my T-shirt. It accentuates her femininity."

"Robert," Trent said. "You'd think bowling shoes accentu-
ated a woman's femininity."

He shrugged. "What can I say? I'm a connoisseur."

When the waiter came to clear their plates and take their
dessert orders, Jaunie patted her stomach. "None for me. I'm
stuffed."

"Come on, Jaunie, don't make me look like a pig." Geri
passed her the dessert menu. "You haven't lived until you've
tried the Swiss mocha cheesecake. Split a piece with me."

Jaunie sighed. "Okay, if you insist."

Robert closed his menu. "Well, I'm in for a piece of that.
What about you, buddy?"

"No, I think I'll just have some coffee."

When the waiter came back with their orders, Geri looked
at her gold Mickey Mouse watch. "Oh, my! It's later than I
thought. I promised Sammy I'd be home in time to watch
Seinfeld with her. I gotta run."

Jaunie reached for her purse. "We can get the waiter to wrap
up this cheesecake."

Geri waved her off. "No, sweetie, you stay and enjoy it. I
don't need the extra calories anyway." She turned to the men.
"You'll make sure Jaunie gets back to her car, won't you,
fellas?"

Robert nodded. "Sure, girl, you go ahead."

Jaunie stared at the huge piece of cake she now had all to
herself. "Thanks a lot, Geri."

Soon after Geri had gone, Robert's pager went off. When
he returned from making his call, he pulled out his wallet and
threw a wad of bills on the table.

"Sorry, guys, gotta jet. Sharice is picking me up for our
date. Can't keep the lady waiting." He shoved his cake toward
Trent. "You'll finish this for me, won't you, buddy?" Before
another word could be said, he was out of there.

Jaunie looked across the table to Trent, who was shaking his head. She nodded. "Are you thinking what I'm thinking?"

"Yeah," Trent said. "I think we've just been set up."

"My car's over there." Jaunie pointed to her blue Honda in the corner of the parking garage. They'd lingered over coffee and cheesecake until early evening had faded into late night.

Trent turned off his ignition. "I'd better walk you over."

She grabbed her purse and stepped onto the concrete with a groan. "Oh, I feel like I'm going to explode. I'll kill Geri for sticking me with that whole piece of cheesecake."

"I know the feeling. Robert's going to get an earful."

Jaunie unlocked her car door, then turned around to say good night. "It turned out to be a good day, didn't it?"

"Yes, it did." Trent removed his hands from his pockets and opened his arms.

She moved into his embrace, resting her head on his chest and winding her arms around his waist. For a long time, he just held her, squeezing gently. She needed this. It was nice— a hug between friends. Just as it had been nice to sit across from him in the restaurant and talk about little things, silly things, without the pressure of finding Andrew or the tension of their past hanging over them.

Slowly Trent's hands began to move up and down her back, rubbing circles around her shoulders, kneading her spine with his thumbs. She sighed from the soothing pressure of his massage. His hands moved over her hips, and she began to notice the change in the embrace—and in her body.

She raised her head. "Trent, I . . . mmm."

His mouth stole her words. His heated lips moved softly, dragging and pulling against hers. He tasted dark and sweet from coffee and dessert.

Trent's hands smoothed over her slim skirt, stopping at the hemline midthigh. Though his hands had stopped moving, sensation still danced in the paths traced by his fingers. Each time she breathed his cologne, a new ribbon of desire curled in her abdomen.

She was immersed in these sensory pleasures when Trent gripped her waist, lifting her onto the hood of the car. He stepped between her legs, bringing his lips to her throat, while his thumbs massaged her breasts through her linen dress.

She teased the pads of her fingers on the soft prickly hairs at the back of his head as his tongue dipped into the cleavage of her square neckline. His lips worked their way up her throat with gentle nibbles. Finally his mouth found hers again, and she felt his fingers graze the edge of her panties.

The sound of elevator doors opening jangled her nerves like a fire alarm. The sharp click of high heels echoed through the garage.

Quickly Trent scooped her off the car, and she scrambled behind the wheel, fumbling to push down her skirt. He jogged to the passenger side, and Jaunie popped the lock so he could jump in.

They sat silently as the woman got into her car and drove away. Reality had quashed the moment, and now Jaunie felt like a soda can that had been shaken hard. Her hormones were jumping inside her like carbonated bubbles with nowhere to go.

"Whew, that was close, huh?" Trent's voice faded into nervous laughter.

She nodded, trying to calm her internal fizzing.

After a long silence filled with deep breaths and straightening clothes, Trent turned to her. "It's not working, is it?"

She peered at him from the corner of her eye. His face was shadowy, but she could see the tension in his jaw. "What's not working?"

"We agreed to keep our hands off each other." He rubbed his palms on his slacks. "That's . . . not working."

She smiled, her cheeks heating as she imagined what they must have looked like clenched on the hood of her car. "No . . . I guess not."

"Right," he said, and the nervous, slightly embarrassed

laughter in his voice changed to something that sounded like fear. "I—I *can't* do this, Jaunie."

She looked at the sweat dotting his brow, and her fizzing bubbles went flat. His fingers were clenched in his lap, and his Adam's apple jerked each time he swallowed hard, which he did frequently.

"Are you okay? You look—"

"No, Jaunie, I'm not okay. I thought we could just be friends—that I could control this—but every time I get near you, I want to touch you."

Jaunie stared at her lap, not really sure why that was a problem.

"Resisting you is harder than I thought it would be. You're a temptation. I'm afraid if I keep seeing you, I . . . We've already gone too far—today in your office, and just now—the more I see you, the more I'll want—"

"Listen to yourself." Jaunie shook her head, trying to understand his desperate tone. "Resisting *temptation?* You make it sound like I'm some kind of sweet that will rot your teeth or—or a drug that you're addicted—"

"That's it. That's what it's like for me, Jaunie. An addiction. Women go to my head faster than liquor, and Erika wasn't the first one to play me for a sucker."

Jaunie shuddered, remembering her role in his bad memories.

"And she wasn't the last. Like an idiot, I kept going back for more. And you know what?" He looked over at her. "I'm not a stupid man. I mean, I run a successful business, I do well on the stock market—and, hell, my friends come to *me* when they're in a jam. But when it comes to women, I don't know what's good for me. I *can't* tell the good from the bad."

"So you plan to stay away from them all, is that it?"

He laid his head back against the seat. "Something like that."

Jaunie sat still as his words shifted inside her head. Trent had a serious complex about women. His fears were real, and she knew from experience that they were valid. Of course he didn't want to get hurt again. How could she make him any promises? Before she'd met him, her idea of a serious relationship was six months and an expensive piece of jewelry. She'd learned about relationships from her mother, and since her mother was still hopping from man to man, she couldn't rely on that example.

Maybe if she believed she could make this work, she would have tried to change his mind. If she'd had any faith that she could go against what her mother had taught her to be, she'd push past his insecurities and make him face what was between them.

But she didn't. So she had to accept this.

"All right, I understand," she said softly.

His hand covered one of hers. "Before I go, I want you to know that the time we spent together was special to me. I haven't let myself get this close to a woman in a long time. I don't want you to think I took that lightly."

She turned her head toward him. "It was special to me, too."

She looked away and he removed his hand. Seconds later he was gone.

Jaunie blinked and her office slowly came back into focus. Once again she'd been daydreaming—about Trent.

It had been almost a month since he'd decided he needed distance. Now running into him was pure hell. He always looked more handsome in person than her imagination could paint him, and he was painted on the canvas of her mind every night. Unfortunately—or fortunately—they didn't run into each other often. Robert said they were working hard these days and spent a lot of time at construction sites. He'd also mentioned that Trent was going out of town more often, scouting out new business. Usually Robert handled that area, but Trent was showing more interest in traveling lately. Jaunie didn't mention that the reason Trent wanted to be away from the nation's capital as often as possible was because she was in it.

"Ms. Sterling?"

Jaunie stared suspiciously at the intercom. Why was Mel

putting on that formal accent? Well, she'd play along. "Yes, Ms. Winters?"

"There is a gentleman here to see you, madame."

Now she was really suspicious. "He's not a salesman, is he, Mel?"

"No, Ms. Sterling, he knows you—but he'd like you to be surprised. Since you were between meetings, I took the liberty of scheduling an appointment for him."

Jaunie's heart pounded in anticipation. It wasn't—*couldn't* be—Trent. Could it? He wouldn't—

"Jaunie, are you still there?"

"Yes, Ms. Winters, just trying to guess who it could be. Send Mystery Man in."

The door opened, and Andrew bopped into the room, wearing baggy orange shorts and an oversized tank top that featured Michael Jordan leaping through the air. "Bet you never thought you'd see me again," he said, taking a seat in front of her desk.

"Andrew! Now this is a pleasant surprise." She cocked her head. "Everything's okay, isn't it?"

"Yeah. It's cool."

Jaunie studied him. He looked a lot happier than he had the last time, but she needed reassurance. "Your mom's doing okay?"

He shrugged. "She's good."

"And your stepfather?"

"Crudhead's chilling."

Jaunie raised her brows. "You're getting along with him then."

"Nope."

"But you just said—"

"He doesn't speak to me at all, and that's just the way I like it."

She frowned. "He ignores you? Your mom doesn't say anything about that?"

Andrew's face broke into a sly grin. "She hates it. They fight about it all the time."

She held up her hands. "Wait a minute. When I asked if everything was okay, you said it was cool . How can . . ."

He nodded, lifting his brows in a look that said, *now you're getting it.* "Momma sticks up for me now. They fight all the time. Pretty soon she's gonna dump that sucker."

Jaunie twisted her lips. "Well . . . I'm glad . . . everything's, um, working out."

Andrew bobbed his head, swinging his legs.

She propped her chin on her palm. "So what have *you* been up to?"

"Man, I've been bored out my mind. All the kids in this new neighborhood are stuck up. Scuzhead tried to send me to some snotty summer camp, but I told him to fu—"

"Andrew!"

"To, uh, fu-get it. Anyway, there's nothing to do. Today I just jumped on the bus and came down here to see what you guys are doing." He reached for a stack of papers on her desk. "You spying on anybody today?"

She took the papers out of his hands. "Nope, I'm between cases right now." This morning she'd spent forty-five minutes checking assets for an attorney, but she doubted that would interest him.

Andrew swung his legs, looking around. "Where's Trent's office? Is he out spying on anybody?"

Jaunie's heartbeat sped up at the mention of Trent's name. "Oh no. Trent doesn't work here. He's a contractor. His office is across the hall."

"Oh," he said, sounding disappointed. "Well, let's go see him."

"I . . . uh, sure. You go ahead. It's the door directly across from mine. Payne & Douglas Contracting."

Andrew popped out of his seat. "Aren't you coming?"

She reached for the stack of forms she'd already filled out and began flipping through them. "I . . . well . . . I have to . . ."

"Come on, please." He widened his eyes. "Come with me."

Jaunie was thrilled to see Andrew. Even though they hadn't

had any contact for weeks, he and Patrice were on her mind frequently. He'd come all this way, and she didn't want him to feel unwelcome.

She stood. "Okay, let's go."

"Cool," Andrew said, bouncing his way across the hall.

Jaunie trailed behind, silently hoping this was one of those occasions when Trent was out of town. She could introduce Andrew to Robert, then they could leave.

No such luck. Andrew pushed open the door, and Trent was standing in the outer office saying goodbye to a client.

Jaunie grabbed Andrew's shoulders to keep him from moving forward. "Looks like he's busy. Maybe we should—"

"Hold on." Trent motioned for them to go into his office. "I'll be with you in a sec."

Reluctantly Jaunie followed Andrew, who was clearly eager to look around. Once inside the office, Andrew immediately seated himself behind Trent's desk and began playing with his computer.

She crossed her arms and leaned against a file cabinet at the opposite wall. "Don't touch that, Andrew."

He looked up. "Why? I know how to use a computer. We have them at school."

"Yes, but that doesn't belong to you."

"It's okay. He can't hurt anything."

Trent's voice startled her, causing her to bump the cabinet, knocking off a roll of blueprints that had been stored on top. They unrolled in a heap at her feet.

"You, on the other hand," Trent said, rerolling the drawings, "are another story."

She stepped away from the cabinet and stood awkwardly in the middle of the room. She crossed and uncrossed her arms, uncertain how to carry herself. "Andrew wanted to drop in and say hi, but if you're busy, we can leave."

"I can spare a few minutes." He put the roll back on top of the cabinet and moved over to Andrew. "Hey, little man. How's it hanging?"

Andrew grinned up at him. "Just going with the flow. You

know what I'm saying? I tried to kick it to this honey dip at the mall yesterday, but she wasn't trying to hear my rap. But I saw that new Wesley Snipes movie. It was all that. Ice Cube has a new album out. You heard it yet?''

Jaunie didn't hear Trent's response. She was floored by Andrew's newfound animation. Trent asked a casual question and got a response that beat the heck out of the ''it's cool'' she'd wrung from the boy.

Obviously the night Andrew spent at Trent's apartment had been enough for them to build a substantial rapport. She knew Andrew didn't have a decent father figure, or even a brother in his life. In fact, it seemed he didn't have many friends since moving to a new neighborhood. It was only natural that he'd be drawn to Trent.

But she couldn't help feeling a bit left out.

To make matters worse, Trent was less than ten feet away from her, and he looked wonderful. He must have just gotten a fresh haircut. On top his hair clung to his head in smooth waves, and the sides were shaved close. The cut made the strong lines of his face more prominent. He was so handsome—damn it! Why couldn't he have gained a few pounds and let his hair get nappy?

It wouldn't have helped. Why was she torturing herself this way? She should go back to her office. She stepped back, cracking her head on the wall. ''Ow!'' She rubbed the sore spot.

Trent turned toward her. ''Are you okay?''

''Besides feeling stupid? Yes.''

He moved closer and touched her arm. ''Are you sure? That was a pretty loud thump.''

''I'm sure. I have a hard head.'' She rubbed her moist palms against her long denim skirt.

He gave her a soft smile. ''I doubt that.''

She smiled back at him.

''What's wrong with you two?''

''Huh?'' they said in unison. Jaunie wondered if Trent temporarily forgotten Andrew's presence as she had.

"You're both acting goofy."

Trent drew back. "What are you talking about?"

Andrew squinted at the computer screen. "You got any games on this thing?"

"Uh? I don't know. My partner, Robert, has a lot though."

"So what's the deal? You two have a fight or something?" Andrew asked.

"What? Why do you think we had a fight?" Trent asked.

"Because she's been bumping into stuff, and you're rubbing your head like you've got a headache or something."

Trent stared at his fingers, which had been worrying his temple just moments before. "I—uh—"

"Well . . . we . . ." They both stumbled at once.

"Yo, Trent!" Robert poked his head into the room. "Can I borrow your keys to the men's room? I can't find mine."

Trent reached into his pocket. "Did you look in the plant stand?"

"Yep."

"The minifridge?"

"Yes."

"What about the file drawers?"

"I'll look there next."

Trent dropped his keys into Robert's waiting palm. "Don't lose these."

"No problem. Hi, Jaunie . . . and who's this?" Robert walked toward Andrew.

"Andrew, this is my partner, Robert."

"So you're the guy who has games on his computer?" Andrew raised his brows eagerly.

"Yep." Robert grinned. "But so does Trent. I loaded all the same stuff on his computer. Let me show you."

While Robert helped Andrew, Trent walked back over to Jaunie. "So how have you been?" he asked softly.

The look that passed between them said so many things. They were staying apart on purpose, and judging by her feelings at that moment, distance was absolutely necessary if they were going to keep his "hands-off" policy. His eyes mirrored her pent-up need.

"I've been good." She looked down, fingering the sleeve of her ribbed blue tunic. "You?"

"Not as good as I thought I'd be."

Jaunie caught her breath. Was he implying what she thought he was? "Well, what would make you feel better?" She hadn't intended for her words to sound so provocative.

Trent's eyes became hooded. "I think . . ."

They both noticed how quiet the room had become at the same moment. They looked over and found that Robert had already gone, and Andrew sat watching them with fascination.

He shook his head as he turned back to the screen. "Two words for you guys. Knockin' boots."

Jaunie frowned at the telephone. "Are you sure you can't make it for lunch, Patrice?" The day Andrew first stopped by for a visit, Jaunie had called Patrice, and the two women had talked for hours.

They'd become good friends over the past few weeks. Patrice needed someone close to her own age to confide in, and Jaunie had never had any real girlfriends growing up. She could relate to the vulnerability she saw in Patrice. Now, on slow days, Jaunie would pick up Patrice and take her out to lunch or shopping.

"I'm sure," Patrice answered. "I've got a lot on my mind. I don't think I'd be good company."

"What's wrong?"

There was a long pause before she finally spoke. "I'm so confused. I want to do the right thing, but I don't know what that is."

"Are you talking about Richard?"

"He and I are still arguing. I did as you suggested, and asked him to go with me to a marriage counselor, but he refuses. The worst part is that he ignores Andrew completely. Richard gives me enough money to buy Andrew whatever he needs, but he won't acknowledge him. This isn't the way I'd imagined it when I married him. I mean, I only did it for Andrew in the first place.''

So dump the jerk! "What are your options?"

"Do you think I should leave him?"

Yes! Run now, run far! "Do you?"

"I don't know. I married him for better or worse, but he's so cold! I tell him that we'll never be a real family if we go on like this, but he doesn't seem to care. I keep thinking we should be able to work this out somehow."

Impossible! Give it up and leave! "What more could you possibly do, Patrice?"

"I've tried everything I know, but what will happen to Andrew and me if I leave Richard?"

A fresh start! Happiness! "What will happen if you don't?"

"I don't like Andrew living in all this confusion. I want him to have a loving, happy home like we had when his father was alive. But if I leave, where will I go?"

"Didn't you say you have a cousin in Virginia?"

"Rachel? Yes, she lives in Alexandria."

"Would she let you stay there until you and Andrew find a place of your own?"

"Maybe . . . but I don't have a job or a car. How would we make it without Richard's money?"

"How did you make it before?"

"Well, the house Darrel bought was paid for. After he died, I didn't have to worry about mortgage payments. My receptionist job at the clinic was enough for Andrew and me to eat, and the bus took us everywhere we needed to go. Richard sold that house when we got married."

"What did he do with the money from the house?"

"Kept it, I guess. I couldn't complain, he bought me a big beautiful new home." Patrice sighed. "And Andrew's just about to start school. I'll have to pull him out and find one in Virginia. It's so hard for him to adjust to all these changes. How can we go from having nice things back to having almost nothing?"

Jaunie bit her lip. She couldn't ask her friend to plunge her life into near poverty just because Jaunie didn't like her husband. No matter what she thought, it was Patrice's decision to make. "I guess it would be a struggle at first. You know I'd help in any way I could, but it probably wouldn't be as much as you'd need."

"I can't keep living this way. What am I going to do?"

"I wish I could tell you, Patrice, but you know what's best for you and Andrew. Take some time and think about your choices. Whatever you decide, I'll stick by you."

"Thanks, Jaunie, you've been a good friend to me. I have a feeling it will work out. Do you want to have lunch tomorrow?"

"I can't. Geri and I are taping the *Dirk Preston Show.*"

"That's tomorrow? Great, you'll have to call and tell me all about it. I can't wait to see you on TV."

Jaunie sighed. "Yeah, well . . ."

"I'll talk to you soon."

"Okay, take care." Soon after Jaunie hung up, she heard knuckles faintly scraping her office door. Was that a knock? "Come in?"

After two light pounds, her door swung open. Geri waddled into her office, wearing a long tie-dyed smock dress and dark glasses. Her skin was bright crimson.

"Geri, what's wrong with you? You look like a lobster!"

"Oy gevalt! I was trying to get a tan for the show tomorrow, and *this* happened."

Jaunie rushed around the desk to examine her friend. "Geri! You told me you never tan. What made you think this time would be any different?"

"I bought this new lotion called All Tan. It was supposed to help even the fairest skin obtain a rich golden brown."

Jaunie rolled her eyes. "Well, that's what you get for wasting your money on gimmicks. Now you'll have to do the show in a rich apple red."

Geri's frizzy hair bounced as she shook her head. "Can't do the show, hon."

Jaunie's stomach pitched. "You have to!"

"Uh uh. Look." Geri pulled off her sunglasses, revealing a strip of white skin in the shape of her glasses outlined by her red skin. She looked so ridiculous, Jaunie would have laughed if she wasn't so close to tears.

Jaunie took a deep breath. There had to be a way. "Okay, Geri. Remember that episode of *I Love Lucy* where Lucy did pretty much the same thing? She tried to get a tan for a celebrity fashion show but fell asleep in the sun and got so burnt she could barely move. Lucy had to do the show to get the dress she wanted for free, so sunburn and all, Lucy did the fashion show anyway."

Jaunie looked at Geri, who merely stared at her as if she were crazy. Jaunie knew she was going off the deep end, but she pressed on anyway. "That was a whole fashion show. On the *Dirk Preston Show,* all you have to do is sit still and answer a few questions."

"You've never had sunburn, have you?"

Jaunie looked down at her brown skin, which provided a natural barrier against the sun. "No, I haven't."

"Jaunie, even if I could put my ego aside and accept the fact that everyone will be asking, 'Who was that masked woman?', I still physically couldn't do the show. My skin stings everywhere, I can barely move, and I'm feeling hot flashes that have nothing to do with menopause."

"All that won't go away by tomorrow?" When Geri gave her a cockeyed look, Jaunie said, "Maybe they can reschedule for when you're better."

"I'm sorry, kid. I know you didn't want to do the show in the first place—forget about on your own—but this is important to the Center and to me. You have to do the show tomorrow by yourself."

"I can't!" Jaunie panicked, sitting behind her desk then popping back up again. "I just can't. I'm sorry, we're just going to have to call them, because I can't." She sat down again.

"Sweetie, love, ouch!" Geri had automatically tried to perch on Jaunie's desk before she realized she couldn't. Instead she leaned stiffly on her arm. "Why are you so worried? You'll be fine."

"I'm sorry, but I'm not going to do this show alone."

"Jaunie, you've seen the *Dirk Preston Show* more than I have. You know he's not into that sleazy tabloid TV. He discusses issues concerning everyday people. Besides, he's full of that good old western charm, and he's always kind to his guests. He wears cowboy hats on every show to remind everyone that he's just a country boy at heart. He's a family man. You'll be in good hands."

Jaunie took a deep breath as her panic began to ebb. "I guess you're right. Every time I've caught the show, Dirk Preston was easygoing and charming. The guests looked at ease. I'm overreacting. It's important to get the word out about missing children. Don't worry, I'll do it—and I'm sure everything will be fine."

Chapter Eleven

The assistant producer of the *Dirk Preston Show* approached Jaunie in the green room. "Are you nervous?"

Jaunie could barely keep her hand steady on the cup of coffee she held. "More than a little bit."

"You'll be fine." The green-eyed blonde gave her a warm smile and touched her arm. "You were a model, right? So you're used to being in front of the camera."

Jaunie's eyes widened. She hadn't mentioned modeling in the pre-interview, had she? Oh, well, her nerves were so frayed, who could remember?

"You look *fan*tastic," the woman said, referring to Jaunie's slim, ankle-length, teal dress. A row of tiny pearl buttons ran from breast to hem, and the light crepe material clung to her figure elegantly.

At times like this, as during her modeling days, Jaunie clung to fashionable clothes and makeup like a security blanket. When she became a private investigator, she forced herself to choose conservative clothing and not to wear makeup, not only to help others see beyond her looks, but to force herself to face each new day raw and without pretense.

But today she needed an extra dose of confidence, so she styled her hair to fall in huge waves around her face and dusted her lids with shimmering teal eye shadow. Her Cairo Rose lipstick made her lips moist and kissable, but it was doing nothing for her nerves.

"Thank you." Jaunie put down her coffee before she spilled it on the dress the young producer had admired.

"Well, I just came back to let you know what to expect."

"Okay," Jaunie said, breathing deeply.

"You're the first guest, so after Dirk goes out to introduce the show, he'll say a few words about the new format, and then—"

"I noticed the new set. Is that what you mean by new format?"

"The set's great, isn't it? We're trying a lot of new things this season. It's going to be *fan*tastic!"

Jaunie clasped her hands in front of her. "Well, I think I'm ready. Dirk passed through on his way to makeup. He seemed really nice. He wanted to make sure he pronounced my name right, but I barely noticed his accent."

The producer grinned. "I guess you didn't catch the article on Dirk in the *Troubadour*. It revealed that he was raised in suburban Chicago, not on a ranch in Texas."

"What?" She never read the tabloids. She knew about their lies firsthand.

She giggled. "Yeah, they thought it would create a huge scandal, but it raised our ratings thirty percent! Everyone tuned in to see if Dirk was a fake. It was *fan*tastic."

Jaunie drew her brows together. She'd just discovered the man who was going to interview her in five minutes was a complete phony, and this woman thought it was *fan*tastic?

"Anyway, we'd already planned for Dirk to ditch the cowboy hat this year, so it all worked out. Like I said, Dirk will introduce the show, then he'll introduce you. You'll walk out through the audience and take your seat on stage, okay?"

"I've got it."

"Good luck." She squeezed Jaunie's arm and left the room.

A couple of minutes before the taping, Jaunie was positioned backstage so she could just turn a corner and walk down the aisle when Dirk introduced her. The crowd's excitement suddenly escalated, and she peeked out to see Dirk take the stage, carrying a microphone.

A wave of dizziness swept over her. She'd seen the new set when she arrived that morning, but then the studio had been empty. Now an audience filled the seats, and Jaunie's old pre-fashion show anxieties kicked in. The stage sat in the center of the studio, surrounded by the audience on all sides. One empty stool waited for her midstage. No angle would protect her from prying eyes.

She turned to watch the backstage monitor. Dirk paced the walkway surrounding the octagonal stage. He wore a sophisticated gray suit—a big leap from his casual western shirts and jeans. He paused to run his hand over his lapel. "Well, folks, as you can see, they're giving me a new image this year. What do you think?"

He flashed his trademark good-ole-boy grin, and the crowd erupted in hoots and cheers of approval. One woman shouted, "We love you, Dirk."

He ran a hand through his light brown corporate haircut. "I kind of feel naked here without my cowboy hat, but they gave me this great haircut, so I guess I'll be okay."

More cheers sounded from the audience.

"They did let me keep one thing though." Dirk hiked up the leg of his slacks to reveal a pair of black, snakeskin cowboy boots.

The crowd went wild. No matter what happened during the rest of the show, he'd won over the audience.

"We've got a great show for you today, and we're going to discuss some very important issues."

Jaunie took in another shaky breath. Why was she so nervous? Clearly all this talk of format changes and new images meant the show was turning in a more serious direction. Dirk was losing his hokey cowboy gimmick to attack real issues. The topic was missing children, for heaven's sake. There was no way he could bring such a heartbreaking subject down to the level of some of the sleazy talk shows on the air.

"She's a private investigator from Sterling & Treymaine Investigation Agency in Washington, D.C. Please welcome our first guest, Ms. Jaunie—that's a beautiful name, isn't it?—Ms. Jaunie Sterling."

As Jaunie made her way down the aisle toward the stage, the distance seemed to grow. This experience so resembled runway modeling, she had to resist the urge to place a hand on her hip and pivot. She could feel her mind automatically blanking out, retreating from the staring eyes, hot lights, and Dirk Preston theme show music.

Jaunie blinked. This was a talk show. She had to talk. She had a message to deliver. Taking shallow breaths, she climbed onstage, took her mike from the stool, and clipped it on the way they'd shown her.

"Hi, Jaunie."

She searched the sea of faces and found Dirk floating in the crowd. "Hi, Dirk."

"Now, Jaunie, you're here with us today to discuss your work—most importantly with missing children. Can you tell us how this all got started?"

"Certainly. Before she became my partner, Geraldine Treymaine was my first client. Her child had been abducted by her ex-husband, and she came to me for help. At that point we got involved with the National Center for Missing and Exploited Children."

Jaunie explained then how she and Geri tracked down Sam, and then she talked about the Center. As statistics rolled off her tongue, she began to relax. Dirk was charming, and before the first commercial break, they even flashed the NCMEC's hotline number, 1-800-THE-LOST, on the monitor.

When they came back from the break, Dirk turned to his audience. "This is fascinating, isn't it, audience? I bet you're looking at Jaunie's beautiful face and wondering how she became a private investigator." He turned back to her. "Why don't you tell them? Isn't it true that before you became a P.I., you worked as a model for the Madeline Temple Agency?"

Jaunie raised her brows. "Uh, yes, it is."

Dirk propped his boot on one of the stage steps, resting his elbow on his knee. He gave her his toothy grin and winked at her. "How does one go from being a glamorous model to investigating crimes?"

Jaunie felt her cheeks warm. "Well, most investigators come from backgrounds in law enforcement or the military, but if you're willing to go through the proper training—"

"Didn't you get your training working as a decoy for Intimate Investigations? Jealous women would hire you to come on to their husbands and lovers to see if they were cheaters?"

Jaunie's mouth went dry, and she felt as though she'd been knocked in the chest with a bag of ice. "Y-yes, that was the kind of work that agency specialized in, but when I started my own agency, I chose to work with missing children because—"

Dirk was no longer listening. He was taking a question from the audience. A round-faced young woman, wearing a denim jacket, stood up. "Um, yeah, did you ever sleep with any of those men you had to come on to?"

Jaunie's jaw dropped. "No! Of course not. I was never alone with any of those men. But that's not what I came here to talk about."

Dirk had moved the mike to a tall, dark-skinned man, wearing a football jersey. "Man, that's not really fair, you know what I'm saying? I've never cheated on my lady a day in my life, but you think if a fine honey like her steps up to me, I'ma say no? Shooooot. Of course, I'd cheat. But it's not my fault. It's hers!" He sat down to a burst of applause and catcalls from other men in the audience.

Jaunie tried to protest, but she was drowned out by the Dirk Preston theme music.

"When we come back from the break," Dirk said. "We'll have a special guest to shed some new light on this topic."

When the camera broke away, Jaunie looked around for

someone she could complain to. This show was getting out of hand. Instead all she saw were the staring eyes of the audience members on all sides. She felt almost dizzy, perched on the stool with the crowd all around her.

People were still calling to her and asking obnoxious, prying questions. Some men were leering, and some women were cutting their eyes at her. She looked for Dirk, but he was off to the side, talking to a man with a clipboard.

Jaunie considered getting up and walking away. She wanted to put an end to this experience. But she was glued to the stool, and her legs were mush. She couldn't find the strength to propel herself from the seat, up that long aisle and through the sea of curious faces. Before she knew it, Dirk was back, center stage, playing to the camera.

"Okay folks, just as I promised, we have a surprise guest. Jaunie's former boss from Intimate Investigations. Please welcome, Alan Warren."

Jaunie watched the aisle, but she saw no sign of Alan. How could he do this to her? It wasn't until he was right behind her that she realized he'd entered from the opposite direction. She hadn't even noticed that a second stool had been placed alongside hers.

"Welcome to the show," Dirk said as Alan situated himself on the stool.

"Dirk," Alan said curtly. He reached over and squeezed her hand. "Are you okay?"

She glared at him, feeling betrayed.

"Jaunie, they didn't tell me this was an ambush," he whispered. "They said you knew this was what the show was about."

Jaunie's pulse raced. *This is what the show is about?* Not missing children? How dare they set her up like this! Jaunie fell into a daze as Dirk asked Alan questions about working with her. To Alan's credit, he tried to take some of the heat off her.

"Actually Jaunie came to work for me because I asked her to—as a favor. She'd just retired from a successful modeling

Get **4 FREE** Arabesque
Contemporary Romances
Delivered to Your
Doorstep and Join the
Only New Book Club
That Delivers These
Bestselling African American
Romances Directly to You
Each Month!

No Obligation!

LOOK INSIDE FOR DETAILS ON
HOW TO GET YOUR FREE GIFT.....
(worth almost $20.00!)

WE HAVE 4 FREE BOOKS FOR YOU!

ARABESQUE

(If the certificate is missing below, write to:
Zebra Home Subscription Service, Inc.,
120 Brighton Road, P.O. Box 5214, Clifton, New Jersey 07015-5214)

FREE BOOK CERTIFICATE

Yes! Please send me 4 *Arabesque* Contemporary Romances without cost or obligation, billing me just $1 to help cover postage and handling. I understand that each month, I will be able to preview 4 brand-new *Arabesque* Contemporary Romances FREE for 10 days. Then, if I decide to keep them, I will pay the money-saving preferred subscriber's price of just $16.00 for all 4...that's a savings of almost $4 off the publisher's price with no additional charge for shipping and handling. I may return any shipment within 10 days and owe nothing, and I may cancel this subscription at any time. My 4 FREE books will be mine to keep in any case.

Name _____

Address _____ Apt. _____

City _____ State _____ Zip _____

Telephone ( ) _____

Signature _____ AR0398
(If under 18, parent or guardian must sign.)

Terms and prices subject to change. Orders subject to acceptance by Zebra Home Subscription Service, Inc. . Zebra Home Subscription Service, Inc. reserves the right to reject or cancel any subscription.

ZEBRA HOME SUBSCRIPTION SERVICE, INC.

120 BRIGHTON ROAD

P.O. BOX 5214

CLIFTON, NEW JERSEY 07015-5214

AFFIX
STAMP
HERE

career, and I was short on employees. She wasn't thrilled with the idea, but she let me talk her into it.''

Dirk nodded politely, then went straight to the audience for the hard-hitting questions.

An overeager heavyset man asked, ''Do any of the girls that work for you sleep with the men you send them out to hit on?''

Alan wrinkled his brow with distaste. ''I am not a pimp, and my employees are not prostitutes. Women want to know if their husbands can be trusted. I just help them find the answer, which is usually no.''

Jaunie watched the spectacle through distant eyes. A haze of anger and humiliation fell over her as she watched Alan deftly deflect the questions Dirk and the audience asked. Some even tried asking her questions, but after the first attempt, Jaunie responded that she'd come to discuss missing children, and then politely ignored further questions.

When the next commercial break finally came, Jaunie left.

Trent and Andrew entered the lobby of the Meridian building, carrying double-scoop ice cream cones.

''Hey, who's that guy with Jaunie?'' Andrew asked, looking over at the elevators.

Trent followed his gaze in time to see the elevator doors close on Jaunie and Alan Warren. ''Some guy she used to work for. He's an old friend.''

''Oh,'' Andrew said, satisfied.

But Trent wasn't. What was that guy doing here anyway? He punched the button, and they waited for the next elevator.

Trent knew it was foolish to be jealous. He'd insisted on keeping distance between them, but the day she and Andrew had stopped by his office, his client had assumed they were his wife and son. For an instant, he'd felt a swell of pride and had wished they *were* his family.

That was dangerous ground. If he ignored his survival instincts, he'd find himself sucked into the quicksand of his conflicting feelings for Jaunie. Until he could keep his mind on friendship, he had to stay away.

By the time he and Andrew got back to his office and finished their cones, Trent's lunch break was over, but an idea had begun to form in his mind.

"Hey, Andrew, now that Jaunie's back, do you want to go over and see her?"

"Nah, she's got her friend over there. I don't want to get in the way," he said, spinning his chair.

"I'm sure you wouldn't be in the way. She'd love to see you."

"That's okay. I'll catch her next time."

"No, no. I think she'd be hurt if you didn't at least stop by and say hello."

Andrew stopped spinning and grinned suddenly. "All right, man. I get it."

"Huh?"

"I said, I get it. Don't worry, I got your back. I'll take care of it."

"What are you talking about?"

"You want me to go over there and check that brother out. Make sure he's not putting moves on your lady. Don't worry, it's cool." He got up and moved to the door.

"Wait, Andrew, I never said—"

"Don't bother denying it, my man. I'm on it. I'll let you know what's up."

With that, Andrew disappeared, leaving Trent confused but strangely satisfied.

Jaunie popped two aspirins into her mouth, then drained the glass of water Alan had given her. "Don't worry, it's just a stress headache. I'll be okay."

"But I feel so bad," Alan said, his handsome features etched with concern. "I would have told you what was going on, it's just that—"

Jaunie held up her hand. "I know, you thought I knew.

You've already apologized. Besides, it's not your fault.'' She sank into her chair, pulling her hair off her neck and pressing her palm to her forehead. ''I should have listened to my instincts. I knew it was a bad idea, but it was so important to Geri and the Center. I didn't want to be selfish.''

Alan gave her a tender look. ''For as long as I've known you, you've never been selfish. You couldn't be if you tried. I'm sorry you had to go through this.'' He reached across the desk, signaling that she should give him her hand. When she did, he caressed her skin with his thumb. ''What can I do to make this easier for you?''

She squeezed his fingers. ''Your friendship is enough, Alan. It helped having you there. At least I didn't have to face that ugly crowd alone.''

Alan started to speak, but a knock at the door cut him off. The door opened before she could say come in.

''Hey, J, what's up?''

''Andrew!'' She got up to give him a hug. ''Hi, sweetie. It's good to see you.''

She knew she was behaving a bit mushier than Andrew was used to, but she felt ridiculously glad to see him. He was proof that she'd done something right in her mixed-up career.

She needed to see as many friendly faces as possible. Alan had been sweet enough to take her to lunch after the taping, but she'd been too upset to eat.

''So who's this dude?'' Andrew asked.

Jaunie sat down again. ''This is Mr. Warren. Alan, this is my friend, Andrew. I've mentioned him to you.''

''It's nice to meet you, Andrew. My son, Jimmy, is about your age.''

Andrew dismissed Alan's outstretched hand with a shrug. He moved to Jaunie's desk and began playing with her calendar, effectively blocking her view of Alan. Alan had to look around Andrew's head to see her.

''Andrew, why don't you ask Mel for an extra chair so you can sit down, too.''

Andrew grinned pleasantly. ''No thanks, I'm fine.''

Alan started to say something, but Andrew started laughing out loud at one of the cartoons on her *Far Side* calendar. "This is a good one. Read this," he said, holding it out to her.

Jaunie took the calendar but didn't read it. Instead she stuffed it in a drawer so Andrew couldn't play with it. "What were you going to say, Alan?"

Alan tried again, but this time Andrew grabbed two pencils and started beating her desk like a drum while he rapped a song.

Jaunie reached out to still his hands. "Andrew, hush for a minute. Alan's trying to talk."

"Sorry," he said innocently. He reached across the desk to put the pencils away and knocked the mug of coffee Alan had been drinking into his lap. "Oops! My bad."

Andrew apologized but looked a little too satisfied to be truly sorry.

Jaunie handed a fistful of tissues to Alan. "I'm sorry, Alan. Andrew doesn't usually act like this."

He blotted his pants with the tissues. "It's all right, Jaunie. But I think I'll leave and let you and Andrew finish your visit."

"Alan, please don't—"

"Don't worry about it. I'll call you later."

After Alan left, Andrew jumped into the empty chair, swinging his legs.

Jaunie dropped into her chair. "Andrew, why were you so rude? What's going on?"

He shrugged. "I just didn't like him."

She arched her brows. "Why not?"

He shrugged again. "He's too much of a pretty boy. You need to go out with a guy like Trent instead."

She shook her head. "Is that what this is about? Andrew, Alan is married. I'm not going out with him—or Trent, for that matter."

"Oh. Sorry."

"It's okay," Jaunie said sadly.

Andrew looked anxious. "Hey, I didn't mean to mess up your day. I'm really sorry."

"No, Andrew, it's not you. I just had a bad morning. Seeing you actually makes me feel better."

His dark eyes filled with concern. "What happened?"

She sighed. "I taped that talk show I told you about today."

"Hey, that's cool!"

"No. It was awful. The host was nosey, and the audience asked rude questions. It was a nightmare."

Andrew scrunched up his face. "That sucks. Did a fight break out?"

"No, thank God."

"Well, did you cuss them out?"

"No." But it would have been nice.

"Did you at least cry or something?"

"Absolutely not." But it had been a close call.

"Aw, that means you won't get on that show where they show the best clips from all the talk shows."

Jaunie rested her forehead on her palm. "That's quite all right with me."

Andrew was silent for a long time. Jaunie wanted to be more sociable, but her head still throbbed. Maybe she should go home. She wasn't going to be of any use for the rest of the day.

"Jaunie?" Andrew asked hesitantly.

She looked up, feeling guilty for being such poor company. "Yes, Andrew?"

"I'm sorry those punks couldn't see how cool you are." He looked away, embarrassed. "You're cool with me."

"Thanks, Andrew. That means the world to me."

He stood. "Well, I gotta go."

"Okay. Thanks for stopping by."

He was halfway out of the door, when he turned back. "Oh, and my mom wants you to call her."

Patrice had sounded so upset on the phone yesterday. Jaunie wondered if she'd made any important decisions. She'd call her when she got home. At the moment she wasn't in any shape to be helpful to her friend.

She tried to smile. "Thanks, Andrew, I'll give her a call."

* * *

Trent was working on a cost estimate for their newest project when Andrew came back. "Come on in," he said, when he noticed the boy standing in the doorway.

Andrew took a couple steps forward. "I have to be getting home, but I wanted to tell you . . ."

"Something wrong? What was going on over there?"

"Nothing much. Dude left soon after I got there, but Jaunie's pretty down."

"Down? Why?"

"She did that talk show thing this morning. I think they dissed her or something."

"Dissed her? What did she say?"

Andrew turned to look at the clock. "Sorry, Trent, I've gotta jet. You should go talk to her, though. See ya."

The kid left before Trent could say anything more. Should he go over there? He was probably the last person she'd want to see if she was upset. The two of them could barely form complete sentences when they were in each other's company.

He tried to go back to his spreadsheet, but his conscience kept nagging him. What had happened on that show? Maybe she needed someone to talk to.

Yeah, right. Like he'd be helpful. Two seconds alone with her and he'd be all over her.

Again Trent tried to concentrate on the numbers in front of him. Again his conscience interrupted him. This was his chance to be a real friend to her. According to Andrew, she'd had a rough day. If he went over to check on her, at least she'd know he cared about more than getting into her—

Did he care about her? For him, caring was just one step away from loving, and loving was imminent disaster.

No, Jaunie *was* his friend. How could he not care about a woman with such a big heart? She'd constantly go that extra mile to help someone, and it had nothing to do with money. Andrew's life had completely changed thanks to her. She wasn't one of those people who paid lip service to a cause. She volunteered at the Center, and she never refused to help anyone who needed her.

He did care about her—as a friend. There was a fine line between love and friendship, but the line *was* there. He just had to make sure he stayed on the safe side of it.

He went across the hall and poked his head through the doorway. She was sitting at her desk, staring. "I know I'm probably the last person you want to see, but can I come in? Andrew told me you had a rough day."

She looked up at him but showed little reaction. "I'm okay. In fact, I was just about to leave."

He waited for her to get up and gather her things, but she made no effort to move. "What happened this morning to make you so upset?"

She sighed wearily. "I won't bore you with the details."

He stepped into her office and shut the door behind him. "I wouldn't be here if I wasn't interested. And I don't mean just idle curiosity. Andrew said you were feeling down, and I was concerned."

She nodded, apparently accepting the sincerity of his words. "It was that talk show. That stupid talk show. I knew it was a bad idea. Why didn't I follow my instincts and cancel?"

Trent frowned, taking a step forward. "That's the, uh, somebody Preston show, right? Weren't you talking about missing children?"

She looked at him and laughed sarcastically. "I tried, but foolish me, why didn't I realize that my former career as a decoy is far more interesting than the ongoing search for missing kids?"

Trent blinked. "Are you telling me that—"

"They set me up," she said, nodding. "They let me talk about the kids for five minutes, then it was on to 'This is Your Life, Jaunie Sterling' complete with a special guest from my past, Alan Warren."

Trent swore under his breath.

"Thank God, he tried to make things easier for me, but the show was past saving. Every time Alan sidestepped one of

Dirk's invasive questions, Dirk retaliated by going to the audience. They never let him down with their snap judgments and prying questions. The whole experience was pure hell.''

He reached across the desk for her hand. He wasn't sure if she would let him touch her, so he left his palm open, waiting. She slipped her fingers into his palm. They were ice cold, so he closed his hand around them, letting her share his warmth.

"Before my father died, he used to say to me, 'Little girl, the past always comes a knocking on your front door. When it does, make sure you're glad to see it.' " She pulled her hand away and began rubbing her upper arms. "I guess he knew even then that I take after my mother.''

Trent didn't know what to say. He'd heard her mention her mother once before, but it hadn't been a pleasant reference. "What happened today wasn't your fault.''

She looked at him incredulously. "Of course it was. I don't know if they'd planned this all along, or if it was something they cooked up after Geri canceled out, but the point is, they were looking for a juicy topic, and they found it in my past. My mother would be proud.''

He shook his head in confusion. "What do you mean?''

"She's the queen of the melodramatic. She'd think what happened today was fantastic because I managed to get the whole show to center around me. Her only complaint would be that I didn't mention her name.'' She slapped her palm to her forehead. "When this show airs, I won't be able to face anyone.''

"Jaunie, I'm sure everyone will understand—''

"No, they won't. You'll see for yourself. They make me out to be some hot siren tempting men from the path of righteousness. No matter what I said, they were convinced I slept with some of those men like some kind of glorified hooker.'' She looked at him coldly. "You ought to be able to relate to that. You've made it clear that I'm only good enough to be the object of your lust.''

Trent jumped up and rounded the desk, tilting her chin in

his hand until their eyes met. "Do you really believe that's what I think of you?"

She stared at him in shock.

"Answer me! Is that what you think?"

She looked away. "No . . . I—I don't know why I said that."

He pulled her to her feet, giving her a gentle hug. "Good," he said quietly. "Because we're friends, and I don't want you to forget that. Okay?"

She nodded against his chest, and he bent to kiss her forehead. "Friendship is a lot more lasting than a fleeting emotion like lust."

Then he slowly backed away and left the office before she could feel the rising contradiction in his pants.

Chapter Twelve

Jaunie leaned against her car, which was parked in front of Patrice's house. "Is this the last of your things?"

Patrice nodded, laying a worn blue comforter on top of the boxes in the trunk. "Yes, we didn't come with much. Richard made me throw out all my old furniture when we moved here. I'm not—Andrew, what are these Sega cartridges doing in here? I told you we're not bringing any of the things he bought for us."

Andrew looked over from where he was bouncing a basketball on the curb. "Aw, come on, Momma! I doubt pukehead will even know it's missing."

"Don't you argue with me, child." She handed him the keys. "Now you go on in that house and put these things back."

They'd planned to be gone before Richard came home from work, but since Jaunie couldn't get away from the office as early as she'd expected, they were cutting it close. As it happened, Richard was just pulling into the driveway when Andrew came out of the house.

With a groan, Patrice got out of the car. Jaunie stayed but

rolled down the window so she would know if Patrice needed her help.

Patrice grabbed Andrew's arm and directed him toward the car. "Go on, Andrew. We'll be leaving in a minute."

Richard stopped the car halfway up the drive and walked over to Patrice. He nodded toward Jaunie's car. "Where are you going?"

Jaunie couldn't see Patrice's face, but her voice sounded shaky. "There's a note for you inside, and when I get where I'm going, I'll call you."

"Where are you going?" he asked again.

Patrice hesitated.

Jaunie heard Andrew whisper, "Come on, come on. Tell him, Momma."

"To . . . live somewhere else."

"Yes!" Andrew shouted, then covered his mouth when he realized they could hear him.

Patrice turned around and motioned for Andrew to sit back from the window, but Richard's eyes remained trained on Patrice.

Through the rearview mirror, Jaunie could see the change in Richard's eyes as he realized that Patrice was leaving him. They deadened. His expression was just as blank as it would be if she'd said she were going to the grocery store.

"You really think you can do better without me?"

"I . . . I have to . . . try, I guess.

He nodded. "Go then." His tone was indifferent as he turned back to his car.

Patrice didn't move. She was frozen with what Jaunie knew had to be disbelief. The only wife the man had ever had was leaving him, and he hadn't even blinked an eye.

When Richard reached his car, he turned around to find she hadn't moved. "Go! I'm not about to argue with you. You had nothing when I married you. If you can't appreciate what I've done for you, get out of my life so I can find someone who will." His words could have been chiseled from a block of ice.

With a startled cry, Patrice ran back to the car. Jaunie put the car in gear, and as she pulled away, she could see Richard looking after them.

"I can't believe you have so many clothes." Patrice said, staring into Jaunie's walk-in closet.

Simone pulled out a slinky evening gown and held it up to her chest. "Six years of modeling *does* have its advantages. My girl will never go naked."

The three women had gotten together to find Patrice something to wear for the interview Simone had set up at her husband's dental office.

Patrice smoothed her hands over the clothes as she moved toward the back of the closet. "These are all designer originals, aren't they?" She pulled out a Giorgio Armani ensemble. "Richard used to take me to all those expensive boutiques and point them out to me."

"Yes. Actually that champagne-colored suit would be perfect for your interview. Take it. I hardly ever wear any of these clothes. Take anything you like. Most of the things I wear regularly are in front."

Patrice's eyes went wide. "Oh, no, I couldn't."

"Please! You'd be doing me a favor. I keep meaning to pack a box for the Salvation Army."

Patrice shook her head. "No, I don't look right in clothes like this. Richard finally stopped buying me designer things because they didn't hang right on me."

"Nonsense!" Simone said, placing her hand on the hip of her narrow-skirted denim dress. "Anyone can wear designer clothes if you've got the right at-ti-tude." She snapped her fingers as she began to strut across the room. "If you walk with confidence, Calvin Klein *himself* will try to take credit for designing your rags."

Jaunie grinned. "I think Simone should have been on the runway all those years instead of me."

Simone draped her arm across Jaunie's shoulder. "You know it, girl!"

Jaunie saw Patrice eyeing the Armani suit wistfully. "Simone, put her hair up in a French twist, while I look for some shoes."

Twenty minutes later, Patrice stared at her reflection in disbelief. "Is that really me?"

"Absolutely, dah-ling," Simone said after a final stroke with the lip brush.

"See, Patrice, you didn't believe me. You were already a step ahead with your smooth skin and pretty features. You should see what some of those models look like backstage before all the makeup and hairspray."

Patrice smiled into the mirror. "I think I'm ready for that Armani."

Patrice tried on the suit and looked so good in it, she was inspired to try on half the contents of Jaunie's closet. Jaunie and Simone tried on clothes and fixed each other's hair.

Later, when Jaunie's bed was heaped with discarded clothing, the three women were sprawled around the room, wearing evening gowns and smeared lipstick as they devoured a bag of chocolate chip cookies.

"Ooh," Simone moaned from her position on the floor. She propped her head against the closet door, knocking one of many jeweled clips from her copper curls. "We have to do this more often. I've forgotten what a joy it is to get away from the rugrats and act like a kid myself."

"Yeah." Patrice slouched on the makeup chair, looking almost comical in a blue velvet ballgown with cookie crumbs on her chin. "I don't think I've ever had so much fun."

On the floor Jaunie rolled onto her stomach, heedless of the yards of pink gauze that tangled around her legs. "This is just like a slumber party, only in midafternoon."

Patrice sat up, her hair already falling out of the French twist. "Speaking of midafternoon, isn't that Dirk guy on now? Does your show air today or tomorrow?"

"Tomorrow," Jaunie said bitterly.

"Wait a minute!" Simone waved her hand in the air. "You didn't tell me you were on the *Dirk Preston Show*."

"And I definitely had my reasons," she said, giving Patrice a mock glare.

"I know you said it was awful, but you really aren't going to watch it?" Patrice asked.

"No! And if you two care about me at all, you won't either."

"Jaunie? What are you talking about?" Simone asked.

Quickly she filled her sister in on the low points of her talk show experience.

Simone rolled her eyes. "Television is going downhill. I can't even let my kids watch it in the middle of the day if I'm not around."

"Don't worry, Jaunie," Patrice said. "It's just a little cable show. I'd bet no one will see it anyway."

Trent walked into his hotel room in Richmond, unknotting his tie. He'd spent the last hour pretending he hadn't noticed his client's daughter flirting with him over brunch.

He rolled his eyes in misery. Trying to think about another woman when Jaunie was on his mind was like drinking orange juice right after he'd brushed his teeth—he knew he should like it, but it left a bitter taste in his mouth.

He stretched out on the dark floral bedspread. Maybe he'd take a nap. He closed his eyes and the telephone rang. "Hello?"

"Turn on the TV!"

"Robert?"

"The *Dirk Preston Show*, turn it on, man. Jaunie's going to be on."

Trent turned on the TV with the remote nailed to the nightstand and flipped channels. "I can't find it."

"There's a commercial on right now." Robert described it so Trent could find it.

"How are you watching this? Where are you?"

"I'm at the job site, talking on the cell phone. I brought a portable TV. It's coming on. You'll be back tomorrow?"

"Yeah, I've got another meeting tonight and a breakfast meeting tomorrow. I'm driving back after that."

"All right, man, later."

Trent hung up and turned up the volume. Jaunie looked incredible and his lower body automatically tightened in response. The interview went well until after the first commercial, when Dirk's questions became sharper and he started using the audience against her. Trent gritted his teeth. Jaunie looked like a woodland creature staring at the barrel of a hunting rifle.

Soon Trent was pacing the room, hands clenched at his sides as he watched the show. If the lamps hadn't been nailed down, he probably would have thrown something at the set when Alan Warren came on. They'd set this up to be as uncomfortable for Jaunie as possible.

When the show returned from a break and Jaunie was gone, Trent started to turn off the TV, but an audience member caught his attention. He watched the show for a few more minutes, then snapped off the set, remembering how vulnerable Jaunie had been after taping the show.

He needed to see her. Two months of distance had done nothing to lessen the attraction between. Whatever his problems were, keeping them apart wasn't the solution.

He picked up the phone to call his client. Jaunie might need more than just his friendship tonight.

Jaunie cringed when the telephone rang again. The answering machine was picking up the calls, but she'd already changed the tape twice.

With a morbid curiosity, she'd listened to every message from reporters, relatives she hadn't spoken to in years, and crank callers. Men had called offering her company for the night, others claimed to be victims of her former career, alternately wanting revenge or reunions.

Her friends were the most persistent. Alan, Robert, Geri, Patrice, and Simone had all called more than once, worrying if she were okay. Even her mother called to tell her she'd looked fabulous and should consider hosting her own show.

Jaunie flopped facedown on the couch, pulling a pillow over

her head. She'd made the mistake of going to work that morning. By the time the show aired, the office telephone was ringing off the hook, and small-time rag magazine reporters had started arriving. Geri sent her home after profusely apologizing for getting her into this mess.

Jaunie didn't blame Geri. There was no way she could have known how this would turn out. But she hoped her celebrity would die down quickly. She'd come home and locked herself in her bedroom, trying to ignore the intermittent ringing of her doorbell.

The answering machine clicked again, and Patrice's voice came over the speaker. "Jaunie? I don't blame you for not answering the phone, but—"

"I'm here," she said into the receiver.

"Thank God, I've been so worried."

"I'm all right. Just keeping a low profile. It's amazing how many people watch midafternoon cable."

"I can't believe they dogged you like that. Dirk Preston used to be such a great host. What happened to his cowboy hat?"

"He's a phony. Thanks for your concern, Patrice, but I'm not in the mood to talk. Can I call you tomorrow?"

"Sure, honey. I just wanted to let you know that you have people on your side. Not everyone feels like Richard does. I know you—"

"Richard?"

Patrice was quiet for a minute. "I didn't mean to bring that up."

"You talked to Richard? He saw the show?"

"Yes, but I don't know how he ended up catching it. He always thought I was foolish for watching soap operas and talk shows all the time."

"What did he say?"

"It's not important. I don't even know why he called. He knows it's over. I told him your sister got me a great interview, and Andrew and I don't need his money."

"What did he say about the show? You said not everyone feels like Richard."

"He was just overreacting."

"Patrice, please, what did he say?"

"He said he didn't want me spending so much time with you—as if he has a say in who I spend time with anymore."

"Why?"

"He just said that maybe your morals weren't—why am I telling you this? It doesn't matter. We both know that he's a jerk. Who cares what he thinks. I didn't call to bring you down. I wanted you to know you have people who care about you. Okay?"

"Thanks, Patrice." Jaunie hung up the phone feeling numb. What if future clients took Richard's attitude? What if they didn't respect her ability to find their children because of her work at Intimate Investigations?

The phone rang again and without thinking, Jaunie picked it up. "Hello?"

"Jaunie?" asked a deep male voice.

"Yes?"

"I'm afraid I might cheat on my wife. Will you come over here and test me? I like to . . ." What followed shocked Jaunie so much, it took her a minute to get the phone into the cradle properly.

Shaking, Jaunie backed away from the phone. Hot tears rolled down her cheeks, and she sank to her knees on the carpet, burying her face in the material of her robe. She'd worked so hard to pull her life together, and she'd been proud of her accomplishments, but now they were meaningless.

Jaunie didn't know how long she sat there, letting her tears flow, but the sound of the doorbell startled her. She huddled on the floor, hoping the persistent ringing would stop.

"Jaunie? I know you're there. It's Trent. Can I come in? Please?"

Trent! She looked down at herself. She wasn't wearing anything besides her satin robe and nightgown. Though she tried to keep a low profile during the day, Jaunie was more than a bit indulgent with her sleepwear. The lilac material was clingy, and the hems were trimmed in lace, but the robe was long enough to cover—

"Jaunie?" Trent called again.

She stood, running her hand over her hair, which was undoubtedly mussed. How could she let him see her like this? She'd been crying and—

"Jaunie, please let me in. Just for a minute."

Trent had gone out of his way to make it clear there wouldn't more than friendship between them. Regardless of what she was wearing, the sight of her red nose and puffy eyes would keep his mind strictly on friendship.

She opened the door, and Trent sighed in relief. "Thank God. I was worried. Geri told me she'd sent you home hours ago."

She moved aside so he could come in, then shut the door behind him.

He stopped in front of her. "How are you?"

"I'm fine. Really. It was nice of you to come by and check, but I'm okay now." She added credence to her statement by sniffing loudly.

He reached out to stroke her face. "You've been crying."

She looked down at her bare feet. "It's been a rough day."

He nodded. "I caught the show. Definitely a setup—anyone with any sense can see that."

"Tell that to my answering machine that's filled twice over with messages from people who want to hear the story behind the story."

He pulled her over to the couch and sat her down. "Tell me what happened."

She rested the back of her head on the couch. "They won't leave me alone. All day long people have been calling and ringing my doorbell. Reporters have started showing up at the agency. For some reason they think an ex-model, former decoy, private eye is a story. But no one cares about missing children. Now I've shamed the NCMEC by connecting their name to this tacky hype Dirk Preston started."

Trent looked at her incredulously. "Is that really what you think?"

"Of course. No one heard the message, they just want to dissect my life and display the juicy details."

"Did you watch the show today?"

"No way! I was there, remember? It wasn't an experience I wanted to relive."

"Then I don't think you have an accurate picture of how you went over. You were dignified and focused. You made a constant effort to rise above their pettiness, making *them* look bad, not the other way around."

"That's nice of you to say, but I'm pretty sure—"

"Do you know what happened after they came back from the commercial and you were gone?"

She raised an eyebrow suspiciously. "No, what?"

"Dirk made excuses for you and tried to go on to another guest. An older woman stood up in the audience and gave him hell."

"What? What did she say?"

"She said she didn't blame you for leaving because a chronicle of your former careers has nothing to do with the work you came to discuss. Her own daughter ran away at thirteen, and she didn't see her again until the girl was in her thirties. That stopped the audience cold. The woman said if there'd been resources like the Center, maybe she would have been reunited with her daughter sooner. She said Dirk and the rest of the audience should be ashamed of themselves for running you off when what you had to say might have really helped people."

Tears were running down Jaunie's face. "At least one person understood. Thank God." She tried to cover her face with her hands, but Trent pulled her into his arms, giving her a much needed hug.

"It was a lot more than one person," he whispered, rubbing her back soothingly. "After the woman sat down to an explosive round of applause, other people stood up and agreed with her before Dirk went to break again. After that, I got the feeling that he'd lost the audience's respect."

Jaunie sniffed, and a new wave of tears began to flow. He continued to rock her gently. "I'm surprised that no one else told you this."

She lifted her head. "I didn't really give anyone a chance. My friends all said positive things, but I thought they were just being kind. Now that I think about it, not all of the messages from strangers were negative. Some said good things, but I guess I only focused on all the requests for interviews and crank calls."

"Crank calls?"

"Yeah, you know—men wanting to know if they can hire a private investigator to do strip searches."

He squeezed her shoulder. "I'm sorry you had to deal with that. You don't deserve it."

"Forgive me for crying like this. I never cry." She sniffed as more fat tears slid from her eyes.

"Hey, you're entitled. In fact, what you really need is to relax. Rest."

"I can't relax. I'm much too tense."

"I have an idea." He got up from the sofa and dropped a pillow on the spot he'd vacated. "Just lie here and close your eyes. Instant relaxation coming right up."

"What are you going to do?" She had ideas of her own, but so far Trent hadn't shown her anything more than brotherly affection. It was nice, in a way, but it would have been nicer if he'd at least noticed her state of undress.

"I'm going to help you relax." He guided her head to the pillow, then waited for her to close her eyes before she heard him move away.

The stress and crying must have worn Jaunie out, because she dozed off soon after she'd closed her eyes. She didn't wake until she felt Trent's hand gently squeezing her shoulder. She opened her eyes to find him smiling at her.

"You must have been tired after all, but I think you'll appreciate this anyway. Come on." He took her hand and helped her up from the couch.

"What is it?" she asked hazily.

He led her toward her bedroom without answering. Her heart started beating faster. Could this be—

He stopped halfway down the hall, in front of the bathroom door. She furrowed her brow when he pushed open the door and nudged for her to enter.

Trent had found two mismatched candlestick holders and candles in her kitchen and had placed them on the sink counter. He'd also laid out fresh towels and a washcloth. The bathtub was filled with a steamy bubble bath, and on the shelf beside the tub was a glass of red wine.

She turned around to face him, overwhelmed. New tears formed in her eyes. "You did all this? How did you find everything? How did you know?"

He smiled. "I figured that if you were anything like my sister, a hot bubble bath would be just the thing. When I found several bottles of fragrant foam bath under the sink, I knew I'd guessed correctly."

She turned slowly, taking it all in again, unsure of what she was supposed to do next. Was he going to bathe, too?

That *would* be just the thing.

She hid her disappointment when he kissed her on the forehead and closed the door behind him when he left.

The dim, almost dark, effect of the candles gave the room a private and alluring atmosphere. Jaunie slid out of her robe and gown and stepped into the warm rose-scented bubbles. Her muscles liquidated instantly as she breathed a deep sigh. But it was more than just a sigh to exalt the pleasure of the warm bath. It was a sigh of freedom, of truly letting go. As she sank back against the tub, she released her worries, her hangups, her unshed tears and her self-doubt. They floated from her body and dissolved in the magically soothing water. She felt purified and brand new—at least for tonight.

Would Trent be waiting when she left the bath? Or would he leave her alone to rest?

She sipped the wine he'd poured for her and closed her eyes. Sensual thoughts began to surface. The heat sensitized and the bubbles teased her skin. Knowing she was bare under the elusive sweet-scented water, and that Trent wasn't far, stirred her imagination. She drained the wine-glass.

Trent knocked softly on the door. "Is everything okay?"

"Yes," she called back. "I was just about to get out."

"Okay. I just wanted to make sure you didn't fall asleep in there."

Jaunie smiled. He was being so attentive. She didn't know what inspired this new tenderness within him, but she hoped it lasted.

She dried herself, dressed, then blew out the candles. She met him in the living room, where he reclined on the sofa, drinking a glass of wine of his own. He looked so at home. So comfortable. So right.

He looked up at her. "There you are. Feel better?"

"Much. Thank you." She moved closer and he stood.

"Ready for bed?"

Oh, no! Was he going to tuck her in and leave? She searched for a way to make him stay, but she was so relaxed, her mind was blank.

"Come on," he said, taking her hand. He led her to her bedroom and opened the door.

She stepped inside, turning quickly, expecting him to say good night. She was surprised when he followed her inside, closing the door behind him.

He moved forward, placing his hands on her waist, then he bent his head and kissed her. It was a soft liquid kiss, unlike any they'd shared before. His lips moved very slowly on hers, drawing out each gentle stroke. With a quiet sigh, he lifted his head.

Hope grew inside Jaunie like a new spring bud. Did this mean he wanted to stay? "Trent?" she whispered, needing to know for sure.

"Yes?"

"Does this—I mean, I thought you didn't want—"

He tugged on a strand of her hair. "I don't know about you, but I was lying to myself when I said that there was only friendship between us. Trying to keep my hands off you is like trying to stop a moving train with my bare hands.''

He pulled her closer. ''Is this what you want, too?''

''Yes.'' The word seemed inadequate to express the range of emotions she was feeling, but it was all she could manage at that moment.

He picked her up and laid her down on her bed. Then he moved over her, hands braced on either side of her body, as he brought their lips together.

This kiss was deeper, but just as slow as the first one. His tongue plunged into her mouth, like a diver searching for buried treasure. He moved his head from side to side, gradually tapering the kiss with smaller ones.

Jaunie tried to deepen the kiss again, but Trent moved his lips to her forehead, his mouth caressing the sensitive spot between her eyebrows. It was both tender and affectionate, filling Jaunie with warm anticipation.

He kissed both temples, then both cheeks and the tip of her nose. She reached up to hold him still so she could kiss him on the lips again, but he ducked his head and kissed her chin. Then he captured her hands and pinned them to the bed, while he moved his mouth to her earlobe.

Trent sucked the entire lobe into his mouth. She melted into the bedspread, realizing that he knew exactly what he was doing. He traced the rim of her ear with his tongue and flicked her lobe with his lower lip. Hot sensual tremors vibrated inside her. She shifted restlessly beneath him.

He held Jaunie in utter suspense as he treated her other ear to the same teasing. His lips moved on to her throat, alternately sucking and nipping, to the place where her neck met her collarbone. He dropped tiny kisses from one side to the other, making her moan with impatience.

When he reached her collarbone a second time, Jaunie began to loosen her robe to give him access to her breasts. He ignored her invitation, working his way back to her mouth. This kiss, both searing and intense, sustained the impact of her anticipation.

Trent sat back on his heels, and Jaunie waited for him to start removing his clothing. Instead he reached for her hand, tenderly kissing its back, then flipping it over to lick her palm. He sipped his way to her wrist, tickling her skin with tiny flicks of his tongue. Pushing up the sleeve of her robe, he dropped a trail of kisses to her elbow. Jaunie half giggled, half sighed with pleasure. He repeated the action on her other arm.

Finally! He parted her robe. Jaunie's breasts were aching for attention, but instead of focusing on her needy nipples, Trent dipped his tongue into her navel through her gown.

Jaunie's hips bucked, and she groaned. He placed kisses across the surface of her stomach, and Jaunie thought she'd go wild. He had yet to touch her most obvious points of pleasure, but tension was building at a frenzied pace inside her. Trent prolonged the torture by skipping from her stomach to her knees. He kissed, sucked, and bit the tender skin behind each knee, then moved on to her ankles. When he lifted her foot and kissed her instep, Jaunie couldn't take any more.

"Trent," she said breathlessly. "What are you doing to me?"

He leaned over her so that they were face to face. "I just wanted you to know that I'm interested in you as a whole person, not just the overtly sexy parts."

"Oh, Trent." Jaunie pulled his face down for a deep kiss. At that moment she could no longer deny that she was in love with him.

Chapter Thirteen

Trent heard the tender words leave his mouth, and knew they should be cause for concern, but he could worry later. Right now Jaunie deserved his full attention, and she was going to get it.

He reached for the lacy hem of the gown that had tested his willpower all night. He couldn't believe he'd lasted this long. The only thing that had kept him from behaving like a barbarian when she'd opened the door wearing that tempting ensemble was the knowledge that he had to be there for her. She'd needed him. And now he needed her.

He dragged the silk slowly over her legs, lightly grazing the skin of her thighs and tantalizing her stomach. Jaunie moaned and squirmed, but she didn't try to stop him. She was naked beneath the gown and robe. His eyes were filled with the beauty before him. He blinked, knowing his imagination had never been this good.

She reached out to him, groping his shirttail and fumbling with his belt buckle. Her hands were making him restless, and he didn't want to lose control. He wanted this moment more than he wanted anything else, and it had to be right.

She forced his shirt open, and Jaunie pressed kisses to his chest. He fought the urge to let his libido take over. He didn't want his mind to blank out, leaving him a slave to the hot colors, smooth sounds, and sweet sensations of sex. He wanted to think clearly so he could love her properly.

Ignoring the primitive callings from below his waist, he let Jaunie strip off his shirt, then he moved from the bed, pulling off his pants, so only his briefs confined him. Thank God, he was still thinking clearly enough to find the protection he'd brought with him.

Trent returned to the bed where Jaunie waited eagerly. He made himself go slowly as he prepared her for his entry. He lowered his head to her breasts as his fingers explored her. He heard her murmur "finally" as his tongue circled her nipples.

He kissed the area between her breasts, then moved up to lick her neck. He heard his own harsh breathing and knew he couldn't hold on much longer.

His groan was loud and guttural when Jaunie grasped him in her hand and helped him put on the condom he'd given her. She nearly sent him over the edge with her hands.

The fight was over when he sank into her dark, velvet softness. Hot, wet, smooth. The first stroke was heaven.

Deeper. Faster. Her legs around his waist pulled him closer. Tight. Sweet. He felt her body quiver beneath his.

Silky, damp skin. His body thrust in sudden release.

Jaunie. His lover.

Jaunie woke the next morning to the knowledge that the weight of a lifetime of worries had been released. Without waking Trent, she put on her robe and tiptoed to the bathroom.

As she brushed her teeth, she glowed with an emotion she thought she'd never experience. Love. It had finally happened to her, and it was everything those sappy poems, gushy movies, and romantic novels had made it out to be.

She must have done something right, because the man who'd

made her believe in love—who'd made her crave these elusive, mysterious feelings—was lying in her bed this morning.

Trent *had* restored her faith in love, and by some miracle, she hadn't destroyed his heart all those years ago as she'd feared. The tenderness he'd shown her last night proved that.

She smiled at her reflection. All the Dirk Prestons, Richard Lincolns, nosey reporters, and crank callers of the world couldn't touch her now.

Today Jaunie Sterling was in love, and she'd just bet that Trent loved her too.

Trent had fallen off the wagon.

More than that, he thought, rolling onto his back. Last night he dove off the wagon headfirst and had never looked back.

Last night, like an alcoholic on a drinking binge, he'd cast all warnings aside and had given in to temptation. And he didn't regret a second of it. No other woman had gone to his head so quickly or affected him so strongly. Jaunie was potent. He had to be careful.

It was too late to pretend he didn't care about her, but it wasn't too late to regain his sobriety. He wasn't in love—yet.

Staying away from Jaunie now would be impossible, but he could stay away from love. It was love that impaired his ability to think clearly and make rational decisions. It was love that took his pride and made him weak. Only the pounding hangover of love could make him hit rock bottom.

Love. He'd never touch the stuff again.

Jaunie was reaching for the play button on the answering machine when Trent came out of the bedroom, looking for her.

"What are you doing?" He wrapped his arms around her from behind, pinning her arms to her sides.

"I was going to listen to my machine. Look, it's only ten thirty, and I've already got eleven messages."

He stepped back, pulling her away from the machine. "Don't do that. Why spoil a perfectly good day?"

"It's okay. I can handle anything today."

Trent squeezed her close, nuzzling her cheek. "Handle it tomorrow."

She giggled, enjoying the attention. "Oh, yeah? And what am I supposed to do when the world comes looking for me?"

He turned her around in his arms. "Let's both blow off work today. Robert's not expecting me until this afternoon, anyway. I'll just tell him not to expect me at all. Can Geri get along without you?"

Jaunie rested her head on his bare chest, tucking her hands into the waistband of his briefs. "I'm between cases right now. What did you have in mind?"

"Let's get away for the day. Why don't we check into an expensive hotel and concentrate on relaxing? The hotel I stayed in yesterday was a dump. I'm in the mood for a little pampering—what about you?"

Jaunie smiled. "Let's go for it."

They were registered at the Ritz Carlton in Pentagon City by afternoon, then hit the mall for lunch. After a few people stopped Jaunie to ask if they'd seen her on TV, she and Trent bought sunglasses and hats and walked around the mall, making a game out of being incognito.

For dinner they ordered ridiculously expensive meals from room service, and after feasting like kings, Trent made long, slow love to her. Later, when they were lounging in each other's arms, watching TV and cuddling, Jaunie began to wonder about their future together. Her feelings for him were clear, and she wanted to say the words out loud.

She rolled onto her side, facing him. "Trent?"

"Yeah, babe," he answered absently, his eyes still trained on the television set.

"I . . ." She couldn't just blurt it out. How should she lead up to it?

Several minutes passed before Trent noticed she hadn't finished her sentence. He was engrossed in a sitcom rerun. When the commercial came on, he touched her leg. "Did you want to say something?"

"Yeah . . . actually I did." She reached for the remote and turned off the sound. Trying to collect her thoughts, she took his hand in both of hers, cradling it in her lap.

He raised his brows. "Is something wrong?"

She smiled, bringing his fingers to her lips. "Nothing's wrong. I just wanted to tell you—"

He pulled his hand from her grasp to stroke her cheek. "If nothing's wrong, then why are we talking?" He pulled her to his side and smoothed her lips with his.

Jaunie let him lull her with his kisses, but when they parted, she sat back on her heels. "I just thought we could plan—"

"Plan? This is supposed to be a break. Relax." He turned her back toward him. "Let me give you a massage."

"That does feel good," she said as his hands brushed over her skin, and his lips nuzzled her neck and shoulders. "But I really—"

"We both needed this time away. Let's not waste time with words." He leaned her back so his lips could cover hers, and seconds later she was lying under him.

For the moment Jaunie let herself be distracted. She had the rest of her life to tell him she loved him.

After two weeks Jaunie's world began to calm, and she had to face the truth she'd been avoiding: Trent didn't share her feelings. She'd seen him often since their stay at the Ritz Carlton, but a pattern had emerged. Each time she tried to discuss the future or her feelings, he became withdrawn or distracted.

Trent had no interest in a serious relationship, and she knew why. He'd been hurt. Hadn't she helped one woman in particular hurt him? Of course he didn't want to risk that kind of pain again. He'd told her as much. Now she couldn't blame him for not feeling what she wanted him to. He'd never made her any promises.

Her faith in love was still new and untested. Maybe it wasn't as strong as she'd thought. She didn't have the power to change Trent's heart, so she'd have to settle for what they had.

At least things had finally started to settle down around Sterling & Treymaine. The phones had tapered off to calls from people who genuinely needed the services of a private investigator, and curious strangers had stopped popping in out of nowhere. Jaunie was starting to breathe easily again, hoping she was no longer the news of the day.

She'd spent most of the morning driving around downtown D.C., trying to serve a subpoena to a bike messenger who'd witnessed a mugging. The man didn't stay in one place long enough for her to catch up to him. Finally she'd had to rent a bike and ride right up alongside him just to serve him the papers.

Jaunie sank into her chair, propping her feet up on her desk. Her calf muscles would thank her later for the unexpected exercise. After a quick massage, Jaunie dropped her legs, her heels dragging something to the floor with them. She bent to pick it up. It was an envelope with her name printed on the outside. No stamp or address. She'd started to open it when Geri poked her head in.

"Are you busy, sweetie?"

Jaunie dropped the envelope on her desk. "No, what's up?"

Geri cleared off her favorite corner and sat down. "While you were out, you got a new case."

"Me?"

"Yes. Apparently one of Robert's clients needs an investigator, and he told him to ask for you. I'd be offended, but Sam stayed home sick today, and I couldn't leave her alone overnight anyway."

"Overnight? What's the case?"

"Surveillance."

"Oh, Lord, Geri. Just don't tell me I have to spend the night in the car."

"Not the *whole* night, sweetie. Mr. Goodman owns real estate downtown, and some property he just bought is being vandalized at night. He wants us to watch the house and report back to him. If you spot the vandals, just follow them. He suspects they work for one of his rivals.''

''Well, it sounds simple enough.''

''Here's his number. Give him a call. I think he wants you to start tonight.''

Geri left her office and Jaunie called Mr. Goodman. He seemed like a nice man concerned about his business interests. The only thing that worried Jaunie was that the property was in Southeast D.C., not the best place to be after dark. But she was a professional, and this was her business.

After Jaunie got off the telephone, she remembered the envelope. She picked it up and opened it. It took her a moment to recognize the photo inside as one of her old modeling publicity shots.

The photo had been ripped apart at clean angles and then pieced back together with cellophane tape. The sharp angles that cut through her face resembled the pattern of broken glass.

She stared at the mutilated photo, searching for a logical explanation. She turned over the envelope. Her name was printed in large block letters, but she didn't recognize the handwriting. The envelope must have been hand delivered.

Dropping the photo on her desk, Jaunie carried the envelope out to the reception area. ''Mel, where did you get this?''

Mel cocked her head to one side, her blond hair fanning over her shoulder. ''I've never seen it before.''

Jaunie frowned. ''You didn't put this on my desk?''

''Nope.''

''Has anyone been in my office while I was out?''

''No. Is something wrong?''

''No. Thanks, Mel.''

Jaunie went back into her office and stared at the photo again. This was obviously someone's idea of a sick joke. For all she knew, the envelope could have been hidden on her desk for days. The office had been so crowded with unwelcome strangers, anybody could have snuck it in while no one was looking.

She dropped the envelope and the photo into the garbage.

Hopefully this was the last of the backlash from her unforgettable television debut.

Dressed in black leggings and a dark hooded jacket, Jaunie prepared to leave for surveillance duty. Mr. Goodman wanted her at the house by midnight, and it was already after 11 P.M. She'd just picked up her car keys when the doorbell rang. "Who is it?" she called.

"It's Trent."

She jerked open the door. "Trent! What are you doing here?"

He came inside. "I drove straight over from Baltimore." He dropped his overnight bag and turned to her, looking her up and down. "Am I interrupting something? Planning a cat burglary?"

The only thing Jaunie had any interest in stealing was Trent's heart, but she couldn't tell him that. "Actually I was just on my way out. I have to work a case tonight."

He drew his eyebrows together. "Where will you be?"

Jaunie felt illogically defensive. "Well, dressed like this, I'm clearly not going out to pick up men."

She started to move past him, but he caught her around the waist, pulling her into his arms. "Hey, hey, haven't we gotten past this yet? I wasn't trying to check up on you."

She bowed her head. "I'm sorry. I knew that. I have to watch a vacant house tonight. Vandals have been showing up and making custom alterations on the property."

Trent lifted her chin. "Are you going out there alone?"

"Yeah. It's no big deal, I only have to watch the house. If anyone shows up, the owner doesn't want me to confront them. I just have to follow them and report back to him. He thinks he knows who's behind the break-ins."

"Do you want some company? I could go along for the ride."

Jaunie reached up and gave him a quick kiss. "No, but thanks for the offer. You really look beat."

"I hate the idea of you sitting out in the dark all by yourself—

but you're right, I'm whipped." He pulled her closer. "In fact, I'm in no mood to drive back to my apartment. Do you mind if I crash here tonight?"

"Of course not, but I probably won't be back until early morning."

"Well, just wake me when you come in. I'll tuck you in before I go to work." He pressed his lips against hers, and Jaunie wrapped her arms around his neck. Their bodies melted together. Each time they tried to part, they were drawn back together again.

Finally she pushed against his shoulders. "You're making me wish I could stay home and play hooky."

Trent gave her another kiss. "If you do, I think I have just enough energy to—"

"No." She leaned up for one last kiss. "I'm going to be late. We can pick up where we left off"—she gave him a deep kiss that left him grasping for her as she backed out of his reach—"when I get home," she finished, closing the door between them.

Two hours later Jaunie squirmed within the confines of her Honda. She was cramped and bored, and she missed Trent.

She reached out to change radio stations. WKYS had switched from the energetic club music that had been helping her stay awake to mellow slow jams. Such music would not only make her sleepy, it would intensify the ache she felt in her heart each time she thought of Trent sleeping in her bed—without her.

After two trips through the range of radio stations, she resigned herself to the fact that everyone played slow songs at 2 A.M. Friday mornings. She slouched in her seat and stared at the house she'd been sent to watch. There was nothing to see.

This wasn't the best part of town for just hanging out, but as far as Jaunie could tell, even the lowlife scum had gone home to bed by now. The streets were quiet, and her eyelids were getting heavy.

Stifling a curse, she pushed her body upright and cracked a window. A cool, late September breeze would come in handy right now. She'd taken a long nap this afternoon to prepare for the job, but her body didn't seem to care. If it could have its way, she'd be in bed at that very moment—with Trent.

She turned up the radio, hoping to drown out her thoughts. But as a woman's sultry voice filled the car, Jaunie knew it was time to give up the fight. The woman was singing about what she wanted from a man.

> *Dark eyes to haunt the night.*
> *A warm smile to melt my heart.*
> *Strong arms to hold on tight.*
> *A man with soul to love me right.*

Of course the song was about Trent. Having him in her life was bittersweet. Her toes curled every time she thought about him sleeping in her bed, waiting for her to come home. But the image was spoiled by the truth. They'd made no plans and had no discussions about what their relationship was. Jaunie only knew what it wasn't—permanent.

Trent didn't love her now. Why should he? What did she have to offer him? Her lifestyle wasn't the picture of wholesome living and domestic bliss. Look at her! She was sitting in the middle of Southeast D.C. at two in the morning, waiting for thugs to show up. And with a past in which she'd made a living off other people's infidelities, who knew what the future held? It was no wonder she didn't inspire the hearts and flowers routine with Trent.

What would she do when he got tired of her? She'd planned to make the most of her time with Trent, but the more they were together, the deeper she fell in love with him.

Jaunie stared at the dark house across the street. It looked lonely—just like her heart. When an old Barry White song came on the radio, she knew she couldn't take any more. She opened the glove compartment and began searching for something, anything, to play instead. Within seconds she began discarding cassettes. Anita Baker? No. Mariah Carey? No. Babyface—

Behind her a cracking sound broke the night. She looked up to see shards of glass flying into the car from the small corner window. Now the high-pitched tinkle of splintering glass came from all sides.

Jaunie covered her head and crouched on the floor of the car as the world shattered around her.

Chapter Fourteen

The piercing explosions ended with a sudden burst of silence, but Jaunie didn't move right away. She could feel pieces of glass covering her head and back. Keeping her head lowered so it wouldn't fall into her eyes, she crept from the car. Other than tiny cuts on her palms, she was unharmed.

Shaking off bits of glass and standing on trembling legs, she looked around. The streets were as quiet and empty as they'd been last time she'd looked. With disbelieving eyes she stared at her Honda. The front windshield was covered with a dense spider webbing of cracks. All that remained of the other windows was scattered inside the car and on the street around her. Only a few jagged edges were left in the window frames.

How could this have happened? One minute she'd been searching her glove compartment for cassettes, the next minute it seemed some supernatural force had blown out her windows. Why hadn't she seen anyone or heard their approach?

Had it been the vandals she'd been watching out for? Had they been watching out for her? How was she going to get home? Glass covered every surface in the car. Even if she managed to clear that away, seeing through the windshield would be impossible.

Jaunie gripped her upper arms, trying to still her trembling limbs. What was she going to do? It was after two in the morning, and she was standing in the middle of Southeast D.C., where someone could walk up and blow her away in a minute. At least she had the gun Alan had made her get.

Alan! He would know how to handle this. Of course he was probably sick of bailing her out of trouble. But who else could she count on? She could call Trent, but not only did she hate to wake him, she hated to worry him. He'd raised a fuss about her sleeping alone in a suburban neighborhood, when she was looking for Andrew. This would make him crazy. Trent would take this story better after she was safe at home. At least Alan was used to this kind of thing.

Jaunie opened the car door and spotted her bag on the floor of the passenger seat. Balancing one leg inside and grabbing hold of the steering wheel for extra support, Jaunie gingerly reached across the glass-covered seats and snagged her bag. Dragging it outside and overturning it, she picked her cellular phone and her gun out of the heap of glass and junk.

Alan didn't ask questions, he just came as soon as he could. He waited while she gave her statement to the police, then helped her arrange for emergency roadside service to tow her car. By 4:30 A.M. he was driving her home.

Jaunie held tight to her steaming cup of 7-Eleven coffee and tried to make sense of the night. She hoped the heat cupped between her palms would seep into the rest of her body, which felt only numb and cold. Staring at street-lights as they passed, she couldn't believe the sun would be coming up soon. What would she tell Mr. Goodman? What would she say to Trent?

Alan drove slowly. She felt him looking over at her periodically. "How are you doing over there?"

Jaunie rested her head against the seat as she faced his profile. "I'm okay. I think I just need to sleep."

"I'll have you home soon, but I think we ought to go over

this again. The fact that the police found those blunt objects discarded just a block away proves that someone—''

''Alan, please.'' She tightened her grip on the coffee cup, nearly burning herself when the hot liquid dribbled over the rim. ''Can we do this tomorrow? I need to wind down a bit first.''

''Sure, sure.'' Alan's tone immediately became conciliatory, and he patted her knee. ''You do need to relax. I'm just worried about you, that's all. You've been through so much these past few weeks. I should have—''

''Stop, Alan. You're always there for me. In fact, I'm waiting for you to get sick of rescuing me.''

She felt his warm gaze on her again. ''Never. You know I'd never turn my back on you. I'll always be there when you need me.''

Jaunie smiled. ''Thanks. You don't know how much that means to me.''

They were silent for a while as he drove, then he said, ''I don't like the idea of your being alone tonight. Maybe you'd better stay with Karina and me until—''

''Don't worry, I'll be fine.''

''No. I won't be able to sleep. Karina and I have plenty of room and—''

''Alan, I won't be alone. Trent's at my apartment. You remember Trent.''

''Yes.'' His answer was stiff. After another pregnant pause, his tone took on a forced nonchalance. ''So why didn't you mention this new development?''

Jaunie sighed. If she didn't know better, she'd think he was jealous. Her mind drifted back to that nonsense Trent had come up with about Alan being in love with her. She brushed the thought away. Men were always territorial when it came to a woman's relationship with another man. ''It's still new. I'm not sure myself what it is.''

Alan's laugh was a bit strained. ''Well, if he's sleeping at your apartment, it must be something.''

She'd had enough of this. Alan was a good friend, but she

wasn't going to discuss her love life with him—especially not under the circumstances. "Actually it's more like he stopped by to see me, and I was on my way out. He'd just driven in from a business trip and was tired, so I said he could crash at my place instead of getting back on the road. I only brought it up so you wouldn't worry about me being alone."

Alan was quiet for a minute. "Sorry, I didn't mean to get nosey. Hazard of the business."

Jaunie reached over to squeeze his hand as he pulled up in front of her place. "No, *I'm* sorry. You've been great. Forgive me if I'm cranky. I'm . . . I'm just tired." She gathered her things and reached for the door handle. "I'll call you tomorrow." She glanced at the sky, which was already beginning to lighten. "Well, that is, later on today."

Alan smiled and nodded, but his eyes were serious. "You know I'll always look out for you, Jaunie."

Trent gave Jaunie a long look before he left for work. She'd come in some time in the early morning and had been sleeping deeply ever since. He'd considered getting up and making her breakfast but decided to let her sleep. She looked like she needed it and . . . well, he liked to watch her.

Not every woman was beautiful in sleep or in the first waking moments of morning. How could they be with tangled hair, puffy eyes, and lines from the sheets indented in their skin? But somehow Jaunie managed beauty twenty-four hours a day, and Trent found her most attractive in the morning.

Her mussed hair was sexy, and she'd open her eyes and smile at him with a heavy-lidded gaze that made him want to spend the day in bed.

In her bed last night, he'd slept better than he had in a long time. Even without her there, he'd felt her presence. The pillows and sheets had been fragrant with her perfume. It took a certain amount of trust for a woman to let a man sleep in her bed alone. The knowledge that she trusted him with that kind of intimacy warmed him.

His only problem was that the atmosphere had left his mind fertile for a lot of erotic dreams, which he'd hoped to fulfill when she came home. Trent released his breath heavily. He had to go now . . . but there was always tonight.

With his hand on the doorknob, he backed out of the room, watching Jaunie curl on her side, still locked in the throes of sleep. So beautiful. So easy to lo—

Trent slammed the door shut to cut off his thoughts, but then had to open it back up to make sure he hadn't awakened her. She slept quietly. He closed the door again, more gently this time, but quickened his pace as he left the apartment, trying to outrun the thoughts he wanted to avoid.

Once behind the wheel of his car, he kept his foot pressed to the gas, but traffic was slow that morning. Even though he wove between cars and drove more obnoxiously than usual, he couldn't go fast enough. They were gaining on him. He tried turning up the radio to drown out their approach, but it was impossible to drown out your own thoughts.

Damn! He pounded the steering wheel in surrender. He was in love with her. He could lie to himself all he wanted, but that wouldn't change the facts. He loved her.

Darkness fell over him with the realization. Now he was a sitting duck: hers for the taking. She could pick him clean. He didn't want any woman to have that kind of hold on him again, and now, whether she knew it or not, Jaunie did.

Trent drove the rest of the way to his office slowly, trying to wade through this dilemma. Cars whizzed past him, people honked their horns at him, but he didn't care. His concentration was centered on one question, and he wouldn't let up until he knew . . .

How did one fall *out* of love?

That afternoon Trent didn't go to lunch. He didn't take any phone calls. He barely spoke to anyone while he thought his problem through.

He couldn't let himself love Jaunie. He didn't want to hurt

her, but it would hurt more if he let this go on. He refused to be like Robert, stumbling from one bad relationship to another. The kinds of women he and Robert wanted weren't good for them. He wanted Jaunie. That could only mean disaster.

In the past he'd wrecked his life for less. Erika had bounced him around like a puppet on a string. Some of the others had lied to him or had taken advantage of his generosity. He'd never forget that it had taken him two years to clear off the credit card debt he'd incurred as a result of one sob story in particular.

He'd faced the truth long ago—when it came to women, he was a sucker. And his feelings for Jaunie were the strongest yet. Things were fine now, but one day the power would rush to her head. He didn't stand a chance of resisting her.

He had to get out. Now. Before he lacked the will to try. He hadn't made her any promises. They both would have to accept that it had to be this way.

Heavyhearted with the decision he'd made, Trent left his office to grab a sandwich. As he passed Robert's door, he heard voices. One of them was Jaunie's.

"Are you sure, Robert? Mr. Goodman said he got our name from you."

"I'm sorry, Jaunie, but I would tell you if I knew this guy."

Trent paused in the doorway. "What's going on?"

Jaunie looked at him warily.

"Jaunie was just telling me what happened to her car. She can't reach the guy that sent her out there, and he told her he'd gotten her name from me. I told her I didn't—"

"What happened to your car?"

Jaunie started to open her mouth, but Robert cut her off. "You don't know? Man, someone bashed in all her windows while she was inside."

"What!" Fear and anger rose in his throat. He grabbed Jaunie's arm. "This happened last night? Are you okay? Why didn't you tell me?"

Jaunie put her palms against his chest. "Trent, calm down.

Everything's okay. I wasn't hurt, and I didn't have a chance to tell you. You were gone when I woke up this morning."

"You should have awakened me when you came in."

"You were sleeping so soundly, and I was dead on my feet. It wasn't a good time to go into all of this."

Trent looked up to find Robert watching them, brow raised in amused fascination. "Robert, get out of here. I need to talk to Jaunie alone."

"Sure, bro, but you do realize this is *my* office, right?"

"And?" His tone brooked no argument.

"Just wanted to keep you informed." Robert grinned widely as he backed out of the office. "See ya!" He closed the door behind him.

Trent turned back to Jaunie, who took a step backward, sitting in the chair opposite Robert's desk. She popped back up a second later when she realized she'd sat on top of a tape measure, keys, and other assorted junk that had been piled on the chair.

"Trent, I didn't want to worry you."

He stepped forward. "Of course I'm worried. Exactly what happened?"

"Basically I had the house under surveillance. Nothing much was going on, and I was getting sleepy. So I was searching my glove compartment for some tapes to help me stay awake, and I heard a crash. I looked up and glass was flying everywhere. I crouched on the floor of my car until it stopped. When I finally got out, all my windows were shattered, and there was no one around."

Trent swore. "How did you get home?"

"Alan came and got me. He got a tow truck to pick up my car, so after we talked to the police—"

Trent swore again, halting her words. His heart had just dropped to his gut. Why had she called that guy? "You could have called me!"

"I already told you, I didn't want to wake you. And Alan's in the business—he's used to being dragged out of bed in the middle of the night."

Trent felt rejected. He knew it was irrational, but he hated the thought of her turning to another man when she was in trouble. *He* was the man in her life, damn it!

Trent refused to acknowledge the fact that just moments earlier he'd been ready to end this relationship for reasons of self-preservation. The truth was, he hated the thought of Jaunie with another man—period.

He spread his arms, and Jaunie walked into his embrace. "I wish I'd been there for you," he said, meaning every word. He loved her. He'd just have to find another way to deal with it.

Geri pulled up in front of Jaunie's house around six thirty. "Are you sure I can't do anything else? You know I'm really sorry—"

Jaunie held up a finger. "I swear, if you apologize one more time . . ."

"I know, I know." Geri shook her frizzy curls. "But I really am so—"

Jaunie slapped her palm to her forehead. "Please, stop. I appreciate your picking me up this morning and driving me home, but what happened to my car is not your fault. I don't want you feeling guilty."

"Hey, it's my guilt. I'll feel it if I want to. I should have checked the guy out. I—"

Jaunie stopped Geri with a hand on her arm. "Cases go wrong sometimes. There wasn't any reason for you not to believe the guy was referred by Robert. I talked to Mr. Goodman, or whoever he is, on the phone and he sounded fine to me. We don't know what really happened. It's possible that it was unrelated to Mr. Goodman. Maybe he had to take care of business out of town and will contact me soon. Maybe Robert did meet Goodman somewhere and he just forgot. We won't know until we check it out further."

"Yeah, and you don't believe that hogwash any more than I do. You were set up, and I'm going to get right on this. There shouldn't be too much going on tomorrow—it's Saturday. Why don't you stay home and relax. I'll call if I need you.''

Jaunie smiled. ''Thanks, I really could use the time to catch up.''

''Good. Take care of yourself. I don't want you burning out on me.''

It wasn't until Geri had driven off, and Jaunie was alone, that she realized she had absolutely no food in the house. She stared at the contents of her refrigerator. If she really wanted to, she could scrape something together, but she wasn't in the mood to cook.

She was just about to dial for pizza when the phone rang. ''Hello? . . . Patrice? What's wrong?'' It took a moment for Jaunie to recognize her friend's voice, which was more high-pitched than normal.

''I got the job!'' Patrice squealed into the phone. ''Simone's husband hired me, and I start next week!''

''Congratulations! We'll have to pick a night to celebrate.''

''How about tonight?''

''I'd love to, but it's been a long day, and I think I'm going to turn in early.''

''Please? I have a lot to celebrate today. I'm letting Andrew invite over a few friends, and my cousin invited a few of the neighbors. It won't be the same without you.''

Jaunie didn't want to tell Patrice she was stuck at home without a car. She didn't feel like explaining how her car ended up in the shop. ''I promise I'll make it up to you. Will you take a rain check?''

''Okay, if you insist. But you haven't heard the best news of all.''

''There's more? What is it?''

''I saw Richard today. Girl, he turned three shades of green when I told him your sister was giving me a job. He was so sure I wouldn't be able to make it on my own, and that I'd come running back to him. I didn't know how much I would enjoy this moment until it happened.''

''I'm so happy for you.''

"This is all thanks to you, and I'll never forget that."

When Jaunie hung up the phone, she debated whether to order pizza or just turn in. She hadn't gone to bed until after 5 A.M., and she'd gotten up at ten. She may as well catch up on the three hours sleep she'd already lost.

Jaunie was kicking off her shoes and unbuttoning her collar when the doorbell rang. It was Trent, carrying two paper bags of Chinese food.

"Trent! What a surprise." The thrill of seeing him almost knocked her back. Her heart still raced every time she saw him. She wondered if that would ever stop happening.

He came inside, holding up the bags of food. "Have you eaten yet?"

"Nope," she said almost giddily. Moments ago she'd been too tired to order pizza, now she was about to overflow with adrenaline. She took the bags and placed them on the coffee table, before going into the kitchen for plates and plastic cutlery.

She came back with the utensils and plopped herself down on the floor beside him, eagerly opening cartons. "Mmm, Szechuan shrimp!"

While Jaunie began filling their plates from each carton, Trent leaned back against the couch. That's when she realized Trent wasn't in a casual "let's hang out" mood. He hadn't said much since his arrival.

With less enthusiasm, she poured sesame chicken over steamed rice. He took the plate she offered him but made no move to eat from it.

"I hope I'm not interrupting any plans you may have had."

Jaunie tried to make a joke, hoping to relax him. "Well, I had a date with my pillow, but I have a feeling you'll be a lot more fun."

She waited for his sexy grin or a corresponding innuendo, but he just continued to stare at his plate.

"I stopped by tonight because we need to talk."

Jaunie's heart pitched. She'd known Trent long enough to know that when the man wanted to talk, he wanted to *talk!* And those talks always led to major changes in their relationship.

She looked down at the floor. He wasn't about to propose to her, so that could mean only one thing. She couldn't look at him, and the sight of the food turned her stomach.

Had he grown tired of her already? It was too soon! They'd hardly had any time together. Maybe if he'd given her a month, just a few more weeks, maybe she could . . . She wouldn't beg him to stay with her. But she wouldn't make it easy for him, either.

Taking a deep breath, she looked up. "What do you want to talk about?"

He studied her. His lips parted several times then closed again, as if he wasn't sure himself what he wanted to say. Then finally the words blurted from his mouth. "I don't love you."

Jaunie's head reeled. Whoa! Talk about your sucker punches. She'd known it but—

Trent grabbed her arm, forcing her to look at him. "I'm sorry. I didn't mean for it to come out like that. That's not really what I'm trying to say."

Cold and numb inside, Jaunie shook her head. "Either way, I'd say that just about covers it. After a statement like that, there's not really much left to say."

Trent's fingers kneaded his temple. "No. What I'm trying to tell you is that I *can't* love you."

Jaunie turned away, not really seeing a difference. She only wanted him to leave so she could deal with this. She wouldn't humiliate herself by telling him that she loved him. He would never know.

"I'm just trying to give you a choice. I can't make you any promises of love or commitment. I've told you before that those things don't work for me. All I can offer is what we have now, and since we've never put a label on it, I'm not sure what that is."

Jaunie turned back to him in confusion. "What are you saying? Do you want to keep seeing me?"

"Yes. That's what *I* want, but I can't ask you to continue seeing me without letting you know that I can't—"

''You're telling me I can count my losses now, or we can go on like we have been and . . .''

''And when it's over, it's over. I don't want to hurt you. It has to be your choice.''

Jaunie was stunned. Here she'd thought this was over, but now she was getting a second chance. She respected his honesty. It hurt to hear him say he didn't love her—especially when that was what she wanted more than ever, but she still had hope.

''Okay,'' she said slowly.

''Huh?''

''Okay. I accept that. It sounds fair. Thank you for being honest with me.''

Trent must have been holding his breath, because he exhaled in one long sigh. ''Good, I'm glad we straightened that out.''

''Me, too.''

An awkward quietness followed. They both stared at their full plates, but neither made any attempt to eat. Jaunie's fatigue returned double strength. She slumped, resting her back against the couch. ''I think I'm more tired than I'd realized.''

Trent pushed his plate away. ''Me, too. In fact, I'm not very hungry, either.''

''Maybe we should just call it a night?''

He nodded. ''Sounds like a good idea.''

They repacked the food into the cartons and stored them in Jaunie's refrigerator, then she walked him to the door. After an uncomfortable pause, Trent bent and kissed her briefly on the lips. ''Call you tomorrow?''

''Sure.'' She locked the door behind him and went into the bathroom to prepare for bed. She been in bed for only a minute or two when the phone rang. It was too soon to be Trent. ''Hello?''

''Jaunie?'' It was Alan.

She tried to hide her disappointment. ''Hi, Alan. What's going on?''

''I just wanted to make sure you were okay.''

"I'm fine, but thanks for your concern. Tell Karina I say hello."

"I'll tell her."

"Or better yet, put her on the line."

"I'm . . . not home right now. I'm on surveillance."

"Oh, well, don't let me keep you."

"You know how it is. Nothing much going on yet. I just wanted to call and check in."

"Thanks, Alan." She waited, expecting to say their good-byes, but he paused.

"What do you have planned tomorrow?"

"I have tomorrow off. I think I'll run a few errands. Maybe do some shopping with Simone."

"If you need a ride I could . . ."

"Thanks for the offer, but I can manage."

"Okay. Well, I'll let you get some sleep. Remember, if you need me, just call. I'll be around."

"Good night, Alan."

Chapter Fifteen

Saturday was a lazy day. Jaunie's alarm rang at 9 A.M. so she and Simone could hit the mall for shopping and errands, but she decided to enjoy the luxury of sleeping in. After calling her sister to cancel, she went back to sleep until noon. She couldn't remember the last time she'd slept so late.

Jaunie took a leisurely bubble bath and gave herself a much needed manicure. Then, lounging around in a silk pajama top and socks, she ate the leftover Chinese food and read through the stack of fashion magazines that had collected on her night table. Even though she wasn't in the business anymore, she still loved clothes. After several years of retirement from modeling, she no longer got wistful pangs as she flipped the pages. Modeling had been a bittersweet experience.

By four o'clock she'd begun to feel guilty for slacking off, so she did three loads of laundry, ran a vacuum over the living room carpet, and finally threw a workout tape into the VCR. After what seemed like two thousand variations of sit-ups, Jaunie hit the shower.

Stepping into the steaming mist, she let the hot water beat down over her skin. She had a lot on her mind—mostly thoughts of Trent. Their talk last night told her a lot. She'd interpreted his feelings correctly—he didn't love her. But it had also shown her that he wanted to be with her, despite his certainty that they wouldn't last.

As Jaunie smoothed a scented bar of soap over her skin, she wondered where her pride was. Why was she willing to take whatever leftovers that man would give her? Why couldn't she hold out for the real thing?

She stood on top of the drain and watched the water pool at her feet. This *was* the real thing for her. She loved him. Part of her hoped that in time he would love her, too. She didn't know any tricks or secret spells to make that happen. All she had was hope.

What she shared with Trent was more than her mother had shared with any of her young playboys. But it was also a lot less than what Simone had with her husband. Simone's relationship proved true love existed.

She turned away from the streaming water. Was she wrong not to—

Through the steamy glass shower door, Jaunie saw the shadow of a male form.

"Trent! Is that you?" Had her wistful musings conjured him up?

The figure disappeared from the doorway.

Jaunie turned off the water and jerked on her robe. She raced into the bedroom and groped for the loaded gun she kept in the drawer with her bras and panties.

Clutching the .38 with two shaky hands, Jaunie dripped water down the hallway after the shadow. She reached the living room, and as she rounded the corner, the front door clicked shut.

Rushing over, she yanked open the door. The hallway was empty. Cool air whisked inside her robe, causing goose bumps to rise on her wet skin. Her heart knocked in her chest so forcefully, only the uneven huffs of her breathing could rival it. She was in no shape to go after the intruder. Her hands shook so badly, she feared she'd drop her gun and shoot herself by accident.

Stepping back inside, she checked the entire house before returning the gun to her underwear drawer. Who had broken into her apartment? A thief? Had he been frightened off when he discovered she was home? Her gut feelings told her that wasn't the case.

After dressing quickly, Jaunie checked the front door. The lock must have been picked because there were no signs of forced entry. Whoever had broken in had known exactly what he was doing.

Taking a deep breath, she went back to her underwear drawer and took out her gun. She hated the thing and had protested when Alan insisted she learn to shoot it. But now, knowing she knew how to use it gave her a sense of security.

Curling into a ball on the sofa, she placed the gun on the coffee table where she could grab it quickly. The rapid breaths and trembling had calmed, but her heart continued to palpitate. Pressing her fingers to her eyes, she forced herself to think.

Someone had broken into her apartment. Someone had shattered her car windows. Someone had left a mutilated photo on her desk. Were all these events related? She'd been a private investigator long enough to know that things like this were rarely a coincidence.

A chill of fear gripped her heart. Crank calls and odd looks she could handle, but now someone wanted to hurt her.

No, she thought. She hadn't been hurt. Someone wanted to scare her, probably as a result of her appearance on the *Dirk Preston Show*. But why?

For several hours Jaunie didn't move from her post on the couch. The doorbell rang around seven thirty, jerking her from her fog of worry and suspicion.

"Who is it?" she called through the door.

"Trent."

She threw open the door in relief, remembering too late that her gun lay in plain sight on the coffee table. Not anxious to relive the dark thoughts that would accompany her explanation, she moved to block his view. "Trent! Hi!" she said eagerly.

"Hi." He tried to look past her. "Are you busy?"

Giving him a wide smile, she ran a hand through her hair, trying to obstruct his view. "No."

He smiled back. "Can I come in?"

She moved back an inch. "Sure. What have you got there?"

He held up a video rental and microwave popcorn. "I thought we could watch a video and finish off the Chinese takeout I brought yesterday."

She moved back another inch, giving him a sheepish look. "I sort of ate most of it for lunch. Pizza?"

He moved forward, forcing her to step aside or be run over. "Sounds good."

She grabbed the movie, steering him toward the phone on the table behind the couch. "Good. You call while I straighten up. Number's by the phone."

Jaunie scooped up her gun, holding the movie on top as camouflage. She grabbed a few magazines for good measure and started toward the bedroom.

"What do you want on your pizza?" Trent asked as she brushed past him.

"Anything." She picked up her pace.

"Pepperoni?"

She nodded.

"Where are you going with the movie?"

She feigned surprise as she looked down at her armload. "Oops. Forgot I had it in my hands."

Trent started placing their order but held his hand out for the movie. If she gave it to him, he'd see the gun, so Jaunie pretended not to see his outstretched arm and headed back for the coffee table. With her back to him, she put the video down and dropped the magazines over her gun.

She jumped when Trent came up behind her.

"The pizza will be here in twenty minutes. Are you okay? If you're uncomfortable because of last night—"

Jaunie turned, wrapping her arms around his waist. "No.

I'm fine . . . about *everything*. Do you want a soda? I have some in the fridge.'' She pointed toward the kitchen, nudging him in that direction.

"Do you have any beer?'' he asked over his shoulder.

"Sorry. Only soda.''

He left the room. She'd grabbed the gun and was rounding the sofa, when she saw him returning with two soda cans. Thinking quickly, she dropped the gun in the base of the potted plant beside the couch.

"Thanks,'' she said, taking the soda he offered her and curling up next to him.

He popped the movie in the VCR. "So what did you do today?''

Jaunie sank back against the cushions with a shrug. "Nothing special.''

Sunday evening Trent reclined on Jaunie's bed, wearing nothing but his boxer shorts. Sinking into the softness of her pillows, he listened to the shower running. A sensual heaviness settled into his muscles as he imagined Jaunie's slick curves under the steamy spray. He thought of getting up to join her, but couldn't find the energy to move.

He loved her bedroom. It radiated femininity—from the four-poster bed with curtains on either side to the elaborate black wicker dressing table across from it. Her nightstand and two chairs were the same black wicker with wine-colored cushions. The dark sensual hues of the room suited Jaunie. Trent was surprised at how comfortable he was here.

When he'd first shown up last night, Jaunie had been jumpy and tense, and he'd worried that he'd ruined things between them. But eventually she'd relaxed, and now she seemed genuinely comfortable with him.

At least he'd found a way to save his pride. He hadn't wanted to lie, but letting her believe he didn't love her was the only solution he could find. His problems always started when a woman knew his heart. This way he'd bought them some time together.

Jaunie had been very understanding, and from the way this weekend was shaping up, he'd made the right decision. She entered the room wearing an ice blue robe that just barely covered her bottom.

"That's a really sexy robe."

She sat at the dressing table and began spreading lotion over her skin. "Thank you."

He watched her with increasing discomfort. Shifting on the bed, he tried to slow his thoughts with mundane conversation. "You've worn a different robe every night I've spent here. How many of those things do you have?"

Jaunie grinned at him. "Do you really want to know?"

Trent rolled onto his stomach. "Yeah."

She moved over to the closet and started leafing through hangers. Red, blue, pink, gold, black, silver—she pulled out robes in more colors than he could name. "Damn! All those are just your robes?" He arched his brow wickedly. "Do you have the nighties to match?"

She grinned at him. "Yes." She reached under the bed and pulled out a large plastic bin and placed it on the bed next to him. Inside was every man's fantasy—lingerie in every color and style.

He reached in, letting a lacy purple teddy dangle from his index finger. "Where did you get so much lingerie?"

She smiled a secretive smile. "Are you sure you want to know?"

He paused for a second. He didn't want to know if they were gifts from former lovers. But now curiosity had gotten the best of him. "Yeah."

"Okay, I used to model for the Victoria's Secret catalog. They still give me an outstanding discount, and lingerie is my weakness."

Trent was both relieved and intrigued. He was beginning to feel uncomfortably aroused. "Since I never had the pleasure

of seeing you model, how about a private fashion show?'' He
held out the purple teddy.

She looked away shyly. ''I don't think so. I'm a bit rusty.''

His gaze skimmed her figure. ''Trust me, sweetheart, ain't
nothin' rusty on that body.''

She seemed embarrassed but pleased. It still amazed him
that a woman so beautiful, who'd been exposed to such a
sophisticated lifestyle, could maintain an unexpected air of
innocence and vulnerability. Her lack of vanity was endearing.

She turned back to him, reaching for the teddy. ''Okay, but
I'm only coming out of retirement this one time, just for you.''

She turned her back and slipped into the purple froth. Then
she faced him, dropping the robe. Trent felt like a cartoon wolf
with his eyes bugging out and his tongue dragging the floor.
She was more than sexy. The purple silk hugged her body from
breast to hip, and the V-shaped neckline and french-cut bottom
were trimmed in white lace. She was exquisite.

Jaunie posed and twirled for him, then paused in front of
the full-length mirror behind her bedroom door. ''No,'' she
said critically. ''This isn't right.''

''Oh, I . . . think it is,'' he said, fighting to breathe.

She reached up and untwined the knot of hair secured at the
base of her neck. ''No. You can't get the full effect this way.
Fashion shows are high glamour.''

Now her hair flowed around her shoulders, and she began
sorting through one of the drawers in her dressing table. ''These
aren't the right colors.''

Trent, still deeply distracted by the sight of her in that teddy,
no longer cared about fashion shows. ''What are you doing?
Come here.''

She moved toward him, but to his disappointment she ducked
to retrieve another bin from under the bed.

''Jaunie.'' Trent groaned his frustration. ''Forget about the
fashion show. Come here.''

''No. You wanted me to do this, so I'm going to do this
right.'' She set the first bin on the floor and lifted the lid on
the second bin. It was divided into three sections; the first

was filled with tubes of lipstick, the second with brushes and containers of powders, and the third held a collection of eye makeup.

"Whoa. All this makeup is yours?"

She grinned. "I still get free samples from makeup companies I used to model for." She delved into the tubes of lipstick and pulled out two choices. "What's your pleasure, grape rhapsody or Egyptian plum?"

Trent shrugged. "I don't know. Come here."

Jaunie took the cap off one tube. "We'll go with Egyptian plum."

Trent was rapt as she parted her lips and smoothed the dark-colored stick over them. With a deft, precise stroke she outlined her full lips with the tip, then, pressing the broad side against her lips and pouting slightly, she filled in the outline with the deep plum color. Trent had had no idea that applying lipstick was such a sensual activity. When her delicate pink tongue slipped between her lips to wet them, Trent feared he might explode. She rubbed her lips together then puckered.

"Jaunie! Come here."

Instead she studied her image. "Oh, no. I don't like this. It's too dark." She picked up a tissue and wiped the lipstick off. "I'll try the grape rhapsody."

Trent started to protest, but he found himself captivated by the erotic gesture. This time he noticed the way she arched her back slightly as she bent toward the tube of lipstick and the way her eyelids lowered in concentration as she traced her lips. He noticed the muscles of his groin tightening.

She smacked her lips. "There. Is that better?"

"Much. Come *here!*"

She gave him a teasing look. "Why?"

"So I can kiss you."

She shook her head. "Uh-uh. Now that I've found the right shade, I don't want you smearing it." She reached into the bin and pulled out another tube. "Now it's time to find the perfect shade for you."

Trent started backing up on the bed as she advanced toward him. "Get away from me with that!"

She pulled the cap off the tube, revealing a silvery color. "Relax. This won't hurt one bit."

He picked up one of her pillows and covered his face, but apparently his face had never been her target. He started when he felt her hands on his stomach, then a cool, creamy substance circling his navel. Trent removed the pillow and looked down. Jaunie was surveying her handiwork with pride. She'd drawn a silver heart around his navel.

"Mmm, I don't know. Silver's not your best shade." She reached into the bin. "Let's try again."

This time he held still as she placed a red heart around his left nipple. "Perfect."

Trent grabbed the red lipstick from her and flipped Jaunie over on his lap. She wriggled, distracting him from his purpose. "Ugh . . . keep still."

"What are you doing?"

He took the lipstick and drew a fat heart on her right cheek, which was pleasantly framed with purple silk and white lace. "Just marking my place."

She turned over and wrestled him for the tube. "Give me that."

Rather than surrender, he chucked the lipstick across the room, then reached over her to plunk the plastic bin onto the floor. "Enough games." He caught her face between his hands. "Come here." He pressed his lips to hers and Jaunie's body relaxed in his arms.

Monday morning began hectically as Jaunie and Trent tripped over each other getting ready for work, but something about the new routine warmed Jaunie inside. Trent had stopped by his apartment the night before so he would have everything he needed, and though waiting for him to shave before she could brush her teeth was awkward, Jaunie appreciated the intimacy. It was nice to share a glass of orange juice and a bowl of cereal with him. If she closed her eyes, she could imagine they lived together as husband and wife. What a bittersweet fantasy. For as much pleasure as the dream gave her, that it would never be a reality pained her more.

While Jaunie's mood sank like sugar cubes in her coffee, Trent went out to buy a paper. When he returned a few minutes later, he dropped an envelope beside her on the kitchen table.

"What's this?"

He shrugged. "I don't know. It was on your doorstep."

Her name, printed boldly across the front of the plain white envelope, looked startlingly familiar.

Trent stopped flipping through the paper to study her. "What's wrong? Aren't you going to open it?"

"Maybe later," she said, getting up and going into the living room. She threw the envelope on the coffee table and started gathering her things. She moved quickly, hoping Trent wouldn't notice her shaky hands.

Trent followed her. "What is it? Something you don't want me to see?"

"Something I'm not sure *I* want to see." She'd spent the weekend in denial, giving Trent her full attention instead of facing what was happening to her. Maybe if she didn't open the envelope, she could extend that blissful state. She threw her bag over her shoulder. "Are you ready to go?"

He picked up his duffel bag from the sofa. "Are you okay? Something's wrong, isn't it?"

Jaunie stared at the carpet. The more evasive she became, the more he'd want to know what was going on. "I'll tell you about it when I figure it out myself."

He walked over to her. "Okay. If you answer one last question, I promise to let the whole thing drop."

She nodded for him to continue.

"Does this have anything to do with why you have a gun growing out of your flowerpot?"

Chapter Sixteen

Trent sighed when Jaunie just blinked at him. "Between you and Robert, I find the most interesting things growing out of potted plants."

She reached into the plant and retrieved the gun, brushing soil particles from the metal of the .38 Smith & Wesson. "I'd forgotten about this."

Trent dropped his bag and folded his arms across his chest. "Do you always store your gun amongst the foliage?"

She gave him a conciliatory grin. "Actually I usually store it amongst my cotton underwear."

He arched his brow in response to her feeble attempt at humor. She wasn't getting off that easy. He had the same sinking feeling he'd gotten when Jaunie's car windows had been bashed in and she'd called Alan instead of him. Then her excuse had been that she hadn't wanted to worry him. She'd probably tell him the same thing today, but this time he'd make it clear that avoidance tactics only made situations worse.

"Okay." Jaunie let her shoulder bag slide to the floor. "Um, the gun was in the potted plant because I hid it there when you came over Saturday."

Trent could feel the pressure building behind his eyes. "And *why* exactly did you do that?"

"Because I didn't want you to see it," she mumbled.

He pressed his index finger into the dent of his temple. "Am I going to have to drag this out of you piece by piece?"

She looked down at her watch. "We'll be late for work."

"We both have partners. They can manage on their own for a while."

Nodding with resignation, she took a seat on the couch. "I didn't want you to see the gun, because I didn't want you to worry. I'm a licensed private investigator trained to handle difficult situations, but at times like these, I've found that men focus only on the fact that I'm a woman."

He wasn't going to let her sidetrack him with the "men are so sexist" argument. "Exactly what difficult situations are you referring to?"

She looked at him, and despite her previous speech, he could see the concern in her eyes. She wanted to play the cool P.I. role, but she didn't want to admit she was scared. A cold fist of fear clutched his heart. "If you don't tell me what's wrong . . ."

"Someone broke into my apartment Saturday . . . while I was in the shower."

His fist came down hard on the coffee table. "What!"

"I saw a shadow, and I called your name. Whoever it was disappeared, so I got out and grabbed my gun. By the time I got to the door, he was gone. I kept the gun out, just in case. Then you came . . . I dropped the gun in the planter, and you know the rest."

"Why didn't you tell me this? Damn it, did you call the police?"

"No. Nothing was stolen, and I didn't see the guy's face. I already told you why I didn't mention it to you."

"You didn't want to worry me? That's ridiculous! Of course I'm going to worry. That's what you do when you care about someone. Wouldn't you worry if something like this happened to me?"

"Yes, I'm sorry. I've been through this before—with clients, but it's different when it happens to you. It's hard for me to expect anyone else to care about my problems."

"Well, get this straight. I care. It makes me crazy to find out these things long after they happen. Next time, worry me." He pulled her into his arms.

"You've got a deal," she mumbled into his chest.

Over her head Trent's gaze strayed to the envelope on the coffee table. *That* envelope, which she'd avoided opening, had started this whole conversation. He pulled her back so he could see her face. "What's in the envelope?"

Jaunie sighed, reaching for it. "I guess there's little point in avoiding this now."

"How do you know what it is before you've opened it?"

"I don't know what it is, but I have this feeling. I got a similar envelope at the office last week."

He held out his hand. "May I?"

She dropped it into his palm, and he tore it open, pulling out a photo of Jaunie. It was a close-up of her face—the kind of photo models signed for their fans. "Best wishes, Jaunie Sterling" was written in the bottom left corner. "It's a picture of you, but why is there a hole in your forehead?"

She took the picture from him. Her fingers trembled. "It's a bullet hole."

Trent felt his breakfast sink like stones. "How do you know?"

She stroked the edge of the hole. "These are burn marks from a bullet."

"I don't understand. You've gotten pictures like this before?"

"The last picture was an old pub shot like this one, but it had been cut up and taped back together."

Trent shook his head. His skull felt like it had been stuffed with cotton, and her words weren't penetrating it.

"I'm beginning to think the first picture is related to my car windows. I found the picture the day it happened. It had been taped together in the pattern of shattered glass. That night, all my windows shattered around me."

Trent swore. "This is getting out of hand. We're going to the police about this, do you hear me? Someone's stalking you, and if this is a bullet hole . . ."

Jaunie slipped the photo back into the envelope. "I threw the first photo away because I thought it was just another prank brought on by the *Jerk Preston Show.*"

"Doesn't matter. We're taking care of this today. I'll drive you to the station."

"Let's at least stop at the office first. I want to check in with Geri, and I'm sure you need to talk to Robert."

"Ten minutes at the office, then straight to the police station. Deal?"

"Deal."

"Hey, sweetie," Geri said when Jaunie appeared in her doorway. "How is it going?"

Jaunie leaned against the edge of the desk. "I have a few things to take care of this morning. Do you need me for anything?"

"Nope. I'm just running background checks." She scribbled some notes with her Mickey Mouse pencil. "Dull, dry, and boring. This guy's slate is so clean, you could eat off it. Not even a crazy uncle locked in the attic—even *I* have a crazy uncle."

Jaunie smiled, feeling her mood lift a notch. "I should be back by this afternoon."

"All right, hon. I didn't want to disturb you over the weekend, so I left the Goodman report on your desk Saturday."

"Goodman? What did you find out?"

"Well, the details are in the report, but here's the gist. Goodman doesn't exist, and his real estate firm is a dummy company. The property you were watching Wednesday night is owned by Tricorp, and their people don't know anything about vandalism or Goodman."

"Then the whole thing *was* a setup. It figures."

"You're not surprised? Sweetie, what's going on?"

"I'll tell you the details when I get back, Geri. First I have to go to the police station."

She left Geri with a bewildered expression on her face and went to her office. Without turning on the lights, Jaunie leaned across her desk, searching for the report. As she leafed through a stack of folders, something struck her as odd.

Had her chair been tufted? Squinting at the sporadic indentations in the black leather upholstery, Jaunie yanked the chain of her desk lamp. Her eyes strayed to the wall behind the chair.

Bullet holes.

Stuffing had exploded from the chair's back, littering the carpet like confetti after a New Year's party. Jaunie hadn't been invited to this celebration. But the strategic holes in the headrest and the heart of the chair told her that she could have been the guest of honor.

The gravity of the situation seeped through her numbness with the slow persistence of a leaky faucet. She kept her office door locked. Only Geri had a spare key. If Geri hadn't been in the office since Saturday . . .

Crouching beside the chair, she stared at the holes until the ruined stuffing and leather blurred. That's where Trent found her.

"Jaunie, are you ready—what the hell happened here?"

She looked over her shoulder. "Bullet holes."

Trent studied the damage and swore while Jaunie reached for her telephone. Pressing the speed dial button, she took a deep breath. "Yes, may I please speak with Officer Michael Barnes. Yes, I'd like to report a crime."

Trent leaned against the edge of Jaunie's desk, studying Officer Barnes. He hadn't been sure about the guy at first. The genuine concern and professional respect he'd shown Jaunie made it clear they were friends. But the flicker of interest in Barnes's eyes had nothing to do with professional courtesy.

Trent was worse off than he'd thought. He'd found himself squeezing Jaunie's arm or stroking her hands while she spoke—

silently staking his claim. The transparent gestures embarrassed him, but he didn't regret them. Barnes had met his eyes in acknowledgment. The signals had been recognized and accepted. From then on, Barnes had taken on a strictly business attitude, which he'd tempered with southern charm. Trent ended up liking the guy after all.

He was sinking in deeper every day, but he couldn't worry about himself now. Until Jaunie was safe, she came first.

"You be careful now, Jaunie," Barnes was saying. "We're going to get right on this, but in the meantime you know the drill. Don't go anywhere alone and try not to follow an obvious routine."

Jaunie scoffed. "Routine? I'm a P.I., Mike. I don't know the meaning of the word 'routine.' "

He gave her an understanding nod. "I know. But you realize that's what makes this so interesting. It's got to be someone who knows you well enough to predict where you'll be and when. Give me a call if you think of any more names you want me to run. The airing of that doggone talk show could have brought any kind of lunatic from your past out of the woodwork."

"Here you are, sweetie," Geri said from the doorway, handing Barnes an envelope. "Another copy of my report." The first one had disappeared, most likely taken by the same guy who'd filled Jaunie's chair with lead.

"Thanks, Geri," Barnes said with a nod. " 'Preciate it."

Geri patted his arm. "No problem, hon. If you ever decide to go for an older woman, you keep me in mind."

Barnes winked at her. "You'll be first on my list."

Geri giggled. "What a cutie-pie!" she murmured on her way out of the office.

Officer Barnes turned back to Jaunie. "Before I go, I wanted to congratulate you on bringing Andrew Montgomery home. Do you keep up with the family?"

"Yes, I do."

"How are they doing?"

"Patrice decided to leave Richard. Now she's staying with

her cousin in Virginia. Andrew is thrilled, and I think Patrice is happier, too. She just got a new job with my brother-in-law's dental office.''

"I'm glad to hear that. Next time you see Patrice and her boy, give them my best.''

"I sure will, Mike—and thank you.''

After Barnes left, Trent wrapped his arms around Jaunie. "Now that that's taken care of, why don't we get out of here? Go to lunch or something. You can't work with your office this way.''

Jaunie rested her forehead on his shoulder. "I've taken enough of your day. Robert must be pulling his hair out by now.''

"I checked on him a while ago. He's fine.''

"I have one more errand to run, and I don't want to tie you up. I'm sure Geri will lend me her car for an hour.''

"Don't bother Geri. I'll take you. Just tell me where.''

Jaunie hesitated, and Trent knew he wasn't going to like her answer.

"Alan's office. I want to let him know what's going on. He might help me think of more names. He has records on the men I encountered when I worked with him.''

Trent sighed. That made sense, but he still didn't like it. "Why don't you just give him a call?''

"I told you, you don't have to come. Geri will—''

"I said, I'll take you.''

When the receptionist showed them to Alan's office, he met them at the door, kissing Jaunie on the cheek and nodding to Trent. Alan ran a thumb under his paisley suspenders as he leaned on the edge of his desk. "What's going on?''

"Things that have been happening to me," Jaunie said.

"Things like what happened to your car windows?''

She nodded. "Wednesday afternoon, before the surveillance job, I found an envelope with a photograph inside on my desk.''

While Jaunie spoke, Trent rested his hand on her leg, watching Alan's face for a reaction. Nothing. Trent knew he'd seen the gesture, but Warren focused on Jaunie. Trent was as good as invisible.

He sat back in his chair, studying Warren. Was his dislike of the man irrational? The guy was married, for goodness' sake. What difference did it make if he had a little crush on Jaunie? Nothing would ever come of it, right?

Trent wasn't convinced.

Jaunie tensed beside him. She was describing the break-in. "I looked up and suddenly he was . . . there. When I called out, he ran. I got my gun and went after him, but he was already gone."

Alan, who'd been leaning forward, listening intently, suddenly withdrew, his features becoming shuttered. He moved behind his desk. "So you think this is related to the incident in Southeast and the picture? Could it be a coincidence?"

Jaunie got up and started pacing the office. "No. Nothing was taken, but I got another picture at my apartment this morning. A head shot with a bullet hole straight through my forehead."

Alan swore.

"When I got to my office, I found that someone had unloaded a gun clip into my desk chair. Obviously the first picture was related to my car windows being bashed in, and the second picture was related to this. I don't know why this is happening, but someone is stalking me."

Alan's fist slammed onto the desk with another curse. Trent raised his brows. He remembered having a similar reaction, but Alan almost seemed to take it personally. For a few minutes, he just sat there mumbling curses at himself. Even Jaunie stopped pacing to watch him, a confused expression on her face.

"Alan, what's—"

His head jerked up at the sound of her voice. "I'm going to put a man on you right away. Carlos can take the day shift, and I'll split the night shift with Bruce. You won't be alone for even a second."

He started to pick up the telephone, but Jaunie stopped him.

"I don't *want* a man on me twenty-four hours a day, Alan. I can take care of myself."

Trent started to volunteer to stick close, but Alan didn't give him the chance.

He stood and pointed a stern finger in her direction. "Don't argue with me, Jaunie. You're in over your head here, and I never should have let it get this far.".

"What are you talking about—'let it get this far'?"

"When I saw the damage to your car, I shouldn't have let you out of my sight. I should have *insisted* you come stay with Karina and me. I promised that I'd look out for you."

"Now wait a minute," Trent started. He was concerned, too, but this guy was ridiculous. "I can stay with Jaunie. She won't need your trained dogs to follow her around because I'll already be there. We only came by to see if you could shed some light on who's behind this. You worked with the nutcases she came in contact with when she worked for you, so—"

Alan turned on him with an angry glare. "Man, don't you dare—"

"Okay, that's enough!" Jaunie shouted. "I'm not going to listen to the two of you argue over what's best for me. I appreciate that you both care, but I'm the only one who's going to make that decision."

Alan stepped toward her. "Jaunie, listen to me—"

She held up her hand. "No, you listen. I will not have one of your men following me around all the time. The police have been notified, and I'll be very careful. Whoever is doing this wants to scare me. He hasn't tried to hurt me. If I stop living life because I'm afraid of what he'll do next, then he wins. It'll die down once he realizes I'm not playing by his rules."

Trent nodded smugly. "I'm moving in tonight. That should cover the night shift." He savored Alan's irritated expression.

"No, you won't," Jaunie said, patting his shoulder. "Thank you, but I don't need a roommate."

Trent ignored the answering smugness in Alan's grin.

"I'm pretty sure this stalker is someone I'd set up when I worked here. The police agree that the talk show probably renewed his interest in me." She turned back to Alan. "Would you check into this for me? Search your files for someone who might hold a long-term grudge."

Alan's temper instantly cooled, and his voice softened. "You got it. Whatever you want, you know that, Jaunie."

Trent rolled his eyes.

"Thanks, Alan. I'll keep you updated." She reached for her purse. "And try not to worry."

Trent stood, and Alan followed them to the door.

Alan leaned in close, and Trent narrowed his eyes. "Jaunie, why don't you come to the house for dinner Friday night. Karina would love to see you. We can talk this out and see what we come up with."

"Well . . ." Jaunie looked at Trent then back at Alan.

Trent slipped his arm around Jaunie's shoulder, giving Alan a look that said, *It's your move.*

"Of course, he's invited, too. Both of you, please," Alan said reluctantly.

"Trent? Do you want to go? If you have other plans, I could—"

"I'd love to go. Thanks for the invitation, buddy." Trent pumped Alan's hand with false enthusiasm.

"Then I'll see you both Friday?" Alan asked flatly.

Trent nodded. "Count on it."

"What was *that* all about?" Jaunie asked when they got back to Trent's four-by-four.

"What do you mean?" Trent unlocked the passenger door.

Jaunie waited for him to get in on the other side. "I mean all that macho stuff going on between you and Alan. It looked like you two were trying to one-up each other. Why don't you get along?"

Trent shrugged.

"What is it? If you two really don't like each other, maybe I should cancel dinner."

"It's no big deal," he finally answered.

Jaunie scrunched down in the seat, crossing her arms. "Oh, yeah? Then tell me."

He shrugged again.

"This has to do with the kind of business he's in, doesn't it? You don't approve of domestic investigating."

"That has nothing to do with it. If the guy wrote greeting cards for the president of the United States, I still wouldn't like him."

"Okay, then why *don't* you like him?"

He shrugged.

Jaunie rolled her eyes and slapped the dashboard. "Please don't tell me this goes back to your opinion that Alan's in love with me?"

Trent shot her a quick glance before returning his eyes to the road. "Fine. Then let's talk about something else."

"Why are you still stuck on this? You hardly know him. Alan loves Karina." She tried not to think about the problems Simone told her they were having.

"And I know he has feelings for you. Let's just leave it at that, okay?"

Jaunie didn't say anything else because part of her was afraid he might be right. It was just the kind of cruel joke fate would play. All her life she'd wondered if she would find love, and when she finally had, it came from the wrong man.

Chapter Seventeen

As they approached the door Friday night, Trent felt Jaunie poke him in the back. "And don't forget to smile, even if you're not having a good time."

"I won't," Trent muttered.

On the way to the Warren's, Jaunie had made him swear to be on his best behavior. And he intended to. With all the stress she'd been under, it was the least he could do for her.

Karina answered the front door. "Hi! Thanks for coming!" She gave Jaunie a one-armed embrace while she balanced a wineglass in her hand. She juggled the glass to shake hands with Trent, then led them to the living room. Alan waited on the L-shaped sofa in the center of the room.

After they exchanged greetings, Karina moved over to the bar. "Can I get anyone a drink?"

"Nothing for me," Jaunie said, removing her coat.

"Here, let me take that." Alan practically leaped the length of the room to reach her side.

Reminding himself that he was on his best behavior, Trent joined Karina at the bar. "Do you have any beer?"

She gave him a dazzling smile. "Bottle or glass?"

"Bottle's fine."

Karina was a lovely woman with a petite figure and a stylishly short haircut, but her black dress was a bit short and *way* too tight. Trent found himself studying his reflection in the black lacquer counter to keep his eyes from straying rudely. That dress seemed better suited for the smokey club where Robert liked to hang out.

"Thanks," he said when Karina handed him a beer.

"So Alan says you own your own construction company. That's *impressive.*" Karina leaned forward, resting her arms on the bar, giving him a healthy view of her cleavage.

"Thanks. I share the business with a partner." Trent looked away, upending his bottle. Either she was oblivious to the limitations of that dress or Karina was flirting. He didn't know which, but he didn't want to find out. He glanced toward Jaunie and Alan, who were chatting on the sofa. "Maybe we should . . ."

Karina straightened, reaching for the wine bottle to refill her glass. "Don't worry about them. They can entertain themselves."

Trent raised a brow. Was it his imagination, or did Karina sound a tad bitter? He wasn't sure because she started talking about her work as a registered nurse, and she seemed upbeat, almost bubbly. They chatted politely for a few more minutes, then Karina went into the kitchen to check on dinner.

Trent joined Jaunie and Alan on the couch, and Jaunie pulled his hand into her lap, lacing her fingers through his. The gesture released all the tension that had been building in his gut, and he relaxed. Even Alan wasn't getting on his nerves—as much.

A few minutes later, Karina led them to the dining room. Trent pulled out Jaunie's chair, then seated himself. Karina disappeared into the kitchen again, and Alan followed her.

Jaunie laid her hand on his knee. "See, this isn't so bad, is it?"

He placed his hand over hers and moved it higher on his thigh. He leaned forward, letting his breath ruffle the hair near her ear. "It's okay, but if we'd stayed in, we could have—"

"Shhh—listen." She held a finger to his lips, and he heard the soft but hostile buzz of voices coming from the kitchen.

"They're fighting." Jaunie's voice was filled with disappointment.

Before Trent could answer, Karina stalked into the room, pausing long enough to take a defiant swallow from her wineglass. Alan followed, carrying a covered dish. While Alan arranged the food on the table, Karina sat across from them, flashing a bright smile.

"I hope you enjoy this. I got the recipe from Simone. It's roasted lamb."

"It smells delicious," Jaunie said enthusiastically.

Alan sat down, and Karina filled her wineglass.

The food was delicious, and eventually they got past those initial awkward moments. Jaunie and Karina talked about mutual friends and traveling, while Trent made small talk with Alan about the Washington Redskins. It wasn't a complete success, but the evening was making a valiant effort to revive itself, when Karina let herself get a bit too comfortable at the table.

Jaunie asked Trent to pass her the rolls. When he lifted the basket, he almost dropped it back on the table. Karina slouched over the table, resting the side of her head on her hand. She was gazing at him with droopy eyes, and her cleavage was prominently displayed on the table. Hastily Trent recovered his composure and replaced the basket, opting to pick out a roll instead.

Alan noticed his wife's posture for the first time and whispered brusquely in her ear. Karina instantly straightened up, tugging on the front of her dress. She gave everyone at the table a tremulous smile, then got up and ran from the room.

"I'm sorry," Alan said, getting up from his chair. "You'll excuse me for a moment, won't you?"

Once he was gone, Jaunie turned to Trent, wringing her hands. "This is worse than I'd thought. Simone said they were having problems, but I'd had no idea it was this bad." She gestured toward Karina's glass. "I've never seen her drink like that."

Trent slipped his arm around her shoulder. "Maybe it was an accident. Some people don't know how to limit themselves."

"I don't think so. She seems really unhappy, doesn't she?"

Trent shrugged. "It's hard for me to say. I've never met her before."

"That's right. I'm sorry you have to see them this way. When Alan and Karina first got together, they were so happy. I don't know what could have gone wrong."

Trent squeezed her shoulder, trying to comfort her. He knew what at least part of Karina and Alan's problem was, but he didn't want to upset Jaunie further. Hopefully they could skip dessert and make it an early night.

A few minutes later, Karina and Alan rejoined them. Karina's eyes were red, and she seemed more subdued. Now she was wearing a black sweater over her dress. They all finished the meal in a tense silence, broken by a few weak strains of small talk that faded quickly.

Finally Karina announced that dessert would be served in the living room. Everyone stood, but before Trent could make their excuses, Alan moved to Jaunie's side.

"Karina, Jaunie and I will join you two in the living room momentarily. I have a couple of files in my office that I want Jaunie to look over." As he took her arm, he turned to Trent. "You don't mind keeping my wife company for a few minutes, do you?"

Trent opened his mouth, then closed it. Jaunie looked at him from over her shoulder. "You'll be okay, won't you?"

"Yeah, I'll be fine."

He sat down in the living room while Karina placed a sliced pound cake and a pot of coffee on the table.

"Help yourself," she said, taking a seat on the sofa across from him.

"Thanks." While Trent served himself coffee and cake, Karina took one sip of coffee and put it down. She moved to the bar and poured herself another glass of wine. He wanted to say something but didn't want to embarrass her.

"Mmm, that's better," she said, taking a long swallow. This time when she rejoined him, she sat right next to him—close enough for her thigh to brush his.

The tension Trent had been feeling all evening took the form of a headache, driving through his temple with the force of a power drill. Scooting over on the sofa, he angled his torso toward Karina to make the gesture appear less abrupt. He took a gulp of coffee, then filled his mouth with cake. "This is excellent cake," he said, chewing furiously.

Karina crossed her legs and gave him a tipsy smile.

He nodded and took another bite of cake. Damn it. He wasn't in the mood to deal with this. What were Jaunie and that third-rate, wanna-catch-a-husband-cheating-but-can't-keep-his-own-wife-happy P.I. doing?

Trent put down his cake. He was going to search every room until he found Jaunie, and they were getting the hell out of this house.

He stood and began backing toward the door. "Karina, I think it's time for Jaunie and me to leave. If you'll just point me in the right direction, I'll go get her and—"

Karina stood. "You're leaving already?" She picked up her glass and started toward the bar.

He touched her arm. "Maybe you shouldn't have any more of that tonight." She was surprisingly docile, letting him guide her back to the sofa and hand her a cup of coffee. She didn't drink it. For the longest time, she just stared into it, as if it held the secrets that would put her life back on track.

For the first time, Trent began to actually feel a bit sorry for her. He sat on the sofa on the other side of the table. "Are you okay, Karina?"

She didn't lift her head, but he saw her tears dropping into her coffee. She set the cup on the table and sniffed loudly. "I'm so sorry. I don't know why I'm making a fool of myself like this. I—I . . ." Her voice faded into a deluge of muffled sobs.

Unsure of what to say, Trent alternated between ''Are you okay?'' and ''It'll be all right.'' Finally he went into the kitchen and brought back a wad of paper towels so she could wipe her face. She mumbled a thank you and lapsed back into a sullen silence.

Trent was standing uncomfortably by the arm of the sofa, trying to decide how to handle this unexpected turn of events, when Karina set the coffee down hard, rattling the cup and saucer with her trembling fingers. The wadded paper towels in her lap slid to the floor.

''I don't know what's worse . . .''

Trent blinked. The drilling headache had switched to a jack-hammer, and his brain couldn't keep up with the conversation. ''Huh?''

She clasped her shaky hands in her lap, staring up at him like a child seeking wisdom. ''I don't know what's worse— that Alan is in love with Jaunie, or that he doesn't even know it.''

Trent's mouth dropped open. ''Whew . . . uh . . . I—whew!'' He'd been caught off guard, not only by her frankness, but by the fact that she thought Alan was so out of touch with his own feelings.

''Don't tell me you're surprised.''

Trent crossed the coffee table to sit on the short end of the L-shaped sofa. ''Um . . . I—''

''It's been building slowly over the years. That's why I don't even think he's admitted it to himself yet. He would never hurt me like this intentionally.''

Trent leaned forward. ''Karina, I'm sure it's not . . . um.'' He'd never felt more useless in his entire life. Just a few days ago, he'd been trying to convince Jaunie that Alan had feelings for her. Now, for Karina's sake, he felt honor bound to deny it.

''I don't even think Jaunie knows how he feels. He goes running off the minute she has a crisis, and she thinks 'Oh, what a good friend.' ''

"Karina. Maybe you should . . ." He didn't finish because she seemed to be in a world of her own now.

"I don't know if it would be harder watching him pine after her, acting as if he's satisfied with our marriage, or seeing her end his misery by returning his love."

She stared down at herself. "Look at me—in this stupid dress, trying to compete with a woman who doesn't even know there's a fight—and losing."

Trent shook his head, trying to comprehend what was happening. "Karina, I'm sure your husband loves you. If he has a bit of a crush on Jaunie, it can't possibly compare to—"

"A bit of a crush?" She leaped up. "A bit of a crush! I'll *show* you a crush. I'll show you." Karina scurried from the room.

Trent followed her into the hallway afraid she would do something rash, but when she darted up the stairs, he didn't dare follow. He had to get Jaunie and go. This was too much. He sank onto the sofa, rubbing his temple, trying to soothe the ache hammering in his skull.

Within minutes Karina was back, carrying a shoe box.

"Karina . . ." He stood, shaking his head. "I really should find Jaunie."

She dropped the box on the table. "Just a minute. I want you to see this."

He stared at the box, then at Karina. "What is it?"

"Look inside." She lifted the lid. "I used to wonder what he kept in here. Some nights, when he thought I was sleeping, I caught him going through it. Finally I discovered where he kept it. I wasn't married to a P.I. for eleven years for nothing."

Curiosity spurred Trent to sort through the box. Pictures. The first was a huge color photo of Jaunie, autographed to Alan. He looked back at Karina. "It's an autographed photo. No big deal."

She lifted a brow. "Look at the rest of them."

All the pictures were of Jaunie: newspaper clippings, magazine ads—beginning early in her modeling career and following through the years. A knot twisted in his gut. Karina was right, this wasn't a crush. This was an obsession.

"You see." Karina's hard quiet voice didn't register right away. "Do you see what I've been competing with?"

Unable to find suitable words to respond, Trent continued to pick out pictures, his eyes no longer focusing on the images. He'd known! He'd known there was something wrong with that guy, and this proved it. Alan was obsessed with her. Who knew what he would—

Afraid to leave Jaunie alone with him for another moment, Trent was about to go after her, when an envelope tucked in the side of the box caught his attention. He lifted the flap . . . more photos.

The first of Jaunie standing in front of Hank's Auto Repair. She was wearing the same outfit she'd been wearing Tuesday morning when he'd dropped her off to pick up her car. Trent stared at the picture. This couldn't be an old picture. The morning she'd put on that short-skirted red suit, she'd told him that she'd bought it on a whim because she'd thought he would like it.

Trent sat back and studied the other snapshots. Jaunie outside the grocery store. Jaunie walking to the bakery across the street from their office building. There was even a picture of Jaunie and Trent going into his apartment building. Of course Trent had been carefully framed out of the shot, so only his sleeve indicated his presence.

In some of the shots, it was clear that the photos had been taken from inside a car. Warren had been following her. The implications of that fact were just sinking in, when Karina moved behind him. She grabbed the shoe box and shoved it under the sofa, leaving Trent staring at the table where it had been. Then Jaunie and Alan appeared in the doorway.

Jaunie immediately rushed to his side. "Sweetheart, I'm sorry we were so long. Do you want to visit a while longer or go?"

"Go," was the only word he could manage through numb lips. His mind was spinning with possible scenarios. Should

he grab Alan by the throat and smash his head in? His fists
clenched at his side. Should he grab Jaunie and run? His feet
were already pointed toward the door. Should he call the police?

His mind remained in a fog as Jaunie said their goodbyes
and led him from the Warren's house. Trent didn't know what
to say, so he said nothing. Silence was preferable to telling
Jaunie that one of her closest friends was stalking her.

"Are you mad at me?" Jaunie asked on the drive back to
her apartment.

"No."

"Well, I wouldn't blame you if you were. I know how you
feel about Alan, and I didn't mean to let him keep me away
so long."

Trent almost swerved off the road. "He wouldn't let you
leave?"

Jaunie's hand slapped his knee. "Don't be silly. We were
talking. He took me downstairs so I could look at the client
files he'd brought home. While I was looking through them,
he started talking about his problems with Karina. He was so
upset, I didn't want to leave him like that."

Trent could just imagine the guilt trip he'd laid on her—
probably told her everything but the truth. His marriage was
falling apart because he was obsessed with another woman.
"What did he say to you?"

"Her behavior tonight really bothered him. He wanted some
advice. Karina's drinking embarrassed him."

Trent tightened his grip on the wheel. "Did he tell you what
made her start drinking like that?"

Jaunie frowned. "I don't think he knows. He admitted that
they've been arguing a lot. He thinks Karina did it to get back
at him. I find that hard to believe, because I've always known
her to be so sweet. But then again, did you check out that dress
she was wearing? Something has definitely come over her."

Yeah, Trent thought as he turned down Jaunie's street, something *had* come over Karina—good old-fashioned jealousy.

How was he going to explain all this to Jaunie? The longer he waited, the harder it would be.

Trent parked the car and turned off the ignition. "Jaunie, about Alan . . ."

"I know, I know. You're being such a good sport about this, but I know you didn't like the fact that I went off with him for so long." She leaned across the seat and kissed him softly on the lips. "I promise, when we get inside, I'll make up for neglecting you." She traced his lips with her tongue. "You won't have any doubt that you're the only man on my mind."

Momentarily zapped by the kiss, Trent tried to touch Jaunie's arm to let her know he had something to say, but she slipped away and was out of the car before he knew it.

He followed her to the house, and when he reached the door, she dragged him inside and covered his lips with hers. This was definitely Trent's idea of time well spent, but first he had to . . .

Jaunie's fingers were plowing into his collar while she pressed distracting feather-light kisses all over his throat. His mind clouded, and he had to fight to stay alert. "Jaunie, I need to—"

"I know, honey, I need it, too." She pressed her lips over his again, this time her tongue tangled with his.

Trent grabbed her shoulders. This was important. He had to tell her about Alan. Jaunie's hands slid inside the waistband of his pants, and the thought escaped him again. Jaunie led him over to the couch and pushed him until he fell backward over the arm and landed on the soft cushions. As her body came down on top of him, Trent knew that whatever had been pressing on his mind could wait.

"That was the best pizza ever!" Andrew said, rubbing his stomach.

As they walked away from the California Pizza Kitchen in the mall, Jaunie nodded in agreement, but Patrice was beaming with pride. She'd just bought them all lunch with her very first paycheck.

"It *was* good," Patrice said with a smug grin. "But once I get a few checks under my belt, I'll treat you guys to filet mignon at Houston's."

Andrew wasn't listening because he'd wandered into a record store and was studying a display of the latest rap music, but Jaunie gave Patrice a wide grin. "You've got a deal. Just tell me when and where."

They continued to walk toward the entrance where they'd parked the car, making several stops for Andrew. At that moment he was playing a game of X-men in the video arcade.

"Your birthday's in a couple weeks, isn't it?" Patrice asked while Andrew tried to exhaust the dollar's worth of quarters she'd given him.

Jaunie groaned. "Don't remind me."

"What are you talking about? Don't you plan to celebrate?"

Celebrate? She couldn't remember the last time she'd celebrated a birthday. Besides, she didn't have much to celebrate these days. She was looking on her thirtieth birthday, and the biggest thing in her life was the crazy stalker leaving her mutilated photographs. All she'd ever wanted was a bit of normalcy and stability. The more she sought those things, the bigger a freak show her life became.

She had Trent. But she didn't really *have* him. The man she loved wanted to keep her—no strings attached—as a girlfriend indefinitely. They had something special, but she didn't know what he was feeling. As close as they'd become, it was hard to imagine that he didn't love her, but he hadn't told her otherwise.

When she woke up this morning, Trent had gone to the construction site early, but he left a note on her pillow saying that they needed to have a very important talk when he got back. All morning she'd worried about what it could be. She knew it had to be about their relationship, but the outcome could go either way.

Trent had been pretty upset last night. Maybe he'd decided he didn't want to deal with the relationship any longer. Then again, she'd done a very good job of making it up to him. She knew he'd been satisfied. Maybe he was ready to get serious. She didn't dare hope.

"I don't know, Patrice. I'm not sure I'll be in the mood to celebrate."

"Oh, nonsense. Girlfriend, we're going to throw down on your birthday. So if *you* don't want to plan it, step back and watch me work."

"Oh. Well then, go girl!" It felt good to know that someone wanted to throw her a party.

Andrew joined them again, and they left the mall. Jaunie unlocked the passenger doors for Patrice and Andrew, then moved around to her side. Before she sat down, she noticed a white envelope on the seat that hadn't been there before. Her heartbeat sped up.

Anxious to confirm her fears, she tore open the envelope. Another photograph—this one burned from all four corners into the center; only her face, trimmed in black char, remained.

"What's that?" Patrice asked.

Jaunie closed the envelope and tucked it into the glove compartment. "Just something I'd forgotten to put away."

She started the car and headed straight for Patrice's home. She didn't want to put Patrice or Andrew in danger.

Her stalker was getting a little too close for comfort.

Chapter Eighteen

Jaunie stopped dialing Mike's number when she heard the door. Trent—finally! She hadn't been home long, but the tension that built in her stomach every time she looked behind the sofa was enough to send her screaming like a mad-woman from the room.

She opened the door and surged into Trent's arms before he could move or speak.

"Sweetheart, what's wrong? You're shaking." He backed her into the apartment and closed the door behind him.

She pulled back to look into his eyes. They were filled with concern and tenderness and protectiveness. Seeing those emotions stirred primitive feelings of safety inside her. Earlier she'd wondered if he loved her. She still wasn't certain, but she knew he cared, and that's what she needed at the moment.

Unlocking her arms from around his neck, she pointed to the picture on the coffee table. "I found that *inside* my car this afternoon."

He walked over and picked it up. He stared at it for a long time and then turned back to her with eyes that had gone from warm sable to cold onyx. She'd seen that look before. The recognition of his contempt made her shiver. At least this time, it wasn't directed toward her.

"There's more, isn't there?" He looked around the room. "Where's the little gift that came with this?"

Jaunie raised her brows but didn't question Trent's certainty that the warning—like her shattered windows and bullet-ridden chair—had already come. She pointed behind her couch.

Trent followed her pointing finger and swore softly. Jaunie didn't move when he knelt to get a closer look. She knew what he was seeing. Her new champagne nightgown had been burned to a silken rag. The taupe carpet beneath it was also blackened and burned. It was as though someone had made a campfire in her living room, using her nightgown for kindling.

She didn't want to see it again. The sight sent a cold vein of fear straight to her heart—not because it was a useless destruction of her property, not even because the stalker had found his way into her home again—but because he had known. He bypassed dozens of gowns and picked the one that was special to her. Trent had bought that gown for her last week.

The man who stalked her must have been near when Trent had taken her to Victoria's Secret to pick it out. He knew how to find her car in a crowded mall parking lot. He could slip into her office, fill her chair with lead, and leave without being seen. Her stalker was close and getting closer. The intimacy of this last gesture proved that.

When Trent finally stood, his jaw was clenched with anger. His body was taut, and she could feel heat radiating from him.

"I was just about to call Mike when you got here."

Trent stalked to the door. "Why don't you hold off on that? It's time to end this mess. When you talk to Mike, you can hand over your man with a full confession. Come on."

"What?" Jaunie grabbed her jacket but paused at the door. "Where are we going? You're acting like you know who's behind this."

"I'm pretty sure I do. But I'm only going to explain this once, so I'd rather do it with all the parties present."

Jaunie was full of questions. Who was it? How did he know?

Where were they going? But Trent refused to answer her. Once they were on the road, he drove with a single-minded focus, his face set in deep lines of concentration. Jaunie's heart thundered. She'd never seen him like this. It was scary and exciting.

When they turned onto the suburban streets of Arlington, Virginia, Jaunie began to recognize the area. "Is Alan in on this, too?" she asked when he parked in the drive.

Again Trent didn't answer. He grabbed her hand when she got out of the truck and pulled her toward the front door. He leaned on the doorbell like a man on a mission.

Alan came to the door, smiling brightly when he saw Jaunie. The smile disappeared when he saw the intense expression on Trent's face. "Back so soon?"

"Don't look surprised. One of your employees must have called to let you know we were on our way." Trent's voice was cold.

Jaunie frowned in confusion. "What—"

"Let's talk in my office," Alan said stiffly. "Karina and Jimmy are out shopping, but they'll probably be back soon."

He took them downstairs. Jaunie sat on a long upholstered couch against the wall, watching both men carefully. Alan leaned against his desk and Trent stood. "Okay. What's going on?" She turned to Alan. "Trent thinks he knows who's stalking me. Do you know, too, Alan?"

Alan raised his brows. "I'll be interested in hearing Trent's theories."

Trent smirked coldly. "I'd just bet you would. Well, don't worry. I won't keep you waiting." Trent turned to Jaunie, his expression softening. "Sweetheart, you're not going to like hearing this, and I don't know how to make this easier for you." He took a deep breath. "Alan is the man who's been stalking you."

"What!" Jaunie knew Trent didn't care for Alan, but this was taking things too far.

Alan made a strangled noise of outrage, lunging to his feet as if to strike out. Trent whirled on him, the look in his eyes saying, *come and get it.* They both moved toward each other like tigers looking for an excuse to pounce.

Jaunie jumped between them. "Don't even think of turning this into one those macho ego trips." When they stepped apart, she sat down again. "Trent, will you please explain to me why you think *Alan* is stalking me."

Trent propped his foot on the coffee table, giving Alan a hard look. "Why don't you answer that, Warren? Explain to her why you've been following her? Taking pictures."

"I was trying to protect her, you idiot. In case you hadn't noticed, Jaunie's in danger."

Jaunie stared at Alan. "You've been following me? Alan! I asked you not to do that."

Alan shot Trent a venomous look before his features softened, and he crouched at her feet. "Jaunie, I promised I'd always be there for you. I couldn't take the chance that this guy might get to you before—"

Trent exhaled an angry curse. "Give me a break. The only person she's in danger from is you."

Alan stood, facing Trent. "Why would *I* want to hurt Jaunie? Huh? That makes no sense."

"You don't want to hurt her. You want to scare her—scare her right into your arms. Your wife told me herself how you live for Jaunie's next crisis so you can be her knight in shining armor." Trent moved closer to Alan. "But you obviously weren't counting on me, were you?"

Alan rolled his eyes, turning back to Jaunie. "You're not buying any of this, are you? This guy is nuts. I'm a private investigator. I watch people for a living. Of course I'm going to try to protect you."

"I—uh . . ." Jaunie looked back and forth between Alan and Trent in confusion. This had to be a mistake. Trent was letting his dislike for Alan cloud his judgment. She didn't like it one bit that Alan had gone against her wishes, but she couldn't fault him for trying to protect her. "Trent, just because Alan had me followed when I asked him not to, doesn't mean he—"

Trent wasn't listening, he was watching Alan. "Let's say

you're right, but if he was watching you so closely, how come *he* hasn't seen the real stalker yet?''

"I am close to finding this guy. But he's slick. I think he's a professional. I just need a little more time to—''

"Or maybe it's because you're so busy trying to catch a glimpse of Jaunie in the shower that you were too distracted to notice.''

"I didn't know she was in the shower! I didn't intend—''

Jaunie's head snapped up. "You mean that *was* you in my apartment that day?''

Alan froze, realizing his mistake. "I didn't know you were in the shower. The night before, you told me you'd be going shopping. I watched the apartment all day, and when you didn't come out, I got worried. I knocked, but you didn't answer, so I picked the lock.''

His eyes begged her to believe him. "I was afraid you were hurt . . . or worse. You must not have heard me calling your name. When I realized you were in the shower, I panicked and left. I never meant to frighten you.''

Jaunie's heart iced over. Nothing sounded like the truth anymore. She stared at Alan in confusion. "I came to your office to talk to you about this. Why didn't you tell me then? I would have understood. Why did you go on letting me be afraid?''

"Because he would have had to explain the rest of it—right, Warren?'' Trent cut in.

Alan shook his head. "I don't know what you're talking about.''

Now Trent came to crouch in front of her. "Think about it, Jaunie. Who else knows you well enough and has the training to slip in and out of your apartment and your office without suspicion? Who else would have something to gain by keeping you unsettled? Every time you have a problem, he's the first one there. He kept begging you to move in with him and Karina, so you'd be closer to him. That was his goal all along, Jaunie. He hated it when you got involved with me. He wants to be the only man in your life. He tried to force you closer by keeping you afraid, making you think you need him.''

"That's ridiculous. You're obviously the one who feels threatened. You're so possessive of her, as if she were your property. You strut around like you own her, but you're not man enough to really claim her."

"Yeah? But you'll claim her, won't you. You're so obsessed with her, you don't even care that your marriage is shot to hell."

Alan turned his back and moved behind his desk. "This is stupid. I'm not going to listen to any more of this. Get out of my house."

Jaunie watched the two men argue as she would a Ping-Pong match. She started to speak, but both seemed unaware of her presence.

"Not until you tell her about the photos."

"I don't know what you're talking about."

"Okay, then I'll show her. I bet Karina didn't have a chance to put the box away yet." Trent turned and jogged up the stairs.

"Where are you going?" Alan started to go after him. "What are you—"

He moved over to Jaunie. "Look, whatever he's up to, you can't believe that I would ever try to hurt you. You've known me for years. You know I wouldn't put you through this kind of pain."

Jaunie searched his eyes. She wanted to believe him. But could she? Alan was the man who taught her that *everybody* lies. He's the one who made her promise not to fall for a good sob story or an innocent face. Was she to use the tools he gave her against him?

She was just about to reassure him that whatever mistakes he'd made, she knew he could never torment her just to keep her close, when Trent returned. He laid a shoe box on the table before her.

"Can you explain this, Warren?"

Jaunie watched as his face paled. Oh, no! It could be true.

"Where did you get that?"

Trent regarded him coldly. "Your wife showed it to me last night."

Alan backed away in surprise. "Karina?"

"She knows, Warren. Karina knows about the pictures and that you're in love with Jaunie."

Jaunie lifted the lid on the shoe box. As she sorted through the pictures, sad realization washed over her. All the photos were of her. Pictures from her modeling days, some so old she barely remembered taking them. Pictures she'd given him and he'd taken from afar. Trent had been right. Alan *was* obsessed, but did that mean the rest of Trent's accusations were true?

Her hand began to shake; her vision blurred with tears.

Trent reached over and squeezed her hands. "I'm sorry, sweetheart, but now do you see what I've been trying to tell you? Who else had access to so many pictures of you? He's crazy."

Jaunie stood. "Alan?"

At first she thought he hadn't heard her. He sat at his desk, head in his hands.

"Alan," she said again. "What does this mean?"

He looked up slowly, as though waking from a dream. He stared in her direction, but his eyes weren't focused on her. "What must Karina think of me? Last night . . . the drinking . . . it's my fault. All of it—"

Jaunie started to interrupt him, but she realized Alan was confessing. He seemed wrapped in his own world of guilt.

"Karina . . . Karina. All the time she knew what I'd never even accepted myself. If I'd known, I never would have—"

"Alan, you need to get help." Tears poured down her cheeks. How could someone she'd trusted for so long betray her like this? "And you have to stay away from me."

He blinked, his features twisting. "Jaunie, how can you believe I would do this to you? Maybe I am in love with you, but I would never—"

Trent moved forward. "No! What you feel for her isn't love. It's obsession. You stay away from her, do you hear me?"

Alan grabbed Jaunie's hands, ignoring Trent. "I didn't do this, Jaunie. I can prove—"

She pulled away. "I'm sorry, Alan, our friendship has to

end here. No phone calls. Nothing. I'll get a restraining order if I have to. Please get help—for Karina and Jimmy's sake." She turned to Trent. "Let's get out of here."

Geri walked into Jaunie's office waving a pink message slip. "I'll give you three guesses who this is from, and the first two don't count, hon."

Jaunie took the slip and read it out loud. " 'It is extremely urgent that I speak with you. Alan.' " She ripped it in half and dropped it in the waste bin. "I can't believe he's still trying to contact me. It's been two weeks. I thought he'd finally given up."

Geri sat on the desk and crossed her legs. "Sorry, sweetie. I thought sending Mike over there to warn him about the Order of Protection would do the trick. After all that's happened, he's still trying to claim he didn't send the pictures?"

"He can say whatever he likes," Jaunie said, sliding back in her brand-new recliner. "The fact that I haven't had any more incidents since we found out about him speaks for itself. The police are keeping an eye on him. I didn't press charges for Karina's sake, but if he makes another move, they'll snag him." Jaunie shook her head sadly. He'd been a good friend to her. It was a shame it had to end this way.

"Well, I'm just glad the whole mess is over. Things have finally settled down, and you and Trent seem happy." Geri hopped down from the desk. "See you after lunch."

"Okay." Jaunie sighed. Geri said they seemed happy. Sure they were happy. Didn't they spend almost every evening together? Didn't he make love to her with an aching tenderness each night? Wasn't that all she needed?

Jaunie got up and reached for her coat. It was time to meet Simone for lunch. How could she complain? she asked herself as she got on the elevator. She had so much. The business was doing well. She and Trent were getting along . . . but somehow getting along wasn't enough. She loved him. She wanted to tell him so, but not if the words wouldn't mean anything to him.

Turning up the collar on her tan trench coat to shield against the early November wind, Jaunie walked briskly toward Simone's favorite Italian restaurant. Trent had come right out and told her that he could never love her. Didn't that mean that he wasn't interested in being loved by her in return? Despite his constant attention and affection, she saw no sign that his feelings had changed. They could go on as they had been indefinitely.

Indefinitely. The word echoed through her head as she neared the entrance to the restaurant. Wednesday was her thirtieth birthday, two days away. Patrice was throwing her a huge party at The Ultimate nightclub in D.C. on Saturday, but she was celebrating quietly Wednesday night with Trent. He'd asked her what she wanted for her birthday. What would he have said if she'd told him what she *really* wanted?

Jaunie pushed those thoughts aside as the hostess led her to Simone's table. There was another woman sitting with her sister. Though the woman wasn't facing her, Jaunie had a sneaking suspicion as to who it was.

Simone waved as she approached, and the woman turned.

"Baby! Come give me a hug." She stood, holding out her arms.

"Raven!" Jaunie inhaled the familiar sent of Chanel perfume as she wrapped her arms around her mother's petite frame. "What a surprise."

"I love those funky little shops in Georgetown. That hat I bought will go fabulously with my handbag from Saks, Jandel." Jaunie's mother kept track of her travels by the labels on her shopping bags.

Jaunie and Simone followed her into Simone's foyer, carrying three full shopping bags each. Raven, who had flown in from New Orleans just for her daughter's birthday, was in town only for the day and had insisted on a full-scale shopping spree.

Of course Jaunie hadn't wanted to make her mother feel bad by telling her she'd gotten the dates wrong again and her birthday was still two days away.

"Just drop everything over there. We'll sort it out in a minute," Simone said, ushering them into the living room. "The kids will be getting off the school bus soon, and I have to make their snacks."

Simone dashed into the kitchen, and Raven put her hands on her narrow hips, taking in Jaunie's herringbone slacks, which she wore with tan suspenders and a cream crushed velvet leotard. "Well, I'm glad we got you that Gautier piece. At least you'll have one decent item in your wardrobe."

Jaunie was spared having to comment because Simone's kids, Maya and Wesley, poured through the front door, leaving a trail of scarves, hats, and mittens as they rushed toward their grandmother for a hug.

"Hi, darlings . . . ah-ah-ah . . . you know we mustn't kiss Mother Raven on the face." She gave them each a small squeeze before Simone ordered them into the kitchen.

"Okay"—Simone opened one of the bags on the sofa and started pulling out clothing and shoes—"let's see what's what."

Jaunie looked over Simone's shoulder. "I think that purple belt is mine."

"Oh, dear." Raven studied the delicate mother of pearl bracelet watch on her wrist. "It's almost four. I have to call Harlan to remind him to send the pilot at six."

Simone stopped sorting clothing to look over her shoulder. "What happened to Marco, or whatever his name was?"

"It was Marcus, darling, and he was a deadbeat. I've decided to lay off the young ones for a while. They're not very stable."

"Ohhhh." Simone smirked at Jaunie behind Raven's back. "Well, the phone's in the kitchen."

"That's okay, baby. I'll use mine." Raven reached into her ivory handbag and pulled out a matching cellular phone.

Jaunie and Simone exchanged looks then went back to rifling through shopping bags.

"Mom-meee!" Maya wandered into the room, carrying a peanut butter and jelly sandwich and holding the end of her pigtail. "My braid came out."

"All right, honey. Come here." Simone sat down, pulling Maya between her legs to braid her hair.

Jaunie looked up, and the reflection in the mirrored wall opposite them made her pause. How could three women in the same family make such a startling contrast? Jaunie studied them each with detached fascination.

Raven held the cellular phone to her ear as if it were one of her jeweled accessories. She posed, hand on one hip, cooing softly into the receiver, trying to cajole her latest male interest into granting her wishes. Her black hair cupped her face in a sleek stylish cut, designed for a younger woman. But her heavy layer of cosmetics helped blur the hard lines of age and decadent living. She wore her ivory brocade suit like armor, daring anyone to notice that her frame was a bit too thin or her skirt a bit too short. She was a self-made diva, and she *worked* it for all it was worth.

Jaunie's gaze slid to her sister, Simone, who was now braiding Maya's other pigtail, while the girl explained why Mrs. Shoemaker asked *her* to read her essay in front of the class that day. While Maya chattered, she switched her peanut butter and jelly sandwich from hand to hand, alternately smearing grape jelly on both knees of Simone's mauve leggings. Simone didn't seem to notice as she periodically interrupted Maya's monologue with lectures on why she shouldn't play with her food or talk with her mouth full.

Simone was captured in her daughter's sandbox world. Her eyes crinkled with humor, and an indulgent smile curved her lips each time Maya mispronounced a big word. Simone's hair may have been slightly mussed and her clothes conspicuously stained, but her face was radiant with a profound contentment that only mothers seemed to know.

Finally Jaunie's eyes returned to her own image, an unusual mingling of her older sister's and her mother's opposing worlds. Jaunie's velvet top, Italian leather boots, and solid gold jewelry were a testimony to her mother's taste for the expensive and self-indulgent. But her practical slacks, fresh-scrubbed face, and simple hairstyle better reflected Simone's unpretentious style. Jaunie had grown up in her mother's shadow, but had tried to model herself after Simone in later years.

Now she stood between two possible paths. The road of her life could curve in either direction. Would she end up like her mother, trapped in a never-ending midlife crisis, flitting from one uncertain relationship to another? Or could she achieve what Simone had: the satisfaction and security that came with a devoted husband and children?

With sudden clarity Jaunie realized she faced her future in that mirror. Two possible outcomes. All she needed was the bravery to choose.

"You look beautiful," Trent said, walking into Jaunie's apartment Wednesday evening. "Are you ready to go, birthday girl?"

"I'm not sure." She smoothed her palms against her simple black halter dress. She'd gotten dressed anyway, but after what she planned to say, Jaunie wasn't certain she and Trent would be going anywhere together. "We need to talk."

Trent laid a thin rectangular package in front of her and sat beside her on the sofa. He took her hand in his. "This isn't going to be one of those 'Oh, My God, I'm Thirty' conversations, is it?"

She wished. Jaunie was definitely having an "Oh, My God, I'm Thirty" crisis, but it wouldn't be cured with a little whining or pampering. She was about to lay everything on the line: all or nothing.

"Trent." She pulled her hand back. "What I have to say is difficult for me, so please don't say anything until I finish, okay?"

He swallowed hard, drawing his brows together. "Go on."

"The first thing I want to say"—she moved across the room

to put some comfortable distance between them—"is that I'm in love with you."

Trent opened his mouth but closed it again when she raised her hand.

"I know you already explained why you can never love me. You were very honest about your feelings, and I respect that. I'm not asking that you change. I just need you to understand . . . I don't want to look back on my life and find that I haven't moved forward."

Jaunie took a deep breath. This was more difficult than she'd expected. Trent's face was as stoic as a stone statue. She had no idea how he was reacting to all of this.

"Anyway, I'm thirty years old today. It's time for me to start thinking about marriage and a family. If I can't find those things with you, then I'll just have to start looking—" She broke off, knowing that if she couldn't have those things with Trent, she wasn't sure she wanted them with someone else. But she had to ignore her fears and put faith in their love. Trent had deep feelings for her, she knew it. If she didn't push him, he'd let their relationship continue in this uncertain state forever. She had to believe in their love enough for them both.

"Trent, I want to get married, and if you won't marry me . . . then we can't see each other anymore." Jaunie gripped her stomach with one hand. There—she'd said it.

Trent laughed bitterly, shaking his head. "Let me get this straight. You'll break up with me, if I don't *marry* you? Are you serious?"

She swallowed hard. "You don't know how serious I am."

He swore, blowing his breath out in one harsh stream. He paced the room, looking as though he wanted to throw something. "Fine."

Jaunie went still. "Fine? What does that—"

He jerked around to face her. "Fine! Fine! I'll marry you!"

She moved back. "But you don't sound—"

He released a deep resigned sigh. "If you're asking if this would have been my first choice, then, no, it wouldn't have been," he said quietly. "But what can I do? I love you too much to lose you. I've never been good at doing what's best for me.''

Jaunie regarded him in open shock. Here he was, saying what she'd longed to hear, but it wasn't *quite* what she'd expected.

He snatched the wrapped box from the coffee table and stalked toward the door.

''Where are you going?'' she called.

''Where do you think?'' he tossed over his shoulder. ''To exchange this necklace for a diamond engagement ring.''

Chapter Nineteen

Trent stared into the diamond ring as if it were a crystal ball, the uncertain fate of his romance locked in its shimmering facets. Was marrying Jaunie a mistake?

The enigmatic diamond winked back at him, refusing to relinquish the answer.

"Hey, bro, whatcha got there?"

Trent snapped the blue velvet jeweler's box closed, trying to hide it in his pocket.

"Uh-uh." Robert slouched into the guest chair. "Now don't even *try* to play me like that. I already saw it. Hand it over."

Reluctantly Trent dropped the box into Robert's wiggling fingers.

"Da-yum!" Robert shouted when the box snapped open. "Now that is one *big* block of ice!"

First thing Thursday morning, Trent had sunk a huge portion of his savings into that ring. He'd been hoping the financial commitment would make the reality of the situation sink in.

Unfortunately it just confirmed the extent of his neurosis. Here he was, trotting down that path once again, more lost than ever. He was like a Looney Tunes character, watching an anvil fall from the ceiling, too numb or stupid to jump out of the way.

Robert set the ring down on the desk. "Ah-ight, man, speak to me."

Trent sank low in the chair. "What's to say? It's an engagement ring for Jaunie."

"Yeah? I talked to her yesterday. She said you really tripped out on her the other night. It was her birthday, man. Couldn't you have waited until after midnight to go off on her?"

"She caught me off guard. But I called her later that night, and we talked. I apologized for how I acted. Everything should be okay now."

"You think so?" Robert stroked his goatee. Jaunie wanted me to talk to you. She's worried that she may have done the wrong thing by pushing marriage. You don't want to marry her, do you?"

Trent stared at his friend, whose three failed marriages were a testimony to what could happen when a man rushed into things. "I don't know what I want."

Yes, he did. He wanted Jaunie. He couldn't help himself. She'd been right when she'd told him that she deserved a husband and a family. Trent didn't have a right to hold her back from those things. But when he'd opened up his mouth to tell her he would let her go, he'd found himself agreeing to marry her.

"What are you afraid of?"

"How can you ask me that? Your track record's no better than mine." He gave Robert a second look. "In fact, it's worse. Much worse."

Robert chuckled, propping his feet on Trent's desk. "I'm not going to deny that, man."

Trent opened the box and studied the ring again. "Seriously, Robert. I've made a lot of mistakes in the past. I just wish I could be sure this won't become another one."

"I hear what you're saying. I may have had a bad marriage or two . . ." Robert paused when Trent raised a brow. "Okay, three, but I just *like* getting married. I like the courting, the honeymoon. I was just having fun back then, and I'm not sure my heart was really in it. Look where I met those women: nightclubs, rap concerts, the all-night Bikini Bowling Alley.'' Robert got caught up in a particularly fond memory before he shook it off. "Anyway, the point is, when I finally get serious, I'll find a good woman, and it will last."

"Yeah?" Trent cocked his head. "And when's that going to happen?"

"Well, bro"—Robert dropped his legs to the floor—"it might be sooner than you think. I finally broke down and let your mother hook me up with a woman from her church. She's meeting me at Jaunie's party tomorrow night. Who knows, I may *like* dating nice girls."

Trent shook his head with amusement. "Well, it's about damn time."

Before Robert left, he nodded toward the ring. "So you gonna give that to Jaunie for her birthday?"

Trent looked down at the ring. The brilliant diamond winked at him again. "Yes, I think I will."

And may heaven help him if he'd made the wrong decision.

Jaunie finished her piña colada, as she absorbed the atmosphere of The Ultimate. Huge, strategically placed, geometric shapes emerged from the dance floor in the main room. On top of each, a male or female dancer showcased the latest dance moves. Well-dressed couples crowded the dance floor and clustered at the bars, while club music thundered from oversized speakers.

"Patrice, you've outdone yourself. This place is great." In addition to the main room, there were several smaller rooms with tables for talking or listening to jazz. Patrice had reserved one of the smaller rooms exclusively for Jaunie's party.

"Thanks. It was fun, and it made me feel good to do something special for you, after all you've done for me." She twirled slowly. "And it gave me an excuse to buy this great new dress."

Having a job and being out from under Richard had made Patrice a new woman. She practically glowed in her fuchsia off-the-shoulder minidress, and her hair looked elegant in her new favorite style: the French twist. Apparently Officer Mike Barnes appreciated the changes, because he'd stayed close to her side all evening.

When Mike went to get them fresh drinks, Patrice pulled Jaunie over to one of the many little tables in the dim room. "So when is Trent supposed to get here?"

"Soon. He had to take care of some last-minute errands."

"Good, I'd hate for him to miss this. Everyone seems to be having a great time."

Jaunie looked around. "That's an understatement."

Simone and her husband were goofing off on the dance floor like kids. Even Geri, who'd worried initially about not fitting in, was in the thick of the crowd, dancing her heart out with a handsome young stud. Robert and his date, a lovely woman with a Halle Berry haircut, were talking intently at one of the tables in a dark corner. He'd get up every so often to introduce her around, and then they'd wander off by themselves again.

Patrice touched her arm. "What's wrong?"

"With everyone paring off, I miss Trent even more."

Patrice smiled. "Well, you two are engaged now. You'll have a lifetime to be together. Why are you looking at me like that?"

"I'm not sure about that. Even though he tried to reassure me that he loves me and *wants* to marry me, I still have my doubts."

"No, I'm sure he loves you."

"Yes, I believe he does, but maybe he needs more time."

"Why would you think so?"

"You know my history with him. I've had five years since that first meeting to come to terms with my feelings about love. I know I can trust him because he proved himself right off. Trent still has scars from his bad experiences with women, and I haven't offered him any reassurance that I'm any different.

How can I expect him to let go of all his fears overnight, just because I turned thirty and crave stability?''

''You two need to talk this out.''

''Yes. When he gets here, I'll let him off the hook.''

''Come on, Jaunie,'' Patrice said, when Mike returned with their drinks. ''Let's go back to the dance floor where all the action is. It's your birthday—you should be celebrating!''

''You two go ahead.''

Mike started toward the floor, but Patrice looked like she didn't want to leave Jaunie alone.

So when a tall handsome man dressed in black from head to toe asked her to dance, she said yes so Patrice could enjoy herself without worrying. Why not, she thought as she followed him out on the floor. Trent would be there soon. Why shouldn't she try to have a good time?

Straightening his tie one last time, Trent slipped Jaunie's engagement ring into his pocket. Tonight was the big night. He planned to propose to her in front of her family and friends. He owed her that much after the way he'd behaved initially. He still had his reservations, but he'd rather face potential heartbreak than lose Jaunie altogether.

He'd just picked up his jacket when the doorbell rang. Trent jerked open the front door prepared to brush off whichever neighbor or salesman stood on the other side. Instead his fists clenched at the sight of Alan Warren. He started to shut the door in his face, but Alan pushed his way inside.

Trent turned on him, ready to bodily pitch Warren through the door. ''You son of a—''

Alan pulled an envelope out of his jacket and held it between them like a shield. ''Jaunie's in danger.''

''Don't start this with me. There's somewhere I have to be, and if you get out of my apartment now, maybe I won't hurt you.''

Alan gave him a serious look. He dropped the envelope on the floor and walked up to Trent so they stood eye to eye. ''If you want to hit me, then do what you have to do. But when you're through exercising your ego, you *will* listen to me, because I'm the only person right now who knows who's after Jaunie.''

The fatalistic glare in Alan's eyes tripped Trent's internal alarms. ''What are you talking about?''

Alan bent to retrieve his envelope. He pulled out a photograph of two men and handed it to him. He pointed to a dark-skinned stocky man, standing in the shadows. ''This man is Dre Kane. He has a one-man investigation setup in Baltimore—but, the word on the street is, if you're willing to pay the price, you can hire him out for *miscellaneous* services on the side.''

Trent was getting impatient. ''Yeah. So?''

''He was hired to stalk Jaunie by this man.'' Alan pointed to the older man in the picture. ''Richard Lincoln.''

''Lincoln? Why does that name sound familiar?''

''He's Patrice Lincoln's husband, Andrew's stepfather.''

Trent swore. ''Why would he want to hurt Jaunie? What makes you think he's involved in this?''

''I checked into his background. Growing up, Lincoln was a loose cannon. He lived in a poor neighborhood and got caught up gang banging. His parents were killed in a drive-by shooting, and and his uncle took over his care. Myron Lincoln was a hard-nosed, ex-military man. He brought Richard to D.C. and sent him to Marshall Hall Military Academy. There Lincoln appeared to have straightened up. He thrived because the school fostered a different kind of gang mentality. If one succeeds, they all succeed—if one fails, they all fail. If a member of the team lets you down, it's up to the team to punish him. That's the attitude under which Lincoln runs his company, and it's the attitude he lives by.''

Trent shook his head. ''I still don't see what this has to do with Jaunie. She doesn't work for him.''

''Not anymore, but she did befriend his wife—helped Patrice leave him. Jaunie didn't start receiving the pictures until after the talk show aired. Lincoln considers himself a moral man above reproach. He probably looks down on Jaunie's past career choices. He wouldn't accept being judged by a woman he views as inferior. She interfered in his life. He thinks it's his right to punish her.''

"This is crazy. I think you're reaching here, Warren. You'll say anything to take the heat off yourself.''

"You know, it makes a lot of sense for Lincoln's man to lie low while the cops are watching me. The incidents stop, everyone thinks they've got their man, and Jaunie drops her guard. I can't look out for her myself—you've seen to that. But I have had my men tailing Kane. He's one slick brother, and we keep losing him. But before he dumped my man tonight, he was seen headed for Fifteenth Street, conveniently near The Ultimate.'' Alan shrugged with staged nonchalance. ''You don't have to believe me, but you have to think about it like this: If what I'm telling you is true, Kane is headed in your girlfriend's direction as we speak. By the time you decide to do something about that, it may be too late.''

The DJ cranked out another fast-paced hit that Jaunie loved, so she stayed on the floor for another dance. She could see a female dancer on top of a huge triangle spinning and twisting erotically to the pulsing beat. Jaunie's partner was a good dancer, and she was having a good time, but it wasn't the same without Trent. She glanced at her watch. Where was he? She needed to talk to him.

The crowd on the dance floor shifted, and her partner moved forward, forcing Jaunie farther back on the floor. The music continued to pulse, and her partner kept edging forward, until Jaunie found herself standing beside a five-foot-tall block, where a muscular male dancer gyrated to the beat.

She watched the dancer for a minute, then looked back at her dance partner. He smiled encouragingly, then stepped forward, wrapping an arm around her waist, holding her close. While Jaunie was trying to disengage from the embrace, she felt scuffling behind her. She looked up in time to see the dancer—

who was exchanging curses with a man in the crowd—leap off the block toward his tormentor.

Chaos immediately broke loose as dancers scrambled to move away from the fight and bouncers charged onto the floor. Jaunie was knocked to the ground in the confusion, but someone grabbed her arms and pulled her to her feet. She searched the swarming bodies for her dance partner, but he'd disappeared. She couldn't find any of her friends, either.

The crowd continued to scream and push, and Jaunie stumbled over the glass of someone's broken beer bottle. She was spun through the crowd on a wave of hysteria and finally knocked up against a wall.

Something was pressing into her back. It was the doorknob of the lady's room. Thank goodness! She pushed into the little room and locked the door behind her. She could still hear the confusion milling outside the door.

Liquid ran down her leg. She'd been cut. A small gash arced across her left thigh. She tore off her panty hose and stuffed them into the garbage, forcing her feet back into her low-heeled pumps. She ran water over some paper towels, blotting up the blood that coursed down her leg. Pressing the wet towel over her wound, Jaunie limped to the door and peeked out.

The mob was still swirling around the club in confusion. A wall of curious onlookers ringed the dance floor. The bouncers were trying to direct everyone out of the club, but the crowd hesitated to leave the action. Jaunie couldn't see her sister or any of her friends anywhere.

Slipping out of the bathroom, still clutching the paper towel to her leg, she pressed herself against the wall as she skirted the crowd. She turned a corner and found herself looking down a long hallway that ended at the top of a set of stairs. She followed the stairs to a huge metal door marked EXIT.

Jaunie pushed through the metal door and breathed deeply as the cold November air greeted her heated skin. She was in an alley beside the club. All she had to do was follow the perimeter of the building until she reached the front door. Her friends were probably waiting for her there.

Jaunie had taken only two steps toward the street, when she heard voices. She rushed toward them. At the end of the alley, a dark Cadillac was parked in the adjacent street. She started when she recognized Richard Lincoln arguing with the man she'd been dancing with. Instinct made her back up against the wall and listen.

"Can't find her?" Richard shouted. "How could you lose her? We choreographed this very carefully!"

"It was just dumb luck, man. She slipped. I think I grazed her leg with the knife, but someone grabbed her off the floor before I could try again. That crowd was freaked. I couldn't get near her after that."

Dear God, they were talking about her!

"This is unacceptable. You get back in there and finish what I paid you to do. Do you understand me? I've toyed with her long enough. I want this finished tonight!"

"No problem, boss. You just—"

Jaunie cautiously peeked around the corner in time to see Richard pull a gun out of his coat.

"If you can't handle this matter sufficiently, I'm prepared to handle it myself." The metal glinted in the streetlights. "But if I have to get my hands dirty on this one, I may as well take care of you, too."

Jaunie flattened herself against the cold brick building, shivering more with fear than chill.

"That won't be necessary," the other man said warily. A moment later Jaunie heard a door shut. She peeked around again and saw Richard sliding into the driver's seat of the Cadillac. Unfortunately the car was facing her. She wasn't going to get out that way.

Jaunie turned back and ran up the alley. The opposite side was a dead end, so she tried the door. There was no handle to open it from the outside. The thick metal was sealed to the frame, so she couldn't pry it open with her fingers. She briefly considered pounding on the door, but she didn't want to attract Richard's attention. And she didn't want to be greeted by the thug he'd sent back into the club after her.

How was she going to get out? Richard was parked at the end of the alley, and she couldn't get by without being seen. Jaunie looked up, hoping to find a fire escape or Dumpster to climb on. Nothing. It was just as well. She wasn't exactly Spiderman, and here she was in a party dress and heels—not quite wall-scaling attire.

Jaunie realized she would bleed or freeze to death before she had to worry about Richard finding her. She had to move— *now.* She crept to the end of the alley, and when she reached the opening, she got down on her hands and knees. Maybe she could crawl right past him, and he'd never know she was there.

Unfortunately crawling was slow going, and the street was cover with glass and debris. She didn't have any other choice. Staying as low as possible, she moved out of the alley into the light. All she needed now was for her favorite thug to come out of the club at that moment. She moved close to the car, trying to decrease her chances of being seen.

Slowly she inched forward, trying not to focus on the assorted garbage she was crawling over. Each movement was a test in restraint as she struggled not to moan as bottle caps and glass particles dug into her palms and knees. Finally she cleared the car. Just a little farther and she could stand up and run. She felt like an inchworm crawling up a drain pipe. At any moment an unexpected downpour could wipe her out.

Jaunie was so excited when she neared the main street, she got up and bolted around the corner. Yes! She was home free.

Jaunie dove around the corner as she heard something hit the wall beside her.

Richard was shooting at her.

Chapter Twenty

Trent left his car illegally parked in front of the club. He spotted Robert and his date huddled on the outskirts of a large crowd.

"There you are, man. What took you so long?" Robert called as Trent neared.

"I had to take care of a few errands," Trent answered, distracted by all the people crammed against the building. "What's going on?"

"You know, same old, same old. Some idiot starts a fight, and the rest of us end up on the street."

"There you are, sweetie pie." Geri slid past a cuddling couple to touch his shoulder. She looked around. "Where's Jaunie?"

Trent turned to face her. "I was just about to ask you that same question. Exactly what happened here?"

"Oh, hon, it was the worst. One of those hunky dancers got into a fight with a guy in the crowd. He leaped off his platform, and all hell broke loose. That's when we lost track of Jaunie. She'd been standing right where the fight started."

Trent swore and started pushing through the crowd. "I've got to find her!"

Robert grabbed his shoulder. "Wait a second. What if she shows up, and then we can't find you?"

Trent reached into his pocket. "I have my pager. If she turns up, beep me."

Two huge bouncers refused to let him into the club, and Alan's words reverberated in his head. Too late . . . too late . . . too late . . .

He skirted the crowd, searching for the lavender dress he knew Jaunie was wearing. Afraid to waste time, he circled the club, then struck off to search the back streets. She wouldn't leave her friends unless she'd had no other choice. Even in the confusion, he knew she would have found them if she could have.

Alan's theory had to be correct. She was still in danger, and he prayed he could find her before—

Trent turned the corner, backtracking toward the club again, when a blur of lavender flew around a corner and smacked right into him.

He caught her by the arms. "Jaunie!"

She was taking deep, heaving breaths as she collapsed against him. Her dress was torn, and her hair was wild.

"Jaunie, honey, what happened?"

"Gun—" she choked out between rapid gasps. "Running— from—"

Over her head, Trent saw Richard Lincoln stagger around the corner. Clearly he was a good deal slower than Jaunie, but the gun he raised toward them narrowed the odds.

He jerked Jaunie against the building before Richard could squeeze off a shot, but her body was heavy, and she struggled to breathe. He had to find a place for them to rest.

"How long have you been running?"

"Long time—making circles," she huffed.

Pulling her along, absorbing half her weight, Trent jogged away from the alley. The streets were filled with cars and pedestrians looking for late-night hot spots. That should have been a comfort, but he knew two people could be shot dead in the middle of a crowded D.C. street, and no one would be able to stop it.

"Are you okay, sweetheart?" He could feel her breath calming a bit as he pulled between two buildings. He nudged her back, urging her to keep moving. "I know you need to rest, but not here. I know of a construction site about a block away. We should be able to lose Lincoln there. Then we can find some help."

Jaunie nodded and continued to push herself forward. They had the advantage on Lincoln. As long as they kept moving, he didn't have a target. He wouldn't be able to keep up for long at his age—Trent hoped.

He directed Jaunie past a parking garage. His buddy's construction site, the structure that would eventually be a high-rise, loomed ahead. He spared a glance over his shoulder. Lincoln pursued them with a dogged determination. He was all the way down the street but could see which direction they were going.

Trent refused to let that worry him. By the time Lincoln got there, they'd be long gone. He stopped in front of the eight-foot-tall fence that surrounded the site. "Jaunie, we're going to have to climb over this fence." He shot her a quick look to gauge her reaction.

She stared up at the fence, then kicked off her shoes and began fitting her toes between the chain links.

"Jaunie, you should wear your shoes. There are a lot of things on-site that you won't be able to walk over in your bare feet."

She looked back, her face set with determination as she kept a steady pace, inching upward. "I can't climb with my shoes on."

Trent glanced through the links where a huge mound of construction debris was piled along the fence. If Jaunie fell on the broken bits of brick and metal from such a height—

He wouldn't think of the danger. She wasn't. Picking up her shoes and stuffing one in each of his pockets, he began to climb after her. He refused to look back to see Lincoln closing in on them.

Jaunie didn't let herself breathe until she stood on the other side of the fence, where Trent helped her put on her shoes. That's when he noticed her leg.

"My God, what happened to you?" His hands cupped her thigh as she balanced herself.

"There was a fight in the club, and during all the confusion, I got cut."

"On what, broken glass . . . ?"

Jaunie swallowed, realizing that Trent didn't know what was going on. Here they'd been running from a madman, and he didn't even know why.

"A knife . . . Richard . . . sent someone . . . to—" She felt tears forming in her eyes as the impact of the situation hit her. He'd sent someone to *kill* her. She began to shake. A distant voice at the forefront of her mind warned her that this wasn't the time to lose it.

He stroked her arm. "Shhh, it's okay. We'll talk about it when we're not out in the open like this." He pointed her toward the building. "Go through the lobby and into the stairwell. You can rest there. I'll be right behind you. I want to see if Richard's following us."

Plastic flapped in the wind several floors above her in place of actual walls. She ran through a huge hole—what she assumed would have been the lobby doors—and to the stairwell.

Where had Trent told her to rest? Uncertain, she kept moving down until she reached the basement level. This portion of the building was most complete. This must be where he'd sent her. The dusty hall broke off into several rooms. She poked her head into each one, searching for a good place to hide. Most of them were piled high with rolls of insulation and other equipment. She finally stopped at a dark room at the end of the hall.

She looked around. The walls were covered with electrical

paneling, and huge metal boxes seemed to grow out of the floor.

"Jaunie? Where are you?" Trent called from somewhere upstairs.

"I'm down here," she shouted toward the hall.

She heard him bounding down the stairs, and soon afterward, he appeared in the doorway. "How did you end up down here?"

"This isn't where you told me to go?"

"No, I—never mind." He walked over, pulling a handkerchief out of his breast pocket, and urged her to sit on one of the crates. He knelt in front of her. "How's your leg?"

She glanced down, her mind registering the sting from the gash for the first time. The wound had clotted, but her leg was a mess from streams of dried blood.

He smoothed the soft material of her skirt as he looked up into her eyes. "Have I told you that you look lovely tonight?"

In shock she stared down at her dress, which had somehow become horribly smudged with black dirt, her shoes were scraped and ruined, and she could feel matted hair sticking to her forehead. His tender words cut the fragile cord that had reined her emotions, and tears began to fall uncontrollably.

He reached up to dab her eyes with the handkerchief. "Let it go, baby. You've been through a lot tonight."

She sniffed, gaping at him in confusion. Why wasn't he demanding answers? Why did he just sit there, comforting and accepting? "Don't you want to know what's happening? Why Andrew's stepfather is tracking us through the streets with a gun?"

"Talked with Alan Warren tonight. He told me why Lincoln is after you."

"I haven't had time to make sense out of this whole thing." She felt like her head was stuffed with cotton. "What does Alan have to do with this? Did Richard hire him?"

Trent squeezed her arm. "No, Lincoln hired a P.I. from Baltimore, Dre Kane. Apparently he'll perform special services on the side—if the price is right."

"Why would Richard do this?"

"He's twisted. He blames you for Patrice leaving him, and he thinks it's his place to punish you. He must have seen the talk show and felt that you didn't have the right to judge him."

"What? Are you telling me he hired that man to stalk me all those months because he thinks I made Patrice leave him? Now he thinks that's worth killing me over?"

"I know it doesn't make sense, but Warren says it goes back to something about 'team learning' he learned at Marshall Hall."

Jaunie felt chilled as it began to sink in. Richard's mind was bent. "So Alan was never a part of this, was he?"

"No. If he hadn't put a tail on Kane, I might not have found you in time."

Jaunie dropped her head into her hands. "Oh, poor Alan. I owe him a huge—"

"Shhh. Did you hear that?" Trent whispered.

Footsteps? Trent motioned for her to hide behind one of the crates in the corner. She crouched quietly, afraid that at any moment she'd see the barrel of Richard's gun appear over the top of the crate. She'd left her purse at the club, with *her* gun in it. That would have evened the odds quite a bit.

She couldn't see a thing, but she could imagine him walking around the room. She heard so many noises, she couldn't tell if they belonged to him or not. In the hallway behind her, she thought she heard scraping and dragging. She knew Trent would have called out if Richard had found him. She could only pray that if Richard had to find one of them, it would be her. Above all else she wanted Trent to be safe.

After what seemed like an eternity, she heard movement across the room and finally Trent whispering her name. "Jaunie, come here."

"What's that smell?" She crept out of her corner and found him peeking out of the doorway. She moved up behind him. "Is he gone? Can we leave?"

He looked over his shoulder at her, his expression grim. "Look." He stepped back so she could see past him.

"Oh, my God!" She swallowed hard. "What are we going to do?"

Trent pulled Jaunie away from the door. He knew she was feeling the same shock and desperation he'd felt when he saw the mounds of insulation stacked in the hall. Richard had effectively blocked their way out by setting the pile on fire.

"Help me shut this door!" he called, moving the crates of parts and bolts out of the way. "Before the fire ever reaches us, we'll die from the smoke and fumes. Shutting the door may buy us enough time to find another way out."

Jaunie helped him close the door, but it wouldn't protect them for long. Flames had already begun to lick the outside walls. They heard the snapping of the fire coming toward them.

Jaunie began dashing around the room, pushing around crates. "What do we need? Something to break through a wall?"

Trent scanned the room. "That would be a good start. Normally we'd try to go for the ceiling duct, but since smoke rises . . ." He pushed around the crates, searching for a lower duct. "There," he shouted, pointing to a grate the wall. "Maybe we can crawl out through there."

Jaunie dashed over with a crowbar.

He tugged at the grate. "Damn it! I need a screwdriver to get this off."

Jaunie scrambled around the room. "I see a sledge-hammer but not any screwdrivers."

The smell of smoke was strong. "Look for something flat and thin. Maybe we can find a substitute."

"Try this," she said a few minutes later, giving him a handful of small metal washers.

The metal disks were sturdy enough to turn the screws, but it was difficult for his large nervous fingers to manipulate them well. Jaunie crawled beneath him and began working on the lower screws. It was a long, tedious job, but they were finally able to pull off the grate.

Trent dropped it to the floor, looking over at Jaunie. "Let me go in first. That way if there's a problem, you can turn back."

"Okay." She looked back. "But hurry. The room is already starting to fill with smoke."

Trent stuck his head into the duct, trying to climb in, but felt resistance at his shoulders. He tried again, this time raising his arms above his head, attempting to dive into the narrow metal tube, but again his shoulders wouldn't pass. He swore. "It's no use. I won't fit. Even if I can squeeze in there, I wouldn't be able to move without getting stuck."

He took her arm and pulled her toward the duct. "You try." Her body began to slip in easily, but she backed out before she got all the way inside.

"What's the matter?"

"Okay, now we know that I fit, but what good is that if you can't make it, too?"

Trent scowled. His eyes were already beginning to burn from the acrid smoke filling the room. "You'll go get help. I'll be okay until you get back."

She gave him an astonished look. "By the time I find help, it will be too late. There's not much time before this room is full of smoke, and the fire overtakes it. I'm not leaving you here." She crouched low on the floor, covering her face with the hem of her dress.

He looked at her incredulously. "What are you doing? Get back here and crawl through that duct!"

"No," she said, coughing. "I won't leave you here."

Trent darted across the room, prepared to shove her through the air duct if he had to. He wanted her safe. If that meant she had to leave him, then so be it.

He took her arm. "Don't you dare argue with me. There isn't time—" He choked, his throat burning and eyes tearing from the smoke.

Coughing, Jaunie pushed him away. "I'm not going. Listen to me. Would you leave me here alone?"

He stared at her, open-mouthed.

"I didn't think so. Either we leave here together, or we . . . don't leave."

Trent's heart constricted, and in that moment he knew—truly knew—what it was to love another person. He felt foolish for taking so much time to see it. Jaunie loved him like no other woman on earth ever would, and he'd waited until their lives were at stake to believe it.

The room became more dense with smoke each second, but his life was suddenly crystal clear. He had Jaunie. He loved her. And no matter what happened now, he wouldn't lose her.

He pulled her into his arms. "We don't have—much time—but there's something I've got to do."

He reached into his pocket and pulled out the engagement ring. "I say this completely from my heart, and I couldn't mean it more." He flipped open the box. "Jaunie Sterling, I love you. Will you marry me?"

Tears were streaming down her face as she held out a trembling hand. "Yes!"

He slipped the ring onto Jaunie's finger, and they clutched each other. Then she shoved away from him. It was as if the ring on her finger had life-giving power. She felt renewed determination.

"This isn't over yet. I'm not going to let a little thing like death prevent you from making good on the promise you just made to me." Her brave speech ended in a wave of coughs.

Trent tore off his jacket. "Cover your mouth with this." He pulled his shirttails to his face. "Maybe we can still break through a wall. Help me find a good spot," he said in muffled tones.

They began moving through the crates that blocked the wall opposite the fire. Jaunie could feel the intense heat at her back. She spotted a strip of wooden boards behind a tall stack of crates. "What's this?" she called.

He was instantly behind her. "I don't know. Where's that crowbar?"

She found it, and he began prying at the wood. She helped

as best she could, and after a few tries, they pulled the wood away. She found herself staring at a gaping hole.

"Oh, my God, is that what I think it is?"

Trent whooped behind her. "It's a utility tunnel. Come on." He grabbed her arm, and they ran through the dark tunnel.

The air was musty, but it was a welcome relief to her burning lungs. She took in a deep breath. "Do you know where this leads?"

"These tunnels usually run underground from the building to the sidewalk. See that light up ahead?" He pointed to the fragmented light streaming in from above. "That's from the grates that everyone avoids walking over on the sidewalk. We have to find a way to climb up."

They ran toward the light. Once they reached the grates, they had to go a bit farther until they found the ladder built into the wall of the tunnel. Trent climbed up first, pushing against the metal until it gave way. Once outside, he pulled Jaunie up behind him.

They lay huddled on the street for several minutes, clinging to each other in relief. She buried her face in his chest. "We made it!"

Trent moved beneath her. "Not yet. Look over there."

Jaunie raised her head. Farther up the street, Richard Lincoln stood, back turned, watching the building go up in flames. "Oh, it's *on* now! He's going to hear from me!" She surged to her feet.

"Wait!" Trent tried to grab her arm, but she was moving too quickly.

The gate behind Richard stood open. Obviously he'd shot the lock off. Moving quietly, Jaunie glanced back at Trent. "See that flat board inside the fence? Sneak up behind Richard and whack him, while I distract him."

She heard Trent curse under his breath, but she slipped inside the gate before he could protest. He might not like it, but she knew he'd follow through.

She skirted the perimeter of the fence, then edged toward Richard's field of vision, shielding herself behind a huge piece of machinery. Grabbing the first thing she touched, Jaunie heaved a chipped cinderblock over the top. Taking the bait, Richard fired a shot and then emitted a loud groan.

Jaunie peeked around to see Richard sprawled on his stomach, with Trent's foot planted firmly on his back.

As she ran over to retrieve the gun that had fallen from Richard's grasp, he attempted to buck Trent off.

Trent swung the board in an arc above Richard's head. "If you're smart, you won't try that again. I've had a really bad night, and I'm in the mood to take it out on you."

"Where's that beeping coming from?" Jaunie trained the gun on Richard. "I wouldn't be surprised if he's programmed to self-distruct."

Trent patted Richard's coat and pulled out a cellular phone. "Here's your bomb." Trent tossed it to her.

"Perfect." Jaunie could hear sirens in the distance. No doubt the fire department was on its way. She dialed the police station. When an officer she knew came on the line, she said, "MacAllister, get over to fourteenth and K and pick up this guy whose been trying to kill me. I want to go home."

"Yeah," Trent called. "Tell him we have a wedding to plan."

Epilogue

"Can I buy you a drink?"

Jaunie spun on her bar stool, looking up into the warmest brown eyes she'd ever seen. "I'm sorry, sir. I'm waiting for my husband, but you can sit down and flirt with me until he gets back."

He sat down beside her, his sensual gaze stroking her from head to toe. "You're too beautiful to wait here alone. Any chance I can steal you away from your husband?"

Jaunie laughed, punching Trent lightly in the arm. "So far he's a keeper, but ask me again in fifty years."

"I'll do that," he said, leaning in to kiss her.

She rested her hands on his knees. "Is our room ready?" It was their honeymoon, and they'd just arrived on the beautiful, romantic island of Jamaica.

"Not yet. The desk clerk said it would be ten more minutes. But I can't wait that long to give you your wedding present."

Jaunie arched her brows wickedly. "Oh? Do you think that's wise? We haven't learned all the Jamaican customs yet. They might frown on such things."

"No, sweetheart, *that* part of your present will definitely come later. First I want to give you this.'' He handed her a small velvet box.

She raised the lid and found a single silver key. ''What's this? The key to your heart?''

''No, Jaunie, you stole that long ago. This is the key to our new home.''

''The house in Silver Spring that you . . .''

He nodded. ''Robert always wondered why I put so much work into that house. Part of me must have known that I would share it with someone special.''

She wrapped her arms around his neck, squeezing him tight. ''Robert had better get to work on a house of his own. He and the girl your mother fixed him up with are getting pretty close.''

Trent chuckled. ''Yeah, when we get back to D.C., we'll probably have a couple of weddings to attend. Patrice and that police officer are really tight these days.''

She drew back. ''You're right. Patrice has finally found a man that Andrew likes. I guess this love stuff is contagious.''

''Yeah. Just talking about it is getting me excited.'' Trent looked at his watch. ''Our room should be ready now. Why don't we go get this honeymoon started right?''

Jaunie agreed, lacing her fingers through his. It would never cease to amaze her how far a little faith could go.

After graduating from college with a degree in psychology, Robyn Amos discovered that writing about the suspenseful and romantic lives of the people in her imagination was more fulfilling than writing scholarly research papers. Robyn continues to write about characters from a variety of cultural backgrounds, hoping her stories of romance and adventure will transcend racial stereotypes. PRIVATE LIES is her second Arabesque title.

Robyn would love to hear from her readers:

P.O. Box 7904
Gaithersburg, MD 20898-7904
Robyn*Amos@aol.com*
http://www.erols.com/robyna

Look for these upcoming Arabesque titles:

April 1998
PUBLIC AFFAIR, Margie Walker
OBSESSION, Gwynne Forster
CHERISH, Crystal Wilson-Harris
REMEMBRANCE, Marcia King-Gamble

May 1998
LOVE EVERLASTING, Anna Larence
TWIST OF FATE, Loure Bussey
ROSES ARE RED, Sonia Seerani
BOUQUET, Roberta Gayle, Anna Larence, Gail McFarland

June 1998
MIRROR IMAGE, Shirley Hailstock
WORTH WAITING FOR, Roberta Gayle
HIDDEN BLESSINGS, Jacquelin Thomas
MAN OF THE HOUSE, Felicia Mason, Doris Johnson,
Adrianne Byrd

BOOK YOUR PLACE ON OUR WEBSITE AND MAKE THE ARABESQUE ROMANCE CONNECTION!

We've created a customized website just for our very special Arabesque readers, where you can get the inside scoop on everything that's going on with Arabesque romance novels.

When you come online, you'll have the exciting opportunity to:

- View covers of upcoming books

- Read sample chapters

- Learn about our future publishing schedule (listed by publication month *and author*)

- Find out when your favorite authors will be visiting a city near you

- Search for and order backlist books from our online catalog

- Check out author bios and background information

- Send e-mail to your favorite authors

- Meet the Kensington staff online

- Join us in weekly chats with authors, readers and other guests

- Get writing guidelines

- AND MUCH MORE!

**Visit our website at
http://www.arabesquebooks.com**